"Baby?" a deep voice—even gruffer with emotion—repeated the word.

Her heart rate quickened more as she glanced up into Nick's handsome face. While he looked like every one of the male Paynes, she had no doubt that this man was Nick—for so many reasons.

First off was that quickening of her pulse, that tingling of her skin. Annalise reacted to Nick as she did to no one else. Secondly, and probably the reason she reacted that way, was because he was the most handsome man she'd ever seen. His eyes were bluer than his brothers', his features sharper, his jaw squarer. And finally, the other men had all seen her pregnant and had known that she was. It was clear that Nick had had no idea. Those bluer-blue eyes were wide with shock as he stared down at her belly.

"You're pregnant?"

Don't miss the previous books in Lisa Childs's thrilling Bachelor Bodyguards series.

* * *

If you're on Twitter, tell us what you think of Harlequin Romantic Suspense! #harlequinromsuspense

Dear Reader,

Bodyguard's Baby Surprise is the third book in the Bachelor Bodyguards series. For the past year, FBI special agent Nicholas Rus has been on the outside looking in on the Payne Protection Agency and the Payne family. But when the girl who literally grew up next door to him is in danger, Nick ditches his career to become her very personal bodyguard. Annalise Huxton doesn't remember a time when she hasn't been in love with Nicholas Rus. But, determined to be a loner, Nick has always pushed her away—until one night six months earlier when they made love. Ever since that night, Annalise has been in danger... and pregnant.

The baby is a surprise Nick never saw coming. He never saw his feelings for Annalise coming either until he's afraid that he might lose her—forever. But Nick doesn't know how to give or receive love. So all he can offer Annalise is his protection, especially since he feels responsible for her being in danger. In his years with the Bureau, he's taken down a lot of dangerous criminals who could be using her for revenge against him. If he can't keep her safe, Nick could lose Annalise before he ever figures out how to show her his feelings for her and his surprise baby.

I hope you enjoy this latest book in the Bachelor Bodyguards series.

Happy reading!

Lisa Childs

BODYGUARD'S BABY SURPRISE

Lisa Childs

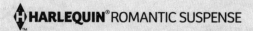

HARLEQUIN® ROMANTIC SUSPENSE

Recycling programs
for this product may
not exist in your area.

ISBN-13: 978-0-373-27989-0

Bodyguard's Baby Surprise

Copyright © 2016 by Lisa Childs

This edition published by arrangement with Harlequin Books S.A.

For questions and comments about the quality of this book, please contact us at CustomerService@Harlequin.com.

® and TM are trademarks of Harlequin Enterprises Limited or its corporate affiliates. Trademarks indicated with ® are registered in the United States Patent and Trademark Office, the Canadian Intellectual Property Office and in other countries.

Printed in U.S.A.

www.Harlequin.com

Ever since **Lisa Childs** read her first romance novel (a Harlequin story, of course) at age eleven, all she wanted was to be a romance writer. With over forty novels published with Harlequin, Lisa is living her dream. She is an award-winning, bestselling romance author. Lisa loves to hear from readers, who can contact her on Facebook, through her website, lisachilds.com, or her snail-mail address, PO Box 139, Marne, MI 49435.

Books by Lisa Childs

Harlequin Romantic Suspense

Bachelor Bodyguards

His Christmas Assignment
Bodyguard Daddy
Bodyguard's Baby Surprise

Harlequin Intrigue

Special Agents at the Altar

The Pregnant Witness
Agent Undercover
The Agent's Redemption

Shotgun Weddings

Groom Under Fire
Explosive Engagement
Bridegroom Bodyguard

Hotshot Heroes

Red Hot
Hot Attraction

Visit the Author Profile page at Harlequin.com for more titles.

For my mother, Mary Lou Childs, who passed away while I was writing this book. She loved babies and dedicated her life to raising not just hers, but her grandchildren, as well. She was an amazing, generous, loving woman who will be dearly missed.

Prologue

Hand shaking, Nicholas Rus pushed the door through the broken jamb. His other hand grasped his weapon. "Stay back," he told the woman who stood behind him—too close. Despite the chill November air, he could feel her warmth.

Annalise was always warm—in temperament and temperature. With her yellow blond hair and bright green eyes, she was like summer sunshine. No matter how many times he had pushed her away and called her a pest when they'd been kids, she had always come back with a smile and a hug. Her hugs were the only ones he'd known in his adolescence.

"I forgot you don't like people getting in your personal space," she murmured. But before she stepped back, she touched him—as if she couldn't help herself. Her fingers brushed across the back of his jacket. Despite the layers of leather and cloth separating them, he felt that touch.

"I don't want you getting hurt," Nick said. "Someone could be in there."

"There was," she said. "I was in there. Whoever did this—" she gestured with a shaking hand at the broken door "—was long gone then."

He wasn't so sure about that. What if the person had still been inside? What if that person had hurt Annalise? Nick shuddered.

"So they're longer gone now," she said.

"You shouldn't be here," he said. And neither should he. He hated this house. He had always hated this house. Not that there was anything wrong with the two-bedroom bungalow; it was the feeling that being inside it had always given him that he hated. His stomach muscles tightened into a tight knot of dread—the same miserable feeling he'd had every time he'd walked through the front door—and even when he'd been a kid, that had been as seldom as possible.

Drawing in a deep breath, he forced himself to cross the threshold. Despite what he said, he didn't protest when Annalise followed him—like she'd always followed him—and flipped on the lights.

"Why's the power on?" he asked. He hadn't paid a bill since *she* had died. He had done nothing with the house—except try to forget about it.

For once Annalise was quiet. But it didn't last long. She reluctantly admitted, "I've been paying the utilities."

"Why?"

"So the pipes won't freeze," she said matter-of-factly, "so it'll be ready when you want to come home."

He snorted. This house, in the lower middle-class area of Chicago, had never been home to him. "I left this place when I turned eighteen." And he had never looked back until his mother had died.

"That was when you joined the *Marines*…" Her voice cracked with emotion.

She had been upset when he'd joined. She'd been only twelve and hadn't understood how badly he'd needed to get away. But that wasn't why she was emotional.

"I'm sorry," he said. That was why he'd come back—not to deal with the house but because he'd known Annalise needed him. Actually, she didn't need him. She needed her brother, but nobody knew where Gage was. He had disappeared behind enemy lines.

"It's not your fault," she said.

Nick blamed himself. Annalise hadn't been the only Huxton who'd followed him around; Gage had, too. He was only three years younger than him, so he'd joined the Marines three years after Nick had. He'd also followed Nick's path after the corps—to college for a criminal justice degree and then into the FBI. The one thing Gage had done that Nick hadn't was reenlist. And that move had probably gotten him killed.

She touched him again, her hand reaching for his—for the one that didn't still grasp his weapon. She was right that he didn't need the gun. There was no one inside the house anymore. The intruders had done their damage—overturning furniture and even smashing holes in the drywall—and left.

"It's not your fault," Annalise said again, as if she somehow knew how guilty he felt about Gage.

She was also right when she'd said earlier that he

didn't like people getting in his personal space; he didn't like anyone getting too close to him. So he pulled his hand from hers to pick up an overturned chair.

"I had nothing to do with this mess," he agreed—though he had created one for himself in River City, Michigan—some three hours north of where he'd grown up.

"The house has been sitting vacant for too long," Annalise said.

She had been dead for almost a year now.

"You should let me either rent it or list it for you," she said. Annalise was a real estate agent and property manager. She'd done well for herself—probably because of her natural warmth. People trusted her.

Even Nick trusted her, and he'd never trusted easily.

She moved around the room, picking up things. The overhead can lights glinted off her pale blond hair and made her pale skin even more luminescent. She looked like an angel.

"Give it away," he said. "Maybe the fire department will take it and burn it down for practice." He liked the idea of burning up all those horrible childhood memories—of coming home from school to find his mother drunk or drugged out of her mind.

If not for the Huxtons living next door…

Annalise and Gage's parents had taken care of him like he was one of theirs. But they didn't live next door anymore. They had retired and left Chicago for a warmer city—in Alaska. They'd found a friendly little town they loved. With Gage gone, Annalise was all alone now.

She sighed. "If you don't want to keep it, let me sell it for you. I can make you some money."

"I don't want it," he said. "The house or the money." He had the only thing he'd ever wanted from his mother: the truth. She'd written it down in a letter he hadn't been given until after her death.

"I took some things out of the house that I thought were yours," she said.

He shook his head. "I didn't leave anything here that I wanted. I don't want any of it."

"Nick…" She obviously didn't understand his bitterness. She couldn't. She was too kindhearted to harbor resentment.

"I'll sign it over to you," he said. "You can do whatever you want with it." Maybe that would keep her busy enough to keep her mind off Gage.

The skin beneath her green eyes was dark—as if she hadn't been sleeping. And her full lips weren't curved into their usual smile. He missed her smile. He had missed her.

"Are you okay?" he asked.

She nodded—too quickly. "Of course. I told you no one was here when I found the house like this last week."

"I wasn't talking about the house."

Her lips lifted now, just slightly, as if she forced the smile. "You're talking about Gage."

He'd tried to bring Gage up earlier, but she hadn't let him. She'd changed the subject. He waited for her to do it again.

"You know he's fine," she said.

"I hope so."

"I know so," she said. And her smile widened as she summoned her faith. He'd never known anyone as optimistic as Annalise. "How about you?" she asked. "Are you okay?"

He was worried about Gage. But he wouldn't admit that to her.

"Tell me about them," she said. "About your family."

She'd been there when he'd read the letter his mother's lawyer had given him. Annalise had always been there. Maybe that was why he'd missed her so much the past several months.

"The Paynes are not my family," he said.

"You all have the same father," she said.

"And they resent me for that." Like she should have resented him for Gage joining the Marines.

"Then they're idiots," she said.

"They're not," he said. And his instant defense surprised even him. But the Paynes were good people who'd been hurt—whom he'd hurt with his mere existence. They had every reason to resent me—to look at him like they did—with anger.

Annalise looked at him now, and her green eyes filled with warmth and compassion and something else—something he'd seen in her gaze and no one else's. "Nick, I know you don't like it, but I have to..." And she hugged him like she always had, her arms sliding around his waist.

But it didn't feel like it used to. Annalise wasn't a child anymore. She hadn't been one for a long time. Her breasts were full and soft against his chest.

"It's not that I don't like it," he said. It was that he liked it too much. Maybe because it had been so long since anyone had showed him warmth. Or maybe because it was Annalise.

But he lifted his arms, and after holstering his

weapon, he slid them around her. She tensed in his embrace and glanced up at his face. "Nick…?"

Then he lowered his head and brushed his mouth across hers. And the chaos wasn't just in the house anymore. It was in his heart, his mind, his body. He knew he was about to make another mess, but he couldn't stop himself. He couldn't stop kissing Annalise.

Chapter 1

Six months later

The soft metallic click echoed in the eerie silence of the ransacked living room. FBI Special Agent Nick Rus tightened his grasp on his weapon, but he knew it was too late. Whoever had broken into his place had already cocked his gun, and the barrel of that gun was dangerously close to his head. Out of the corner of his eye, he could see the metal glinting in the faint light of the lamp overturned on the hardwood floor.

Was this it? He had lived most of his thirty-one years on the edge. As a Marine, he had been deployed to the most dangerous places in the world. As an FBI agent, he had taken on some of the most dangerous criminals in the world. But he was going out in the living room of some River City rental house?

Hell, no. He ducked and jammed his elbow back—into the ribs of the intruder. Then he wrapped the fingers of one hand around the barrel of that gun and shoved it up while he swung his own gun around and jammed it hard into the other man's chest. "Who the hell are you?"

"Your friend—I thought," Gage Huxton murmured before uttering a low groan of pain.

"My friends don't pull guns on me." But then he remembered a few instances when they had. "Well, at least they don't trash my place." He released Gage's weapon and holstered his own. "I've had some bad houseguests before, but you…"

Gage chuckled, but it was rusty-sounding. "Funny. I walked in here just a few minutes ago and found this mess."

Nick picked up the lamp from the floor and shone the light around. The couch cushions and pillows had been slashed, the stuffing pulled from them.

"Looks like somebody was looking for something," Gage remarked.

Nick shrugged. "I can't imagine what." He'd lived such a nomadic life that he had few possessions. "More likely someone is trying to send me a message."

"You piss someone off lately?"

"I've pissed off a lot of someones since I came to River City," Nick admitted. His move to Michigan had been tumultuous for him and for the people his presence had upset. Not just the Paynes but the criminals he'd put away since his arrival in the city.

"Has this been going on that long?" Gage asked. He'd been back in the US only a few weeks—back from the dead, actually, since he'd gone missing on his last deployment and had been presumed dead for months.

Nick nodded. "Yeah. That's why this is my fourth place in just a little over a year." He'd kept moving around, but they always found him—whoever it was routinely trashing his place.

"That's why you're doing the short-term rentals," Gage said.

"I was supposed to be here short-term," Nick reminded him. The Bureau had sent Nick to River City to clean up the corrupt police department. After years of going undercover to expose corruption, he'd become an expert at handling it. But cleaning up the River City Police Department had taken longer than he'd thought it would. It had also made him some dangerous enemies.

"Why would you leave?" Gage asked. "You've got family here."

Nick snorted. "I don't think they consider me family." But he had begun to think of them that way. "Especially Nikki." She was the one who'd told Gage where to find Nick a few weeks ago. She was the one who could track down anyone. He glanced around at the destruction. Did she resent him enough to do this to his place?

"Nikki," Gage said with a wistful sigh.

Nick shoved him again.

"Don't worry," Gage said. "She's your sister, so she's off-limits. That would be like you going for Annalise."

Actually, that would be worse, because Annalise was really Gage's sister. Other than them both being named for their father, Nick had no connection to Nikki Payne. Gage apparently hadn't talked to his sister yet. He didn't know about Nick and Annalise. If he had, he might have pulled that trigger when he'd had the chance.

"You need to call her," Nick said. Sure, she might tell Gage how he'd treated her. But he didn't care about himself. He cared about her and how worried she'd been about her brother.

Gage sighed again—raggedly. "I can't. She can't hear me like this." His voice was raspier than it had once been, but Nick suspected that wasn't what his friend worried his sister would hear. He worried that she would hear his pain—whatever hell he'd endured all those months he'd been missing. "But I sent her an email. I let her know that I'm back—that I'm okay."

He was alive. Nick wasn't sure how okay he was. He wasn't sure if Annalise was okay, either—since he hadn't talked to her for the past six months. He hadn't known what to say. "Sorry" hadn't seemed adequate—although he had told her that, too. He'd made a mess of their friendship. And when Gage learned what he'd done, he would have made a mess of that friendship, too.

So maybe it was fitting that someone kept trashing his place—since Nick kept trashing his life.

Payne Protection Agency, Annalise read the sign and confirmed she'd found the correct address. The body-guard business occupied both floors of the brick building in the industrial area of River City, Michigan. The email had come from here.

Gage.Huxton@PayneProtectionAgency.com

It had to be real. Her brother was alive. And it made sense that he would have come here. Not to the body-guard business per se, but here to River City—to Nick.

Even after whatever he'd been through in the past six months, he was still intent on following Nick around.

She had once been, too. But not anymore.

Nicholas Rus was the last person she wanted to see. Maybe she shouldn't have come here. But River City was nearly as big as Chicago. She was unlikely to run into him. She opened the door and stepped into the brick foyer of the building. Another door led to the lobby, but when she reached for the handle, it escaped her grasp as the door pulled open. A man stepped out, nearly colliding with her. Strong hands caught her shoulders and steadied her.

"Sorry," a deep voice murmured with concern.

She glanced up—into Nick's handsome face. The jaw, the cheekbones, the nose were chiseled, the eyes so bright a blue they were almost startling. But he was staring down at her as if she was a stranger—as if he had never seen her before.

"Are you okay?" he asked.

"Nick?" But it couldn't be. Even Nick couldn't be cold enough to pretend that he didn't recognize her. And she didn't feel the way she usually felt when she saw Nick. Maybe her heart had finally given up on him.

The man's brow furrowed. And he shook his head. "No. You know Special Agent Rus?"

She'd thought she knew him better than anyone else. But she'd been a fool. For so many reasons…

"He's not why I'm here," she said.

"Do you need a bodyguard?" the man asked. "I'm Logan Payne—CEO of Payne Protection."

"He never tires of saying that," another deep voice murmured as a second man stepped into the building from outside. Their faces were identical, but this man's blue eyes sparkled with amusement. "He used to be the sole owner, but our younger brother and I each bought our own franchise. If you want a bodyguard, come see me." He held out his hand. "I'm Parker Payne."

"Which one of you does Gage Huxton work for?" she asked.

"He should work for me." And then there were three. This man had come in behind the other brother. "I'm Cooper Payne, and my team has all the ex-Marines."

"Unless they're family," Logan said. "Then they work for me."

"Gage isn't your family," she said. He was hers. So why hadn't he come to see her since he'd been back? Why hadn't he at least called? Why had he only sent that short, impersonal email?

"He's Nick's family," Logan said. "So that makes him our family."

"Nick's not family," she said.

"Finally someone speaks the truth around here," a female voice remarked. The woman was small, but she shouldered the larger men aside and stepped closer to Annalise. She didn't look like them. Her hair was reddish-brown instead of black, her eyes brown instead of blue. But she was as much a Payne as they were. As Nick must be...

This was the family his mother's letter had told him about—the siblings he'd never known he had.

"Who are you?" the woman asked as she thrust out her hand.

"Annalise Huxton."

The woman's eyes widened. "Gage's wife?"

"Gage isn't married," Annalise said. While her brother hadn't been particularly forthcoming in his email, she doubted he'd met anyone and married her while he'd been missing. Before he'd reenlisted, he had been pretty serious about a woman, but she'd broken his heart, which had probably precipitated his reenlistment. "I'm his sister."

"I'm Nikki Payne," the woman said.

"Nice to meet you," Annalise said as she took Nikki's hand, which was small but callused. And her grip was surprisingly strong. Maybe having all older brothers had made her tough, whereas Gage had always tried to coddle and protect Annalise. Even Nick had, when he hadn't been ignoring her. But Nick wasn't her brother.

She'd always known that, but until six months ago, she'd thought Nick had considered her a pesky little sister. He hadn't ignored or coddled or protected her that night. Instead, he'd broken her heart.

But he'd done more than that...

Much more. She flinched as a little foot struck her ribs, and she pressed her hand over her stomach. That was probably why Nikki had assumed she was Gage's wife. Because she was pregnant.

Maybe coming here—even to see Gage—had been a mistake. He would want to know who the father was. And she couldn't tell him. She couldn't tell anyone.

"Gage isn't here," Logan said. "He left for an assignment this morning."

Even as disappointment flashed through her, she breathed a little sigh of relief. She wanted to see her brother—wanted to see for herself that he was all right. But she didn't want to have to answer his questions any more than he probably wanted to answer hers.

"When will he be back?" she asked. Eventually he would have to know that he was going to be an uncle in a few months. But that wasn't the reason she needed to see her brother. She wasn't even here to make sure he was all right. He was back. He was working. He was probably fine.

Annalise was the one who needed help.

Logan shrugged. "It's hard to say. Days. Maybe weeks. As long as the person he's protecting is in danger."

For her, it had been months. She'd been in danger since that night Nick had showed up in Chicago. That couldn't be a coincidence. He must have gotten her in trouble somehow—in more ways than one. Because someone had spent the past six months stalking her.

Logan Payne had been running Payne Protection long enough to recognize when someone was in trouble. Annalise Huxton was in trouble. The fear was in her pale face, her wide green eyes. She was scared.

He silently cursed himself for sending her brother away. He could pull Gage off the assignment, though. He could bring him back and send someone else.

A small hand squeezed his forearm. "Let me take Gage's place," Nikki said. She must have recognized what he'd seen. She was intuitive. But she was too little, too young, too fragile to do their job.

"You don't work for me anymore," he reminded her. "You went to work for Cooper."

She thought she could manipulate Cooper more easily than him or Parker. But he doubted Cooper would hand her any assignments more dangerous than the desk jobs Logan had given her.

His sister glared at him, and he was used to it. She hadn't been happy with him for a while. So he wasn't surprised that when he split up the protection agency, she'd chosen to leave the franchise he was keeping.

"Annalise needs to see her brother," Nikki said. "He was missing for months." She glanced at Cooper then—and there was no glare on her pretty face.

Maybe that was why she'd asked to work for him—because she'd missed him so much when he'd been deployed.

"It's fine," Annalise said. But the crack in her voice made it sound as if she was anything but fine. "I'll see him when he comes back."

"Will you stay in River City and wait for him?" Nikki asked.

"I—I could check into a hotel," Annalise said. "I haven't yet."

Logan wondered why. Had she worried about her reception from Gage? Or had something—or someone else—made her afraid of staying?

"I don't know how long he'll be gone," Logan reminded her.

"Maybe I could stay at Gage's place," Annalise murmured.

"He's been staying with Agent Rus," Nikki said.

Would his sister ever accept that Nick was their brother? Logan hadn't been happy, either, to learn their father had betrayed their mother. But he hadn't blamed Nick.

Annalise's face paled even more, and she quickly said, "I can't stay there."

From what Logan had been told, Gage had grown up next door to Nick in Chicago—making them as close as brothers. Obviously Annalise hadn't felt any more like a sister to Nick than Nikki did.

"You can stay with me," Nikki offered. She must have recognized what Logan had—Annalise was scared. Or maybe she just liked that Annalise wasn't a fan of Nick's, either.

But the blonde shook her head. "I couldn't impose."

"No imposition at all," Nikki assured her. "Did a cab drop you here?" She glanced around as if looking for bags.

Annalise shook her head again. "I drove my car. It's not that far a drive from Chicago."

"So you're parked out front?" Nikki asked. "I am, too. You can follow me back to my place and we'll get you settled in."

"And I'll see about sending a replacement for Gage so he can come back early," Logan offered. If Annalise was as scared as he suspected she was, she needed family. She needed her brother.

Nikki held open the door for her, and Annalise walked out with his sister. They were gone for only a moment when he heard the scream and the squeal of tires.

As usual, his instincts had been right—Annalise was in danger. And that danger had followed her to River City. He drew his weapon, just as his brothers had, and the three of them rushed out to the street. But they hadn't reacted quickly enough—because gunshots rang out.

They were too late.

Chapter 2

Nick's heart hammered against his ribs as fear and panic overwhelmed him. He flashed his shield and hurried past hospital security—into the ER waiting room. Logan and Cooper rushed up to him.

"Where is she?" he asked. "And how badly is she hurt?" She had to be hurt or they wouldn't have brought her here. His panic intensified and pressed on his lungs, stealing his breath.

Logan shook his head. Was it so bad that he couldn't answer him?

"We don't know yet," Logan said. "A doctor is checking her out."

"What happened?" he asked. What was she even doing in River City? Gage hadn't called her, and it sounded as if his email to her had been brief. Had she come to visit *Nick*?

Six months had passed since that night. Six months with no contact, which had been unusual for her. Before, she had always called or texted or emailed him to see how he was doing. But not this time.

Not after what he'd done…

No. She hadn't come to visit him.

Logan shrugged. "We didn't see it. She and Nikki had stepped outside…" He pushed his hand through his black hair. "But I knew she was in danger."

"How?" Nick asked.

"She looked scared," Logan said.

What the hell did Annalise have to fear? Then Nick remembered that house—his mother's house—and how badly it had been ransacked, like his place kept getting ransacked. He shook his head. It couldn't be related. His mother's house had sat vacant for months. That was why someone had broken into it.

"Thanks for calling me," Nick said.

"I was going to call Gage," Logan admitted. "But Cooper told me to call you instead."

Nick spared Cooper a glance of gratitude. Even though Gage hadn't spoken of it yet, Cooper, as a Marine himself, must have sensed what Gage had been through and understood that he hadn't been ready to see his sister. And how would he handle her being hurt? Even Nick couldn't handle it.

"I'm glad I'm the one you called," Nick said.

"Annalise won't be," Nikki said as she walked into the waiting room through a door marked No Admittance. She had come from inside the hospital, maybe inside the ER.

"Where is she?" he anxiously asked. He had to see her—had to make certain she was all right.

"She doesn't want to see you," his half sister said. Even though she couldn't stand him, she probably wasn't lying.

Because of what had happened—and his silence for the past six months—he could understand if she never wanted to see him again.

But she was Annalise, always so warm and affectionate. Surely she would forgive him...even if he would never be able to forgive himself.

Annalise's head pounded as images flashed through her mind. It had all happened so quickly. She had walked outside with Nikki, only to find two men breaking into her car.

Not again...

Frustrated and angry, she had reacted without thinking. She'd run across the street to stop them. The moment she'd crossed the road, she had realized her mistake. She had gotten too close. One of them had reached out, wrapped a huge hand around her arm and jerked her toward the open back door of her car.

She'd screamed then. And shots had rung out—fired from close range and also from across the street. She had struggled harder, fighting for herself and her baby. She had to get away. If she left with them...

The car started away from the curb, but she was half in and half out, her feet touching the road. She reached up and clawed at the face of the man holding her. He howled and released her, and she tumbled to the asphalt.

She pressed trembling hands over the mound of her belly. What had she done? She had been so stupid to run toward the car—so careless. What if her baby had been harmed?

Her belly shifted beneath her palms as her baby moved. At her last regular OB appointment, she'd had an ultrasound, but the doctor hadn't been able to determine the sex. Annalise didn't care what she was having— just that the baby was healthy. He or she had to be okay.

Annalise had been scared when she'd found out she was pregnant—scared that she wouldn't be able to handle raising a child alone. But she had never been as scared as she was now—not even when that man had grabbed her. Her heart pounded frantically, making the machine next to her bed beep faster. The curtain partitioning her bed off from the rest of the ER rustled. The doctor must have returned with the ultrasound results.

"Is my baby okay?" she asked.

"Baby?" a deep voice, gruff with emotion, repeated the word.

Her heart rate sped faster as she glanced up into Nick's handsome face. While he looked like every one of the male Paynes—with his chiseled features, thick black hair and startlingly blue eyes, she had no doubt that this man was Nick—for so many reasons.

First, that quickening of her pulse—that tingling of her skin. She reacted to Nick as she had no one else. Second, he was the most handsome man she had ever seen. His eyes were bluer than his brothers', his features sharper, his jaw squarer. Finally, the other men had all seen her and knew she was pregnant. It was clear that Nick had had no idea. Those bluer blue eyes were wide with shock as he stared down at her belly.

"You're pregnant?"

She splayed her hands across her belly, but she couldn't hide it from him. So she nodded.

"Is it mine?"

A gasp slipped through her lips—that he would ask, that he wouldn't just know. She didn't sleep around. She wouldn't have slept with him six months ago if she had been involved with anyone else at the time.

Or would she have?

She had wanted Nick for so long—even before she'd known what desire was. When he had finally returned that desire, she hadn't been able to resist and probably wouldn't have even if she'd been in a relationship at the time. But thanks to Nick—and always wanting him—she'd had few relationships. No ordinary man or high school boyfriend or college crush had been able to measure up to the hero she had made Nicholas Rus out to be in her girlish fantasies.

Nick was no hero, though. He was just a man—a man who'd always made it clear he didn't like anyone getting too close to him. And until that night six months ago, he had never let Annalise too close.

Before she could answer him, the curtain rustled again, and another man joined them. His light green scrubs hung on his tall, thin frame. The young ER doctor glanced at her and then at Nick as if trying to gauge the relationship.

"Is she all right?" Nick asked. And his gaze skimmed over more than her belly now. He looked at her face, and his breath audibly caught at the scrape on her cheek. He reached out, but his fingers fell just short of touching her.

"Is the baby all right?" she asked. The baby was all she cared about. She didn't care about her car. It wasn't the first one she'd had stolen.

She'd been so stupid to risk her pregnancy over a damn car...

The doctor glanced at Nick again—as if wondering if he could speak freely in front of him. Damn HIPAA laws. She didn't care about her privacy right now.

"Please," she implored him. "Tell me!"

The baby shifted again. He or she had to be okay, or he wouldn't move like he was. Right?

"Your baby is fine, Ms. Huxton," the doctor assured her. "It appears that when you fell out of the vehicle, you fell on your side."

Nick flinched as if he'd taken a blow.

"Your shoulder took the brunt of the force," he continued, "and it appears you've struck your head, as well. You have a slight concussion."

That explained why her head kept throbbing so painfully. She lifted her fingers to her temple. "But the baby... Is he or she..." They hadn't been able to determine the sex on this ultrasound screen, either. The tiny legs had been crossed again. " ...all right?" She needed that reassurance, needed to know that her recklessness hadn't put her pregnancy at risk.

The doctor reached out, and his fingers did touch her, squeezing her hand. "The baby is fine. Strong heartbeat. Active. All properly developed for twenty-four weeks."

She uttered a sigh of relief. "Then I can leave?"

The doctor pulled his hand away. "I'm not concerned about the baby," he said. "But I do have concerns about your concussion."

"There's no reason for concern." She shook her head but winced as pain reverberated inside her skull. Maybe she did have a concussion. "I'm fine."

"You're not fine," Nick said. "You've been hurt."

He would know. He had done it. But he wasn't referring to his breaking her heart. He probably wasn't even aware that he had.

"The address you provided for your intake paperwork says that you live in Chicago," the doctor said. "You definitely cannot drive that distance, or really at all, for at least twenty-four hours."

A giggle bubbled up inside her, but not wanting to sound or become hysterical, she suppressed it. "I have no car to drive," she said. "It was stolen."

"Is that what happened?" Nick asked. "You were carjacked?" He uttered a slight sigh, almost as if he was relieved.

Surprised by his reaction, she stared at him.

"Logan made it sound like something else," he explained. "Like it wasn't random."

She doubted it was random. After everything else that had happened, it would have been too much of a coincidence. But she wasn't sure how much she wanted to share with Nick. He had already proved to her that she shouldn't have trusted him—with her heart, and maybe not with anything else.

"You shouldn't drive," the doctor repeated as if they hadn't spoken. "And you should not be alone tonight."

"She won't be alone," Nick said. "She's going home with me."

She gasped. "No." But before she could finish her protest—that there was no way in hell she would go home with him—the doctor and Nick both turned to her.

"I'm sure you'd rather not stay in the hospital," Nick surmised—correctly. And of course, he knew the only way the doctor would release her was if he believed she would not be alone.

Damn him. He'd always had an uncanny ability to know what other people wanted or needed—except her. He had never known how much she'd wanted him—needed him—until that one night.

But that night had been an aberration. He hadn't realized how much she'd needed him after that—more than she ever had. Or maybe he'd known and hadn't cared.

What was different now?

The baby? He must have realized the child Annalise was carrying was his.

"She doesn't want to go home with you," Nikki said.

Special Agent Rus flinched as if she'd struck him. She had watched the man take a blow and even a bullet without ever betraying an ounce of fear. But this caused him pain. Annalise Huxton caused him pain.

"She doesn't," he agreed with a glance to the door of the bathroom where Annalise was changing from the hospital gown back into her clothes. They were torn and stained from her tussle with the men and the asphalt. And thanks to Nikki letting them get away with her vehicle, those clothes were all she had in River City.

Nikki flinched now. Maybe her brothers were right. Maybe she wasn't cut out to be a bodyguard. She hadn't reacted fast enough.

"I told her she could stay with me," she said. But now she wondered if that was a good idea—if she could keep the pregnant woman safe.

"I appreciate the offer," he said.

She opened her mouth to point out that she hadn't made the offer to him when he continued, "And I appreciate you saving her from the carjackers."

Her face heated now as it flushed with embarrassment. "I didn't," she said.

"But Logan said you exchanged gunfire with them."

"I did," she said. She had gotten off a couple of shots and might even have hit one of them. "But Annalise got free on her own. She's tougher than she looks." Just like Nikki had always tried to convince her brothers *she* was tougher than she looked. "Maybe that's why she ran toward them when she saw them stealing her car."

"She ran toward the carjackers?" he asked, his face paling with fear as he probably imagined all the horrible things that could have happened—that Nikki had almost let happen.

She nodded. "Just before she did, she mumbled something about *not again*. Her car has been stolen before. Once would be random. But twice?"

When Nikki had joined her brothers in the waiting room, Logan had said he'd sensed she was in danger. Logan was rarely ever wrong—except about Nikki. Or at least she'd like to think so?

"That's why she's going home with me," Nick said, his square jaw clenched with grim determination.

"You didn't know, did you?" she asked.

He arched a dark brow.

"That she's carrying your kid."

His face flushed now, and he shook his head.

"Maybe it's good that you were named after our father," she said. "Apparently you're the most like him." Of course, she had been named for him, too—something she resented nearly as much as she resented Nicholas Rus's existence.

Rus flinched again, and a twinge of regret struck Nikki. Giving him a hard time had become more of a habit to her than anything else. It wasn't like she hated him—like everyone else thought.

Sure, she wasn't happy with how he had come into their lives and turned them upside down—especially Mom's. But apparently Mom had always known that her husband had cheated on her. Was any man worthy of a woman's trust?

Annalise stepped out of the bathroom, and she looked up at Rus with mistrust. Then she gazed at Nikki, imploring. Nikki wanted to offer her hospitality again. But after the incident in the street, she wasn't certain she could keep the woman and her unborn baby safe.

"I want a full report about what happened and descriptions of the men," Agent Rus told her.

She would have bristled at his bossiness. But she understood why he was. He'd been running the police department since coming to River City to clean up the corruption. Apparently he thought she worked for him. But his demand wasn't unreasonable. She intended to do more than fill out a report. She intended to track down the men herself. They wouldn't get away from her again.

"I also want you to come down to the station and look through mug shots," he said, "if you think you would recognize the men if you saw them again."

She nodded in agreement. "Sure. I would."

"I could look at the mug shots, too," Annalise offered.

Nick shook his head. "You have a concussion. You need to rest. Once the doctor brings your release papers, I'm taking you home."

Annalise glanced at her again—with that imploring gaze. And Nikki's stomach knotted. She hated to disappoint Annalise, but she didn't want to endanger her, either. "I'd better get going," she said as she hurried out.

In case her brothers were still in the waiting room, she bypassed it and took the elevator to the underground parking garage. She didn't want to see her family again. She'd already spoken to them once— to assure them that Annalise was all right. They'd been so concerned about her that they hadn't questioned Nikki. And she hadn't looked at them. She didn't want to look at them now. She didn't want to see the *I told you so* on Logan's face, didn't want to see the doubt on Cooper's. She didn't want him second-guessing hiring her.

Tears stung her eyes, blurring the elevator doors. But then they slid open, and she stepped into the parking structure. She had been in such a rush to follow the ambulance to the hospital that she couldn't remember where she'd parked. Which floor had it been?

She walked through the structure, looking for her black coupe. Logan hadn't given her a black SUV like he had everyone else who worked for him—probably because he hadn't wanted bad guys blowing her up when they meant to blow up one of her brothers instead.

She uttered a regretful sigh as she remembered the men who'd lost their lives when one of their SUVs had exploded. Someone had been trying to kill Parker and had nearly succeeded. Tears stung her eyes again, and she blinked furiously. When her vision cleared, she realized what she'd found. Not her coupe but *them*.

Nikki had known she would recognize the men if she saw them again. Unfortunately they glanced up, furtively—from the black SUV they were trying to jimmy open—and saw her.

They clearly recognized her, as well. She reached for her weapon—realizing too late that she'd locked it in the glove box because she'd known she wouldn't make it past hospital security with it.

So she was unarmed and outnumbered.

Chapter 3

Nick cursed himself for not just leaving his SUV parked illegally outside the emergency room entrance. He should have exercised his authority, so that security wouldn't have dared to have his vehicle towed away. But he hadn't been thinking after Logan's call. He'd been so anxious to get to her—so anxious to see Annalise for himself. He'd pulled into the first available spot in the garage and run up the stairs to the ER. Now he struggled to remember where he'd parked.

He didn't want to leave Annalise alone long—waiting in a wheelchair in the lobby. She'd looked so pale sitting there, so fragile. Even pregnant, she was still slight because of her small frame, narrow shoulders, thin arms and long, slender legs. Dark circles rimmed her green eyes, as if she hadn't been sleeping well because she'd been afraid. Logan had noticed her fear.

Nick saw it now, the fear and the vulnerability. Nikki had told him Annalise was tougher than she looked—that she'd saved herself. Of course, she was a Huxton. Gage wouldn't have survived being missing in action for months if he wasn't tough, too.

At least Annalise wasn't alone in the lobby. Or just with hospital security, either. Logan and Cooper stood over her chair, offering more protection than Nick had thought she'd get from some nervous hospital security guard. She was safe.

He wasn't as certain about Logan and Cooper. Annalise was furious. She didn't want to go home with him. And she hadn't wanted to ride in the wheelchair, let alone having to wait in it until he pulled his vehicle up to the lobby doors. His half brothers probably had a fight on their hands to keep her in the chair and make her wait for him.

She might see this as her opportunity to call a cab to take her home to Chicago. Her home was in Chicago; his wasn't. He had never felt as if that house or anyplace else he'd lived was home. The only time he'd ever felt as if he was home was when he'd been with Annalise. When he'd given in to his desire to kiss her, he'd worried that it might have been awkward. They'd known each other so long.

But it hadn't felt awkward. It had felt right and passionate and thrilling. And he hadn't been able to stop. But he'd felt most at home buried deep inside her body.

Had they made a child that night? Twenty-four weeks ago. The doctor had said that was how far along her pregnancy was. However, Annalise had never confirmed her baby was his.

But he knew...

Annalise carried his child. And she hadn't called him. She hadn't told him about the pregnancy. Or that she was in danger.

She probably wouldn't be waiting for him to come back with his vehicle. She had no intention of staying with him. So he quickened his step, running toward his SUV just as he'd run toward the ER earlier.

That was when he heard it—the scream. It wasn't just a shrill cry. It was his name, full of terror and warning. "Nick!"

Someone was in trouble—someone he knew.

"You're in trouble," Logan Payne said.

Annalise laid her palms over her belly. "That sounds like something my grandmother would say."

His face, so similar to Nick's, reddened. "I wasn't talking about your pregnancy."

"Then how do you mean I'm in trouble?"

Did he know how deeply she loved Nick? And how unlikely it was that Nick would ever return her feelings? She had to get over him. If she was going to mend her broken heart, she could never trust him with it. He would only hurt her again.

"Those guys weren't stealing your car," he said.

"Really?" she asked. And his brother Cooper, who also stood beside her chair, furrowed his brow, mirroring her confusion. "Then why is my car gone?"

If she had it, she would have driven herself back to Chicago—doctor's orders be damned. Or better yet, she would have driven herself to Alaska. She had thought she'd needed Gage. But maybe she needed her mom and dad more.

She would have gone to them before, but she didn't

want to put them in danger. Gage could handle it. He could protect her. He had survived being missing in action when everyone else had given him up for dead. She hadn't. She knew her brother was tough. Trying to be like Nick had made him tough.

"You know what I'm talking about," Logan said.

Unable to hold his gaze, she glanced down at the terrazzo floor of the sun-filled glass lobby. "Have you called Gage?" she asked.

"No," Cooper answered for Logan.

"Why not?" she asked. She needed her brother—more than she ever had.

Cooper wouldn't meet her eyes.

And she realized why. Concern filled her. She had been so happy—so relieved—he had come back alive that she hadn't considered what condition he might be in. "He's not all right, is he?"

"Physically he's fine," Cooper assured her.

"And…?"

"Mentally and emotionally, he has some recovering to do yet," Cooper said. "He'll get there. It just takes time—more time for guys who've been through what he has."

"Thank you," she said.

Cooper shrugged off her gratitude. "I haven't gotten him to talk about it. I don't really know what he's been through. The only one who might know is Nick."

Gage had always gone to Nick—had always told him everything. If Nick knew, why hadn't he told her? Why hadn't he called her? Had he been so determined to avoid her after they'd made love that he hadn't even wanted to call to talk about Gage?

"Thank you for not calling him," she clarified. "I

wouldn't want to add to whatever he's going through."
She couldn't imagine the horrors her brother had endured while he'd been missing. Gage was tough, but everyone had a limit.

"Then you'd better be honest with us about what's been going on with you," Logan said. "Your getting hurt might be more than your brother could handle."

He was right. It wasn't that she didn't want to share her troubles with someone. But she wasn't certain whom she could trust.

These were Nick's brothers. She couldn't trust Nick— not after the way he'd treated her. So how could she trust any of them?

"My sister told me what you said when you saw those men jacking your car," Logan said. "This isn't the first time that's happened."

"No," she admitted.

"And it's not the only thing that's happened to you."

Her head began to pound as other memories rushed in, and she squeezed her eyes shut to block them out.

"Annalise?" Logan prodded her.

They hadn't been raised together, but he reminded her of Nick. Even before he'd become an FBI agent, Nick had always been good at asking questions and finding out information. Perhaps Logan should have been an FBI agent, too. He was a natural interrogator, as well.

And she had never been good at keeping secrets. She parted her lips to speak, but someone shouted. She opened her eyes to see a security guard running up to Nick's brothers.

"You guys are with Payne Protection, right?" he asked.

Both men nodded. "What's wrong?" Logan asked.

Because it was clear that something was. The young man was flushed and breathing hard.

"There's a shoot-out in the parking garage! I called 911, but I don't think the police will get here in time. So I need to go down there." His throat moved as he swallowed hard, obviously afraid. "I need backup."

Annalise's heart hammered against her ribs. "Nick's in the parking garage." He'd gone down to get his vehicle to pick her up. Just like her car getting stolen again, it couldn't be a coincidence. Nick had to be involved in that shoot-out.

"I think Nikki's down there, too," Cooper said.

Logan's face paled, and his hand shook slightly as he reached beneath his jacket—probably for his weapon. But his holster hung empty from his arm. He glanced at her. "I told Nick…"

That he would protect her. She had heard him, and she'd thought it was ridiculous that they thought she needed protection inside the hospital. Obviously they'd been right.

"Go," she urged him.

He shook his head and turned to Cooper. "You go."

Cooper was already grabbing the arm of the security guard and pulling him across the lobby.

"Be careful!" Logan called after him. "And make sure they're okay!"

Cooper glanced back and nodded. But he could only do his best—if he arrived in time. Annalise worried that he and the security guard would be too late to help.

Nick couldn't be gone.

She pressed her hands over her belly again. And the baby shifted within her womb. Her child couldn't lose his father before she was even born.

* * *

As Cooper Payne shouldered open the door to the parking garage stairwell, shots reverberated inside the concrete structure. He kept the security guard behind him, shielding him as he would have a Payne Protection Agency client or a fellow serviceman. Fortunately he'd the foresight to leave his weapon with security, so he'd retrieved it before they'd left. He clasped the Glock in both hands, swinging the barrel in each direction he looked.

Where the hell were they? The noise faded to a faint echo as the shots stopped.

His heart stopped, too—for just a second. From his years in combat, he knew why the firing ceased. Because everyone was dead...

His blood chilled, and the hair lifted on his nape. He still kept his hair short, as he had when he'd been enlisted. His brothers wore theirs longer—except for Nick, who had also been a Marine. Nick looked the most like him, and they were nearly the same age.

His half brother was too young to die. Cooper bit the inside of his cheek, resisting the urge to call out to him. To Nikki...

Had she gone down to the parking garage? She hadn't said goodbye. She had simply disappeared from the hospital. Nikki always did that when Nick was around, though. She couldn't handle being near the evidence of their father's betrayal—couldn't stop blaming Nick for what their father had done.

He hoped she had left before Nick had come down for his SUV, and she was safe.

Cooper slowly moved forward, keeping low so he could duck for cover if the firing started again. Because he was staying down, he saw the blood—the droplets of it sprayed across the concrete. Someone had been hit.

How badly? And who?

Then he saw the SUV. Like the Payne Protection company vehicles, it was black, but this one had all the windows shot out, the glass scattered across the concrete like the blood. The government plate on the back confirmed his fears. It was Nick's.

But where the hell was Nick?

He lowered one knee to the ground as he leaned down farther, looking for bodies on the other side of the vehicle. He found more blood—small pools of it. Maybe more than one person had been hit since there was blood on both sides of the SUV.

As he looked around, he noticed a Payne Protection vehicle parked nearby—not one of the black SUVs but Nikki's small coupe. He recognized it from the furry pink dice hanging from the rearview mirror.

The former cops—Logan and Parker—gave her so much crap about those dice. They had warned she might get a ticket for obstructed vision. Nikki probably didn't even like them, but she was too stubborn to remove them now. She was too stubborn to give in.

Even if she'd had the chance to drive off, she would have stood her ground. She would have fought to prove herself. That was why Cooper had hired her for his team. He wanted to convince her to believe in herself.

"What the hell happened here?" the security guard wondered aloud, his voice unsteady with fear.

Cooper shook his head. He hadn't holstered his weapon. He gripped it tightly as he moved around the coupe to the passenger side. The door hung open, and so did the glove box. A box of ammo lay on the concrete next to some spent shells. And some more broken glass. The rear window was broken, and bullets had dented the trunk.

He looked again at the ground—looked for the blood he'd found around the SUV. The search must have distracted him, because he heard a gun cock—a gun too close to him. How the hell had someone gotten the jump on him?

He swung around, pointing his gun barrel behind him—into the pale face of his little sister. His breath shuddered out. "Are you all right?"

She nodded. But she was trembling. So badly that she nearly dropped her gun when she lowered it. "I'm sorry. I didn't know it was you."

He didn't care that she'd pointed the gun at him. "Were you hit?" he asked.

Her curly hair was usually messy, but it nearly stood on end now—almost as if someone had pulled it. There was a red mark on her cheek that would undoubtedly become a bruise, and her sleeve had nearly been torn free of her jacket. She'd been in a hell of a fight.

Concern and anger both gripped him. He wanted to make sure she was okay even while he wanted to rip someone apart—whoever had hurt her.

"We need to get you to the ER." He holstered his weapon now and reached for her. He would carry her there—like he'd carried other soldiers from combat. Nikki looked like she'd been to war.

She stepped back and shook her head. "I'm okay," she said. But her voice cracked on the claim, and her brown eyes glistened as tears pooled. "Thanks to Nick."

Cooper tensed. That might have been the first time she'd referred to their half brother by his first name.

"Where's Nick?" he asked, and his voice cracked now as he remembered all the blood he'd found. Had that been Nick's blood?

Nikki shook her head. "I don't know…but I think he got hit."

The blood had been Nick's—at least some of it.

A tear slipped between her furiously blinking lashes and trailed down the red mark on her cheek. "We need to find him."

Depending on where he had been hit, they might not have much time to find him and get him help before it was too late.

Before Nick couldn't be saved…

Chapter 4

He was a dead man.

Nick had learned long ago that there was no honor among thieves. His own mother had turned on her former boss and lover and testified against him—to save herself from a prison sentence.

Nick had just witnessed that lack of honor again as one of the gunmen, with no regard for his injured partner, had jumped into his vehicle. Or was it the one they had stolen from Annalise earlier that day? The little SUV wasn't the older model sedan she'd had six months ago. But the Honda had an Illinois license plate. Maybe the men were from Illinois, too. Maybe they had followed her to Michigan.

But why? Why would anyone want to harm sweet Annalise?

Nick intended to find out. But the man sped off in

the little SUV, leaving his partner behind. His concern was only for himself. Nick had pursued the vehicle first, running after it as it careened around the corners of the parking structure. He'd fired shots into the rear window, taking out the glass like the gunman had taken the glass out of his SUV, when they'd fired at him through it.

And Nikki...

Rage gripped him as he remembered what he'd stumbled upon when he had headed toward his vehicle. The fight. Those men had hurt Nikki. They had pulled her hair, punched her face. She'd fought. His sister was a hell of a fighter. She had punched back. She had kicked. She had pulled moves he hadn't known she knew. But she'd been outnumbered...

The rage kept him from reacting to his gunshot wound—from one of the bullets fired through the broken window of his SUV. He'd felt the sting of it and could feel the blood oozing from his torn flesh to soak his shirt. But he ignored the pain to pursue the vehicle—until it was clear he wouldn't catch it. The engine revved as it pulled out of the parking garage and onto the street. Horns honked as other vehicles nearly crashed into it. The Honda sped off. One of the gunmen had gotten away.

The other man couldn't.

He had been hit. Nick wasn't sure which one of them had fired the shot, him or Nikki. As well as a good fighter, she was a good shot. If she wasn't, the men might have abducted Annalise outside Payne Protection. Was that why they had come to the hospital parking garage? Had they been determined to try again?

But if they'd been after Annalise, why had they been attacking Nikki? Why had they been standing beside Nick's government-issue SUV?

Who the hell was their real target?

Nikki?

Her coupe had been parked near his SUV—near enough that she had been able to go for her gun. If she hadn't, he might not have survived the onslaught of ammunition the other men had fired at him. Sometimes she acted like she hated him, but she had helped him. Hell, she'd probably saved his life.

And instead of making certain she was okay, he had left her alone. Sure, the other gunman was injured. But he was still armed. He could hurt her.

Of course, the injured man had been running after his partner, too—until he'd seen Nick behind him. Then he had dived between some parked cars. Nick hurried back toward where he'd remembered losing him—between a Hummer and a Cadillac—in the reserved staff parking section.

It was easy to track him. All he had to do was follow the blood trail—the one that wasn't his. His blood was running down his arm and dripping from his fingertips. At least it was his right shoulder that had been hit, since he was left-handed.

He gripped his gun more tightly as he tracked the blood to where it turned from a trail to a pool. But he didn't need a weapon. He found the man leaning against the side of the Hummer. Deep gouges marred his face. Someone had scratched him. Nikki? Or Annalise? His eyes were open. So was his mouth.

But he wouldn't talk. He wouldn't answer any of Nick's many questions. He was dead.

Then Nick heard the telltale metallic click of another gun cocking—near his head. And he worried that he might be a dead man, too.

Annalise had loved Nick too long to lose him now. Not that she'd ever really had him. Even that one night…

They had made love. But he didn't love her. Not like she had always loved him. She couldn't remember a time that she hadn't been in love with Nicholas Rus.

"Where is he?" she asked Nikki.

Tears brimmed in her brown eyes. She shook her head and tousled her already tangled auburn curls around her pale face. "I don't know…"

Logan cursed.

Nikki flinched—either over his reaction or because she was in pain. She had obviously been roughed up. But she had refused medical attention for her injuries. She had rushed into the lobby instead—to fill in Logan on what had happened in the garage.

The men who'd stolen Annalise's car had come back. They had been waiting in the parking garage.

For her?

For Nikki?

For Nick?

Why? What did they want?

Annalise owned nothing of value to anyone but her. After all the times they'd broken into her home and her office and stolen her vehicle, they had to realize that she had nothing they wanted. So why wouldn't they leave her alone?

Unless it really wasn't her that they were after…

The trouble hadn't started for her until after Nick had

been to Chicago, until after that night they had made love in the house where he'd grown up.

"Nick chased them out of the parking garage. And I don't know how he could..." Nikki's voice cracked with emotion as she continued, "I think he was hit. I *know* he was hit."

"Hit?" Panic clenched Annalise's heart. "You think he was shot?"

Biting her lip, Nikki nodded. "He was bleeding. There was blood all over the cement." She shuddered. "But it didn't stop him."

Nothing stopped Nick from going after what he wanted. The son of a drug addict single mother—the odds had been against his making anything of his life. But he had accomplished everything he'd wanted. He'd joined the Marines, gone to college and earned a high position in the FBI. No, nothing stopped Nick.

"So he must not have been hurt badly," Nikki said as if she was trying to convince herself.

But his half sister didn't know Nick like Annalise did. She had no idea how determined—how single-minded—he could be.

"He needs medical attention," Annalise said. How long could he survive with a bullet in him? Even Nick had limits to what he could endure.

"Cooper will find him," Logan assured them.

Then he focused on his sister, and a muscle twitched in his cheek, above his tightly clenched jaw. Annalise recognized the telltale sign of stress and tension. She'd seen that same muscle twitch in Nick's cheek so many times. But she had seen him clench his jaw like that even when he hadn't been stressed or angry. She'd seen it when she'd hugged him. She had thought that was because he didn't like being touched.

But maybe her hugging him had stressed him out. Maybe he'd had to struggle for control of the passion she'd experienced the night they'd made a child together.

"And while Cooper is finding Nick," Logan said, "you're going to the emergency room to get checked out." When he took his sister's arm, she flinched. "Nikki, you are hurt!" And he swung her up in his arms as if she were a child.

Embarrassment flushed Nikki's face with color even brighter than the mark on her cheek. Annalise's heart swelled with concern and sympathy for the other woman. She understood what it was like to be underestimated—like Nikki's brothers obviously underestimated their little sister. She also understood what it was like to be hurt and need their comfort and protection. She could recognize that Nikki was torn between wanting to be a tough, independent woman and the little girl who needed her big brothers.

The wheelchair forgotten, Annalise hurried after the brother and sister as Logan carried Nikki back to the ER. Logan shouldered open the door marked No Admittance. There was no security guard to stop him. They were all in the parking garage—looking for Nick and the men who'd shot at Nikki and him.

Not just *at*.

Nick had taken a bullet. He was bleeding. He needed to be in the ER, too.

"I'm fine," Nikki said as she wriggled in Logan's arms. "I'm not the one who needs medical attention."

She was worried about Nick, too. But then, she'd been there. She knew how badly he'd been hurt.

"You shouldn't be back here," the doctor who'd treated Annalise agreed. "We have critically wounded coming in!"

"Critical?" Annalise uttered the word on a gasp of shock and pain.

A ding rang out, and doors to an elevator at the end of the hall opened. Two men—dressed in scrubs like the doctor—pushed out a gurney. A sheet covered the patient from head to toe.

She couldn't see the man's face. But his legs dangled from the end of the gurney. He was tall and broad. His shoulders hung over the sides.

Her heart pounded furiously with fear and dread. Nick was tall. Nick was broad. But it couldn't be Nick.

It couldn't be.

When he'd enlisted in the Marines, she had been so afraid that she would lose him. And when he'd joined the FBI...

He had been in so much danger so many times and had survived. Today he'd only been going down to the parking garage to retrieve his vehicle—for her. He shouldn't have been in danger there. Of course, she shouldn't have been in danger outside the Payne Protection Agency, either.

Her voice cracking, Nikki asked the question burning in Annalise's throat. "Is he dead?"

The medical professionals ignored her—until the doctor standing beside them asked, "Did you pronounce him?"

One of the doctors nodded.

"There was nothing we could do," the other one said. "He bled out before security cleared the parking garage for us to treat him."

Tears burned Annalise's eyes. Nick had bled to death while waiting for help?

She couldn't bear the thought that he had been alone and hurt. But then Nick was always alone. He insisted that was the way he'd wanted it. That was the reason he'd given for always pushing her away.

Nikki gasped, too, and the tears that had brimmed in her eyes spilled over. "No…"

They had been named for the same man. If they had anything else in common besides their names, they might not have pushed each other away. Now Nikki would never have the chance to connect with the brother she'd obviously resented.

And Annalise's baby would never get to meet his or her father—just as Nick had never had the chance to meet his. Horror and regret overwhelmed Annalise, making her legs tremble and threaten to fold beneath her. Before she could fall, though, strong arms closed around her, holding her up.

"Mrs. Payne?" a young woman asked. She stared across the desk at Penny, her dark eyes wide with concern. "Are you all right?"

She nodded and replied, "Of course."

She was anything but fine, though. Her heart had started pounding faster and harder, thumping inside her chest. She didn't want to betray her fear to the young bride, though. Megan Lynch was already too nervous about her pending nuptials. Too nervous to be getting married.

Penny held her tongue and her opinion. She had once been a nervous bride herself. Maybe, in the way that she somehow knew things, she'd known she would lose her husband too soon. There had been rewards for the pain she'd endured, though: her children.

Panic clenched her heart.

One of her children was hurt. She knew it. Even before the phone rang, she knew it. She had that tightness in her chest and that sick feeling in the pit of her stomach. She was often teased about being psychic. But she was no medium. She just had a very special connection with her children. Her feeling that one of them was hurt had never been wrong.

And it wasn't wrong now. Her hand shaking, she reached for the phone before it even started to ring. She skipped her usual greeting of "White Wedding Chapel. Penny Payne, wedding planner, speaking," and just said, "What is it?"

"Mom," Nikki spoke tentatively—almost fearfully.

"What is it?" Penny asked again.

"I'm fine," Nikki replied.

And Penny remembered the first long trip Nikki had taken with her new driver's license and the phone call she had received from her youngest and her only daughter shortly after Nikki had left. "Mom, I'm fine but…"

Then she'd dissolved into tears over the deer she'd struck and killed. That was partially why Logan had kept his sister behind a desk instead of assigning her fieldwork. She wasn't as tough as she acted. If she had to hurt anyone…

"But?" Penny asked. Nikki hadn't said the word this time, but she'd heard it in her voice.

"Mom…" And just as when she'd inadvertently killed the deer, Nikki broke into tears. Her sobs rattled the phone.

"You're fine," Penny reminded Nikki and herself. Her daughter wasn't hurt. But what about her sons?

Nikki drew in a deep breath. "Yeah, I'm fine. I'm fine." And now it sounded as if she was trying to convince herself.

"Who's not fine?" Penny asked.

Nikki's breath escaped in a ragged sigh. "Nick."

The panic already clenching her heart squeezed tighter. Nikki had never referred to her half brother by his first name. She usually never referred to him at all if she could help it. The fact that she was saying his name now—and with so much emotion…

Nicholas Rus wasn't one of Penny's children. She hadn't given birth to him like her sons and daughter. But she had that same connection with him that she had with every one of her biological children. Sometimes it felt even stronger than that connection—because of all her children, Nick was the most like her. Somehow they both instinctively knew what other people needed.

But about their own needs, they were clueless. Nick had no idea what he wanted or needed. And now he might never have the chance to figure it out.

Chapter 5

Nick's shoulder throbbed. Maybe he shouldn't have refused the painkillers the doctor had tried to push on him. But he needed a clear head now. He needed to focus. There were so many voices—all of them talking at the same time in the way that the Payne family conversed. Only he who spoke loudest was heard. Usually that was Logan—especially since they were in the dark-paneled conference room of the Payne Protection Agency and, as he was quick to remind the others, he was CEO.

But it was Penny Payne's soft voice that cut through the rest of them. "Quiet down," she said in that tone of hers that brooked no argument. That was how she had raised four kids on her own after her husband had been killed in the line of duty. "Nick is hurting."

"Then he should have stayed in the hospital like the doctor told him," Garek Kozminski said.

Nick snorted. "Like you ever followed a doctor's orders." A few months ago, Garek had checked himself out of the hospital with a hole in his leg. That was worse than a hole in the shoulder. At least Nick's gunshot wound had been a through-and-through.

"Like he ever follows anyone's orders," Logan murmured.

Garek flashed his brother-in-law-slash-boss a wide grin. That was how he and his brother Milek had become honorary Paynes; their sister had married Logan. "I get the job done."

Nick couldn't argue that. Garek had helped him bring down one of the most dangerous crime bosses in River City—hell, in the country.

"We need to get this job done now," Nick said. "We need to make sure Annalise is safe."

"And Nikki," Logan chimed in.

Garek's wife and fellow bodyguard—Candace—was still at the hospital with Annalise and Nikki. Annalise would have collapsed had Nick not caught her in the hallway of the ER. He hadn't even noticed his shoulder wound then. His concern had been only for her.

That concern clutched his heart now. But the doctor had convinced Annalise to let him monitor her for a while. And Candace was probably the best of the Payne Protection bodyguards. She wasn't alone, though. Because of the shooting in the parking garage, the police were involved. Nick had requested his best men—the ones he knew he could trust now—to back up Candace and make sure the man he'd let drive off didn't come back.

He silently cursed himself for letting him get away. That guy had been alive and able to talk—unlike his partner, the man Annalise had mistaken for Nick lying on the gurney. Was that why she'd collapsed? Or had that been because of the concussion she'd sustained during the carjacking?

She and Nikki were also giving their statements to Nick's best detective and their descriptions of the man who'd gotten away. With all of River City's finest working the case, they would find him.

But that wasn't enough for Nick. He had to make sure Annalise and his half sister were safe. That was why he'd called this Payne family meeting. While he hadn't been to many of their meetings, it wasn't the first one he had attended, either. But those other times he'd been on the sidelines, just offering his opinion or his warning.

His warnings were probably why he wasn't often asked to the meetings. This one he'd called himself. He wasn't asking their opinions, though. He already knew what he had to do.

He hadn't expected Penny to invite herself along. But since she had silenced the others, he appreciated her input.

Then she added, "We also need to make sure Nick stays safe."

He swallowed a groan and assured her, "I'm fine."

"You lost a lot of blood," she reminded him of what the doctor had said when he'd argued against Nick leaving the hospital. She stepped closer and gently patted the side of his face as she always did her sons'. "I was afraid that we were going to lose you."

They had never really had him. But he didn't point that out—because he didn't want to hurt her feelings. She had done nothing to deserve the pain his mere existence had already caused her.

"It's going to take a lot more than a bullet to bring down Nick," Parker Payne said. He should have known. He'd survived being blown up.

She ignored Logan's twin, leaned forward and kissed Nick's cheek. "Promise me you'll be careful," she implored him.

Her sons groaned in sympathy. They knew what she was asking. For Nick—with Annalise in danger—it was the impossible. He shook his head.

"Nicholas," she murmured.

Logan came to his rescue. "Mom, we need to strategize."

She arched a reddish-brown brow and asked, "Are you throwing me out?"

Logan probably wouldn't dare. But he gently guided her toward the door of the Payne Protection Agency conference room. Their heads close, they whispered together, shooting glances back at him.

Uneasiness lifted the short hairs on the nape of Nick's neck. They were obviously talking about him. He knew it wasn't the first time he'd been the topic of Payne family conversations. But he suspected he wasn't the only one about whom they talked. He didn't want them talking about Annalise, speculating about what their relationship was.

Nikki had already figured it out, though. She knew he'd gotten Annalise pregnant—just like his dad had gotten his mother pregnant. He had never met the man, but Nikki was right: he was the most like him.

Everyone else talked about Nick Payne like he'd been a hero. But he hadn't been any hero to Nick. He'd abandoned him to the care of a drug addict.

Nick wanted to be a hero for his kid. But mostly he

wanted to be a hero for Annalise. When they'd been growing up, she had always acted like he was one—always looked at him like he was one. He'd let her down once already. He didn't want to let her down again.

Logan swallowed the sigh burning in his lungs. He'd made the promise to their mother that Nick had refused to make. After she walked out, he closed the door of the conference room and turned back toward the others.

He would make sure Nick was careful—that he didn't get hurt again. A twinge of panic struck his chest as he remembered the fear that Nick had been the one lying on that gurney, a sheet covering his face. Even when Nick had appeared next to him, holding up a faint Annalise, Logan hadn't been sure the guy would survive. Blood had been dripping from him, running down his arm from his blood-soaked shirt and coat.

He wore a scrub shirt now. Blood had seeped through the bandage and the shirt, though. The damn fool should have stayed in the hospital. But he was stubborn—more stubborn than Logan had ever realized.

"We've got this. We'll make sure Annalise and Nikki stay safe," he assured Nick.

Nick snorted. "You're crazy if you think I'm going to sit back and do nothing."

Logan had to acknowledge that he probably *was* crazy if he thought he could keep Nick away from the action. But he'd made a promise to their mother, so he had to try. He pointed out, "You have your hands full with the River City PD."

"I'm done," Nick said.

After he'd brought down the biggest crime boss in

Michigan—hell, probably the US—he had every reason
to believe that. But it hadn't stopped there.

"The corruption runs even deeper than you thought,"
Logan reminded him. "Every time you've thought you
caught them all, you've found more corrupt officials."

Milek grunted in acknowledgment. Nick had just arrested his wife's former coworker, an assistant district
attorney who'd taken bribes for dismissing charges.

"And that's probably what's put me in this situation," Nick said.

"What situation is that?" Garek asked the question.
"What's been going on, Nick?"

He sighed. "Not long after I took the assignment to
clean up River City PD, someone started breaking into
my place and ransacking it."

"That's why you've moved so often," Parker said.

"But they always find me again."

Frustration gnawed at Logan. Why hadn't Nick told
them what was going on? Because he hadn't been raised
like them—with them—he was used to handling everything alone.

But apparently he hadn't been completely alone. He'd
had the Huxtons.

"So you think whoever's going after you is going
after Annalise now?" Logan asked.

Nick didn't reply. His jaw was clenched too tightly,
so tightly that a muscle twitched in his cheek. But he
gave a sharp nod.

Whoever it was must have suspected he cared about
the young woman. She was Gage's sister. What was she
to Nick? The mother of his unborn child?

He wanted to ask. "Nick—"

"I'm done," he said again with a finality that chilled Logan's blood. "I'm going to quit."

"You would really quit your assignment?"

"Not just my assignment," Nick said. "I'd quit the bureau."

For Annalise?

She obviously meant a lot to him. Why had Nick never mentioned her before? But then, Nick had never shared a lot with them. He'd put his life on the line for them in the past, but he hadn't told them much of anything about his life.

"You don't have to quit your job," Logan said. But he wasn't certain he could reason with Nick. He wasn't just determined; he was mad. And despite everything they'd been through together in the past year, Logan didn't think he had ever seen Nick mad before.

"After bringing down Chekov, you could take over the whole damn bureau," Garek said. "You can't quit—not after making the coup of your career." Garek had nearly lost his life and the woman who was now his wife when they'd helped Nick take down Chekov.

"I don't give a damn about my career," Nick said.

It was clear he cared about only one thing—one person, actually. Annalise.

Logan stepped closer and assured him again, "We'll keep her safe for you."

Nick shook his head. "*I* will keep her safe."

"You're not a bodyguard."

"I should be," Nick said.

Logan couldn't argue that. As good an FBI agent as Nick was, he would make an awesome bodyguard, with his intuition and his protective instincts.

"I want to be," Nick said.

"Are you asking for a job?"

"Would you give me one?"

Logan would have loved nothing more. "On one condition."

"I don't care what you say," Nick said. "I won't be too distracted to protect Annalise. I'll be more focused and dedicated than any other bodyguard you have."

No other bodyguard present attempted to argue. They didn't doubt Nick. Not in this situation.

"I know," Logan said. "That's why your first assignment will be protecting Annalise."

"Then what's your condition?" Nick asked.

"That you work for my franchise," Logan said.

Cooper and Parker both cursed him. Getting Nick on either of their teams would have been a triumph.

Nick hesitated. "But your team…"

"It's the family team." Or what was left of the family since Cooper and Parker had started their own franchises and Nikki had gone with Cooper. Logan felt a pang in his chest that the family was divided. He had the Kozminskis, though. And Gage. And if Nick was foolish enough to give up his career with the FBI, Logan wanted him, too.

"But, Logan—" Nick was going to argue, like he always did, that he wasn't really family. But he was.

So Logan interrupted him. "Can you work for me, though?" It was a valid question. "You've been running the whole River City PD since you came to town. Is being a bodyguard going to be enough for you?"

"Keeping Annalise safe is all I care about," he said. "That's why I'm heading back to the hospital now." When he stood, he swayed on his feet.

Garek caught his uninjured shoulder. "You should check yourself back in."

"He should," Logan agreed. But they all knew he wouldn't. It was clear that Nick's only concern was for Annalise—not himself.

It wasn't until he left that Logan realized Nick hadn't answered his question. Would being a bodyguard be enough for him? But then, Nick probably wasn't thinking about the future. Hell, if he ran into another shootout like the one in the parking garage, he would be damn lucky if he survived the present.

Annalise leaned back in the passenger's seat of the black SUV and drew in a deep breath. She'd felt suffocated earlier. She wasn't used to people fussing over her. She wasn't the one who'd been in the parking garage. She hadn't been in a fight like Nikki, whose cheek had gone from red to purple. She hadn't been shot like Nick.

She shuddered as she remembered the blood soaked into his shirt and coat. She'd felt the clamminess of the blood through her clothes when he'd caught her in his arms. Despite his gunshot wound, he had stopped her from falling.

To the ground.

She'd fallen long before that moment in the ER. She'd fallen for him so long ago that she couldn't remember the exact moment when it had happened.

But she knew why. Because he was Nick.

Because he was strong and honorable and heroic. For the past six months, she had been doubting that and cursing him. Then he'd risked his life to rescue his sister. And then, even injured, he'd caught Annalise.

She'd had only that moment—seeing the dead man

on the gurney—when her knees had weakened. There had been no reason for them to whisk her back into a bed. No reason for them to keep her for monitoring.

When she'd finally convinced them of that, Nick was already gone. He'd checked himself out against doctor's orders. He was gone, just like he'd been the morning after they had made love in his mother's house.

"Will you take me home?" Annalise asked the female bodyguard. Candace Baker-Kozminski was an Amazon—tall and strong and intimidating. But she had fussed, too. And so had Nikki and the River City detective who'd taken her statement about the carjacking. They were all so concerned about her—making sure that answering questions and looking at mug shots wasn't too much stress for her to handle.

Candace glanced away from the traffic for just a moment to meet Annalise's gaze across the console of the black SUV she was driving. "Home?"

"Chicago."

"You can't be alone right now," Candace said.

"I don't think I have a concussion," she protested. The pain in her head was only a dull ache now.

"You can't be alone. You're in danger."

She shivered. She had been afraid before—over the break-ins and the previous car theft. But after they'd tried to pull her into the car, she couldn't deny it or pretend it was all a misunderstanding anymore. She *was* in danger.

"I can bring you home with me," Candace said. "Garek and I have a great security setup. You'd be safe. But I need to check in at Payne Protection first. See what the plan is."

"I haven't hired Payne Protection," Annalise said.

Candace chuckled. "You don't hire family."

"I'm not a Payne." And neither was Nick—at least, not legally.

Candace glanced over again, but at Annalise's belly—like she suspected that she carried one of them. "Your last name doesn't have to be Payne to be part of the family."

Annalise opened her mouth to argue, but Candace continued, "Your brother works for Payne Protection. And every bodyguard becomes part of the family."

She needed her brother. But Cooper was right. She couldn't risk upsetting Gage now. He had already been through too much. And if she tried going home alone and something happened to her...

She shuddered. She couldn't risk that for Gage or for her baby. She had to accept help from the Paynes.

"Okay," she agreed. "But can we stop somewhere first so I can pick up some things? I need clothes and toiletries." Her overnight bag had been stolen with her car.

Candace glanced into the rearview mirror and nodded. "I haven't noticed anyone following us. It should be safe." A few miles farther, she pulled into the parking lot of a department store. "This should have everything you need."

It wouldn't have Nick. She'd once thought he was everything she needed. But Nick would never be there for her the way she needed him. He could be physically present even when he was injured, but she doubted he would ever be emotionally available. He'd shut off his emotions long ago, when he was a kid.

And now he wasn't even physically around. He'd run

off, leaving her to the protection of the Paynes. At least she could trust them.

As she reached for the door handle, Candace cursed.

Annalise's hand trembled. She recognized the frustration and fear in that one word. "What?"

"I was wrong. We *were* being followed." And she reached for her gun.

Chapter 6

Whaat the hell had he agreed to? Sure, Nick wanted to work for Payne Protection. He had actually been thinking about it for a while—had been thinking about how bodyguards protected people. Nick usually just put them in danger.

Was that why someone was after Annalise? Was it his fault?

It had to be. Annalise was too sweet and honest to have angered anyone enough to go after her. But someone was after her.

He'd been too late getting back to the hospital. The Payne Protection SUV had already been pulling away from the lobby doors—with Annalise in the passenger seat and Candace driving. He'd pulled out behind them, but his hadn't been the only vehicle.

It wasn't Annalise's small SUV. That would have

been too conspicuous with its shot-out windows and bullet-ridden metal. That must have been ditched somewhere—for a rental with an Illinois plate. It was a nondescript sedan, something he might not have noticed if not for the plate and the fact that it stayed behind Candace's SUV.

Why hadn't she waited for him at the hospital?

Because Logan was giving the orders. *He* was the boss. Why the hell had Nick agreed to that?

He would do anything to keep Annalise safe...

He'd thought Candace would, too. But instead of heading toward the Payne Protection Agency, she pulled off into the parking lot of a busy department store. Maybe that was smart, though.

Whoever else was following her might not try anything here. But then, he and his partner hadn't hesitated to open fire in a hospital parking garage. What would stop him now?

Nick.

Maybe he was wrong. Maybe it was just a coincidence that it had an Illinois plate. But it wasn't a chance he was willing to take—not with Annalise's safety at stake. So he careened into the lot behind the car.

He'd had to ditch his shot-up SUV, too. It was probably good that Logan had hired him since he now had a Payne Protection company vehicle. It had more horsepower than even his government SUV had had. He pushed hard on the accelerator and headed toward the sedan.

Before he could ram it, shots rang out. But the bullets didn't strike his vehicle. They hit the glass of the SUV Candace drove, shattering the rear window.

Had Annalise been hit?

Rage coursing through him, he continued to drive straight toward the car. But as if the driver had finally noticed him, he gunned his engine. Nick could have chased the car as it sped from the lot. He didn't.

His heart was beating hard and fast with fear and dread. He had to make certain that Annalise was okay. She was his only focus—she and the child she carried.

Garek Kozminski's skin itched beneath his clothes that suddenly felt too tight, too constricting, like all the bars and bulletproof glass of the concrete fortress. He had been in prison before, a long time ago. And he'd vowed to his sister and to himself that he would never go back.

But he had been back—to visit his own father. And now he was visiting the man who'd tried to step into his father's place when Patek Kozminski had gone to prison. But like his father, Viktor Chekov had only wanted Garek to steal for him.

"Bring back memories?" Chekov asked as he settled onto a chair across the table from Garek in the visitor's area.

Too many memories. But Garek refused to admit that to the former crime boss—his former boss. He just grunted. "I didn't come here to get all sentimental with you," he said.

"Have you come to gloat?" Chekov asked. He looked older now than his fifty-five or sixty years. His hair was even grayer. His face was gray, too, and wrinkled. And he'd gotten thinner, his shoulders bowing as if he didn't have the strength to hold them straight anymore. Or as if he carried too heavy a weight on them.

Guilt?

He doubted Chekov had enough of a conscience to feel any guilt. To feel anything.

Except concern for his daughter. That was what had driven him to confess to all his crimes in order to reduce her sentence for the people she'd killed and had tried to kill.

"No gloating," Garek said. He couldn't believe he had once feared this man. But he'd been a kid then—afraid of what the crime boss would do to his younger brother and sister if he defied him. "No reason to gloat."

"You've gotten your revenge," Chekov said. "Doesn't it feel good?"

"Is that what this is about?" Garek asked. "Revenge?"

Viktor's dark eyes narrowed. "What are you talking about?"

"Revenge," Garek said. "You brought it up. Isn't that why you're going after Nicholas Rus?"

A gasp of surprise escaped Viktor's thin lips. "Nicholas? He's in danger?"

"It almost sounds like you care," Garek remarked. And the surprise was all his now.

"I like Nicholas," Chekov admitted. "He's one of the last honest lawmen."

"He's changed that," Garek said. "He's found other honest lawmen. He's cleaned up River City."

Chekov snorted. "I'd expect a naive remark like that from your brother, Milek. Not from you."

Milek was the sensitive one—the artist. No one had ever called Garek naive.

"Nicholas would never make such a naive remark," Chekov said. "*He* knows better. He knows there's no cleaning up corruption. Men will always be greedy for money. For power."

"What about revenge?" Garek asked, steering the conversation back where he wanted it. Motive. "Are men hungry for revenge?"

"Not just men," Chekov said.

Garek's pulse quickened. What was Viktor telling him? "Your daughter…"

"Is locked up in a psychiatric hospital where she can't hurt anyone," Chekov said.

Garek snorted now. "Just because people are locked up doesn't mean they don't have any ability to get things done on the outside."

Chekov uttered a dirty little chuckle. He was probably still ruling his crime empire from the inside despite Nick's best efforts to contain him. Then he shrugged. "*I* would not hurt Nicholas."

"There are plenty of other people who would like to, though," Garek surmised.

Chekov nodded. "I have no problem with Nicholas. He has kept his word to me. He's a man of honor."

That meant more to Chekov than anything else— that a man kept his word. If someone was after revenge against Nick, it wasn't Chekov.

"But some people don't respect honor like I do," he allowed.

"Who are these *some* people?" Garek asked. Not that he expected the mobster to give up names. Chekov was old-school. He would not narc on anyone else—even if he could have reduced his own sentence.

Predictably he shook his head. But then he added, "Tell Nicholas I hope that no harm comes to him."

"You know Nick," Garek said—because it was apparent that Chekov did. "He isn't worried about himself."

"I didn't think Nicholas had anyone else to worry about," Chekov said.

Neither had Garek...until he'd heard about Annalise Huxton. His wife had met the pregnant young woman. Was she carrying Nick's baby?

And even more important, was she in danger because of Nick?

Annalise studied the house. It had a stockade fence around it and bars on the windows. This was where Nick had been staying in River City? Where her brother had been staying with him?

Nick held open the front door for her to walk past him. He'd left Candace to file the police report at the department store parking lot while he'd brought Annalise back here.

She glanced around the stark living room. They had a leather couch and a chair, but both had been duct-taped back together. What had happened to them?

"Are you okay?" Nick asked the question again— just as he had when he'd pulled open the passenger side door of the shot-up SUV.

And just as then, she assured him, "Yes."

But that was only because Candace had pushed her down—below the windows. Otherwise she might have been hit. Glass from the back window had exploded throughout the vehicle and rained down onto the dash above Annalise's head.

She reached up to touch her hair. Nick's hand was already there, fingering through the tresses.

"There isn't any glass," he said as if he'd read her mind.

Sometimes she had wondered if he really *could* read minds. He seemed always to know what someone else was thinking or feeling. It was his own feelings that were hard to read—so hard that Annalise had occasionally wondered if he felt anything at all.

His hand moved from her hair to skim along her jaw. He tipped up her chin so that her gaze met his. He stared at her intently—as if he was trying really hard to read her mind now.

She shivered from his touch and because she knew he could see all. She had never been able to hide her thoughts or feelings. He had to have known that she loved him, that she had loved him for years. But she had finally realized love wasn't enough—not when it was on only one side.

"Were you going to tell me?" he asked.

Maybe he didn't know everything.

"About what?" she asked. Finally she summoned the willpower to step back, to step away from him. His hand fell to his side. But her face still tingled as if he was touching her yet. "My car being stolen before?"

"It wasn't just your car," he said.

She shook her head. "No, my office was broken into," she said. "My apartment, too."

That muscle twitched along his jaw. And he glanced around his place.

"Maybe if I had bars on the windows and a fence, it wouldn't have happened," she mused.

"Those don't keep everyone out," he murmured.

"Someone has broken in here, too?" she asked. And her pulse quickened even more than it already had from his touch. "Are we safe here?"

He nodded. "Gage put up the bars."

"So he didn't feel safe here?"

He sighed. "I don't know if Gage will feel safe anywhere ever again."

She shuddered. What had her brother been through? "Has he talked to you about what happened over there? Where he was those months he was missing?"

Nick sighed again. "He hasn't talked much."

Nick had been over there, too. He had never talked about it, either. But he was Nick. He rarely talked at all—at least, not about himself.

But Gage had once been so gregarious and charming. Even when he'd been missing, she hadn't believed she'd lost her brother. Now that he was back, she was worried that she might have lost the man she had known and loved.

"Seems like neither Huxton has been talking to me like they used to," Nick mused aloud.

"You haven't talked to me, either," she reminded him. Not since the night they'd made love. And he actually hadn't done much talking that night, either.

Kissing…

Touching…

Stroking…

She shivered again.

"You're cold." He picked up a plaid blanket from the duct-taped couch and wrapped it around her shoulders. But he didn't step back. His hands stayed, holding the blanket on her. "Or you're in shock." He peered into her eyes again. "Maybe you should go back to the hospital."

"I'm fine," she said irritably. "And I'm sick of everyone fussing."

"Good thing you didn't meet Mrs. Payne yet." A slight smile curved his lips, and affection warmed his blue eyes. "She fusses." But judging from his tone, he didn't seem to mind it.

Of course, Nick had never had anyone fuss over him except Annalise…

He'd hated it when she'd done it. He'd called her a nuisance and a pest. He'd told her to get a life. They had been kids at the time. But his words had still stung because she'd loved him so much—even then.

"I won't be here long enough to meet her," Annalise said. "I need to go home tomorrow." She had a closing on a home she'd sold and a property management business to run.

His grasp on her shoulders tightened. "You need to stay here where you can be protected."

She didn't feel safe. Staring up into his face, she felt scared. "Nick…"

"You should have called," he said. "Or come to me."

"About the break-ins?"

Finally his hands moved from her shoulders. But they only slipped lower—down her body—to her belly. He cupped it in his palms. "You should have called me about getting pregnant."

The baby shifted beneath his hands as if she felt her daddy's touch. Tears stung Annalise's eyes. This was what she wanted. Nick and their baby. But it wasn't what he wanted, or he would have called her after the night they'd made love. He would have come back to see her.

She was just a pest to him, just the nuisance she'd always been when they were kids. Even more so now that she carried his baby.

But maybe he didn't have to know it was his. "Why would I have called you about that?" she asked.

"Because it's my baby." He said it as if he had no

doubt, as if it was a foregone conclusion. He hadn't looked that certain back at the hospital.

"Why would you think that?" Because she didn't want him to think that. She didn't want him to assume he had to take care of her because of the baby. She didn't want to be a responsibility that he resented.

"The doctor said you're twenty-four weeks along," he said. "It was twenty-four weeks ago."

She closed her eyes as images tumbled through her mind: Nick's blue eyes darkening with desire as he stared down at her. His arms rippling as he dragged his shirt over his head, baring his chest but for a dusting of dark hair over his sculpted pecs. He was so muscular. So handsome, so sexy...

And the way he'd touched her...

The way he'd kissed her...

Her heart pounded, and it was hard to draw a deep breath, hard to focus on anything but her desire for him to touch her again, to kiss her again.

She opened her eyes and his face was close, his head lowered to hers. Anticipating his kiss, she drew in a quick gasp of air.

But he only stared at her—as if looking into her soul. "Are you telling me it's not mine?"

She flinched as the baby kicked her ribs, as if in protest. She couldn't lie to anyone, let alone Nick, and not about this. "I don't—"

The muscle twitched in his cheek as he tightly clenched his jaw. But somehow he managed to ask, "Is there someone else, Annalise?"

Because of him, there had never been anyone else. Even knowing now that he would never return her feelings, she doubted there would ever be anyone else. Like

Nick knew everything, he had to know that. So she began, "Of course—"

But then her cell phone rang. At least that hadn't been in her car when they'd stolen it. It was in her purse. She fumbled inside for it, mumbling, "That's him."

Nick tensed. "Him?"

She nearly laughed at the expression on his face— the utter shock. He thought another man was calling her and that man was the father of her unborn child. Maybe Nick didn't know her as well as she'd thought he did.

She held the phone out to him. "I can't answer it," she said. "I can't talk to him right now." Because Gage would hear it in her voice, the fear that hadn't left her since the man had tried to pull her into the backseat of her vehicle. And she didn't want him to worry.

He had enough problems of his own—more than she'd realized.

"What do you want me to do?" Nick asked.

"Talk to him." He was probably the only one who could. She pressed the green circle to accept the call.

But Nick just stared at her. Maybe she was imagining it, but she thought she saw more than shock in his blue eyes. She thought she saw disappointment. And maybe hurt...

Chapter 7

Did he know Annalise at all? She had grown up next door to him—from a chubby-cheeked little girl to an awkward adolescent. But when he'd left, he had still been a teen himself. He hadn't been there when she had matured from teenager to woman. He didn't know how many boyfriends she'd had or apparently still had.

He wasn't her boyfriend, though. He'd been only a one-night stand. And this guy...

He must be her boyfriend. So why had she handed Nick the phone? Why did she want him to talk to him?

Was this who'd been threatening her? A jealous boyfriend? An obsessed ex? Maybe this guy had found out about the night she'd spent with Nick, and he'd started stalking her.

If Annalise had been any other woman, he would have considered that option first. But she was Annalise. And he couldn't imagine her with anyone else. He couldn't imagine her with anyone but him.

And he kept imagining that.

Her silky blond hair spread across the pillow as she stared up at him, her face flushed with passion. Her already full lips swollen from his kisses. Her arms and legs clinging to his body as he moved inside her.

"Annalise!" a male voice shouted her name.

And Nick realized who'd called her. "Gage?"

"Nick? What the hell are you doing with Annalise's phone?" her brother asked.

He'd been wondering that himself—until now. Now he realized that Annalise hadn't wanted to worry her brother, and she'd thought she might give away something if she talked to him.

"She's here, of course," Nick replied.

"At our place?" Gage asked. Then his curse rattled the phone. "I thought she might show up after I sent that email. That's why I called."

"You've owed her a call for a while," Nick admonished him. But Gage hadn't wanted to worry Annalise any more than she wanted to worry him now. The Huxtons were like the Paynes in how unselfishly they loved each other.

"Then why did you answer the phone instead of her?" Gage asked, his voice even gruffer than usual with suspicion.

Annalise's face paled, and she shook her head. She wasn't a liar. So she couldn't come up with an excuse on the spot. That was why she'd handed Nick the phone: to lie.

"She's…"

What the hell would Annalise be doing if she'd come up for a regular visit?

"She's cooking," he said. She had made a habit of coming over to Gage's and cooking for him when he'd worked for the Bureau. Nick had always been invited over, as well. Maybe that was why he hadn't considered that she could have another guy. She'd always had time for her brother.

And him.

She'd never dragged a boyfriend along. Nick's stomach tensed at the thought of Annalise with another man—the way she'd been with him.

How she'd clung to him and moved beneath him.

The way she'd shuddered and screamed as she...

"What's she cooking?" Gage asked wistfully.

Sweat beaded on his upper lip. She was cooking him—scorching him with just the memory of her passion. "I don't know."

Gage chuckled, and his voice wasn't as rusty-sounding as it had been. "She won't let you in the kitchen?"

"You're the one she doesn't let in the kitchen," Nick reminded him. Gage had no domestic abilities whatsoever. Their mom had been a real mom—like Penny Payne—who'd enjoyed taking care of her family. Gage never had to fend for himself or starve like Nick had.

Nick knew his way around the kitchen. So Annalise used to let him help. But she'd always stood too close, always touched him too much.

Even her innocent touches—her hand on his back as she leaned around him to grab a utensil, her hip bumping his as she dried the dishes he'd washed—had affected him. Made his body tense and needy.

But he'd denied what he had been feeling for her, had denied that need—until six months ago.

"I wish I was there," Gage murmured. He missed his sister.

Nick could understand. He'd missed her, too, so badly, the past six months. His gaze moved down her body to the swell of her pregnant belly. He'd had no idea.

"I thought you weren't ready to see her," Nick said. Annalise flinched.

Gage's sigh rattled the phone. "I didn't think I was."

But he was changing his mind. And Nick couldn't have that yet. He couldn't let Gage come home too soon, before he'd had a chance to explain what had happened that night when he'd lost all control.

Hell, it didn't matter what excuse he used. Gage wouldn't understand. He lived by a code, and Nick had violated that code when he'd crossed the line with Annalise.

"Be sure you're ready before you see her," Nick advised.

Gage sighed again. "You're right. I don't want to worry her."

And she didn't want to worry him. "So you don't want to talk to her?"

Annalise shook her head, tumbling her blond hair around her thin shoulders. As if worried that he might hand the phone to her, like she had him, she stepped back.

"Not yet," Gage said. "Just tell her I called, okay?"

"Of course." He clicked off the phone before Gage could say more—before he could inadvertently make Nick feel worse about keeping so much from him. He should already have told him about that night. And now there was so much more he didn't know—about the danger or the baby.

Nick wasn't sure he knew about the baby, either. So the minute he clicked off the phone, he asked, "Is it mine?"

Hurt flashed in her green eyes. "Of course..."

Of course. She was Annalise. She was too good-hearted, too sweet to have cheated on another man with him. Or was he being a fool, thinking only of the girl she had been instead of the woman she might have become?

He had to know. He had to ask. "Was or is there anyone else?"

Her face flushed, but it wasn't like that night—it wasn't with passion. Maybe embarrassment. Maybe anger. She didn't answer him. She only shook her head.

He reached out and skimmed his fingers over the side of her head, where she'd hit it on the asphalt. "All this—the break-ins, the car thefts—couldn't a jealous ex be behind it?"

He could understand a man not wanting to give her up once he'd had her. It had taken all Nick's willpower to stay away from her the past six months—to avoid going back to Chicago to be with her again.

And again...

She laughed as if the thought was ridiculous. But then, she'd never known how special she was—how beautiful.

Maybe when she looked in the mirror, she still saw that little girl with the chubby cheeks or the adolescent with the pimples. Maybe she didn't see herself the way Nick and every other red-blooded male saw her.

"You can't tell me there was no one else." Not as beautiful as she was, as sensual. The way she'd made love to him.

Her eyes narrowed. "You think I sleep around?"

"You were trying to make me think your baby might not be mine," he reminded her. "Why?"

"I—I didn't want to trap you into anything."

"So you were never going to tell me?" Maybe she wasn't the Annalise he'd thought she was. Maybe she was as selfish and deceptive as his mother had been when she hadn't told Officer Payne that she'd gotten pregnant with his child.

Pain gripped Nick, squeezing his heart in a tight vise. He'd thought Annalise was different. He couldn't trust her any more than he'd been able to trust anyone else.

Her mouth was open as if she was trying to form an answer to his question. Before she could say anything, he shook his head. "I need to check outside," he said, already heading toward the door, "and make sure nobody followed us."

Nobody had. He'd made damn certain of that. Being inside with her was more dangerous than anything he'd find outside. She had just hurt him more than anyone else could have.

Gage stared down at the dark screen of his cell phone. "What the hell's going on?"

He wouldn't have survived to twenty-eight—not with the life he'd led—if he couldn't trust his instincts. And his instincts were telling him something was wrong— really wrong.

It wasn't his current assignment. That couldn't have been any less dangerous than it was. The only threat to the client he had been assigned to protect was in the elderly lady's mind. Probably the onset of Alzheimer's disease. One of his grandmothers had had it. He remembered her paranoia that someone had been stealing her clothes—like anyone else would have wanted to wear the polyester pantsuits that had gone out of style decades before.

Like his grandmother, Mrs. Toliver could have used a nurse, not a bodyguard. He wasn't needed here.

But he suspected he was needed at home—with Annalise. He wasn't surprised that she'd come to see him. He was surprised she hadn't come earlier. And why hadn't she taken his call?

He couldn't believe she hadn't had her phone with her in the kitchen. As a real estate agent and property manager, she said she couldn't afford to miss any calls and lose a client. Why had she missed his call?

And Nick…

He'd been acting strange since Gage had come back. At first he'd just thought he'd surprised him—with being alive and all. Everyone had given Gage up for dead months before.

But Annalise…

She was too optimistic ever to let herself think the worst. Just like she'd always thought she would have a chance with Nick someday. Knowing Nick and how he would never see Annalise as anything but a pest, Gage had told her to give it up. He wished she had listened to him, because now he understood what it was like to love someone and not have that love returned. It hurt like hell. Worse than anything he'd suffered in Afghanistan.

No, it didn't matter where he was. He wasn't safe. Not from those feelings. And he certainly wasn't safe back at the place he was staying with Nick. Someone kept breaking in. Someone was after Nick besides Annalise, for once.

She shouldn't have been there. Shouldn't have been where she might get hurt because of Nick. Gage turned on his cell again and considered hitting Redial. Maybe this time she would answer. But knowing his sister, she wouldn't listen. She never listened to him when it came to Nick.

So he scrolled down to another number and hit that. It was after office hours, but Logan answered right away—almost as if he'd been waiting for Gage's call.

He updated his boss about Mrs. Toliver and concluded, "I'm not needed here."

"I'll let her family know," Logan said.

"So I can come home soon?"

"Are you ready?" Logan asked. There was something in his tone, something that had been in Nick's, too. A caution. Everyone had been cautious of him at first— like they thought he might lose it at any second. They had no idea the control he'd had to learn. He wasn't about to lose it. But now—along with the caution— there was an evasiveness. They were keeping something from him.

And he'd had it. He wasn't losing control; he was losing patience. He didn't need protecting.

"What's going on?" he asked. His instincts were right. He was needed at home.

Annalise's nerves were frayed, and as always when she was nervous, she talked too much. "I could have had someone else drive me."

She'd wanted to—but Nick had refused with just a

shake of his head. He had never been much of a talker, but he'd taken his reticence to another level. Since the night before—since Gage's call—he'd been giving her the silent treatment.

It was going to be a long three-hour drive to Chicago. "I really couldn't postpone the closing," she said. "It's already been postponed a couple of times because of issues with the property that had to be fixed before the bank would give my client financing."

He glanced away from the rearview mirror to meet her gaze. "Are you talking about Carla's house?"

"Your mom's?" He'd never called her Mom or Mother. Just Carla. The woman had never been much of a mother, though.

He nodded.

"If I'd sold hers, you would have to be at the closing, too," she said. That was why she hadn't listed it for sale. She hadn't wanted to see Nick again—unless he'd wanted to see her. But he hadn't even called.

A pang struck her heart, and a little foot struck her ribs. Their baby was active.

"Did you burn it down?" Nick asked—hopefully.

She shook her head. "I rented it." Which had been unusual.

The tenant had paid an entire year's rent in cash, but she didn't think he had even moved in. He hadn't switched any of the utilities to his name. And the number he'd given her was no longer connected.

Weird.

So many odd things had been happening. The strangest had been Nick making love with her that night six months ago. She had given up hope that he would ever be attracted to her. But she must have caught him in a weak moment.

She would have liked to give herself a similar excuse. But she never needed an excuse to want Nick. Even now.

She couldn't stop staring at him—at his strong hands gripping the steering wheel. She remembered how they had looked moving over her body, cupping her breasts…

Her nipples tightened as she remembered his thumbs sliding over them. His thigh shifted as he pressed on the accelerator, the muscles moving beneath his black pants. And she remembered how they had moved as he'd thrust his hips.

Her body began to throb as desire overwhelmed her. Before, she'd had only her girlish fantasies of what it would be like to make love with Nick, of how it would feel. Now she knew.

Nick wasn't looking at her, though. He was totally focused on the street as he weaved between cars. His attention was divided only when he glanced into the rearview mirror. And he kept doing that.

Annalise's stomach lurched—not from his driving but from fear. Even before he said the words, she knew.

"We're being followed."

Would the men never give up? Would they keep coming after her?

And why?

Chapter 8

Damn it...

Nick had been certain he hadn't been followed the night before. So where the hell had the tail come from?

How had they found them?

Or had they already known where he was?

With Annalise in the SUV, he didn't want to drive too fast—too recklessly. But he either had to lose the tail or...

But that would be even more dangerous—doubling back—catching him. He would be armed, as he'd been in the hospital parking garage and department store lot. He would fire more bullets. And maybe this time he wouldn't miss Annalise.

Nick's shoulder throbbed. The bandage, stiff with dried blood, pulled at the stitches beneath it. He would have blamed the wound for keeping him awake last night. Or the danger.

He'd sat up on the couch, his gun nearby, just in case he'd needed it. But he wouldn't have been able to sleep even if there was no threat. No injury. He wouldn't have been able to sleep because Annalise was in the house. And his body had throbbed in a place other than his shoulder. It had throbbed with desire, with need.

He couldn't be distracted, though, not with her safety at stake. Hers and their baby's. But would they ever be safe until whoever was after them was caught?

He jerked the wheel to do a quick lane switch. Then, at the last moment, he took a sharp turn. He hadn't lived in River City all of his life, but he'd been there long enough that he knew it well. He knew the back alleys and the side streets and the deserted areas of the city where the economy had yet to rebound.

Maybe that was his fault. He'd shut down so much of the corruption that some areas weren't doing the business they once had. There weren't as many street corner drug dealers or prostitutes. Whoever was after him might think it was his fault, too. They might blame him for their business not doing as well. And they wanted to shut him down.

Why go after Annalise?

Had they followed him that night to Chicago—to her? When he had spent the night with her, maybe they'd thought she meant more to him, more than he was willing to admit she did.

He focused again—on the street and the rearview mirror. The black vehicle was back there yet. And because it had nearly lost him, it was going faster, making the tail more conspicuous.

They were definitely being followed. He took another sharp turn and another.

Annalise gripped the passenger door and the console.

"Are you okay?" he asked. Was he endangering her? Or the baby?

She nodded. "Did you lose him yet?"

"No."

"He's that good?"

"He is." And realization dawned. He knew who was behind him. He pulled over into a dead-end alley and stopped the SUV.

Annalise glanced fearfully around. "What are you doing?" Her green eyes widened as the other vehicle pulled into the alley behind them. "We're trapped."

He shook his head, even as he drew his weapon. He didn't think he would need it, but he had learned to take no chances. Except for that night.

The night he'd gotten Annalise pregnant.

He reached for the driver's door handle. But before he could push it open, Annalise clutched his arm. "Nick!"

"It's okay," he told her. But it wasn't. He stepped out, walked back to the other vehicle and pounded on the driver's window.

It rolled down, and the blond-haired bodyguard leaned out. "How the hell did you make me?"

"You're not that good," he said.

Milek Kozminski chuckled. "I'm the best."

"I made you," he reminded him.

And color flushed Milek's face. "You wouldn't have if it hadn't been for the other car."

"Someone else was following me?" Panic clutched his heart, and he tightened his grasp on his gun and glanced around the alley. But there were only rusted dumpsters and their two vehicles.

Nobody else.

"You lost that tail easily," Milek said.

At least there was that. "That's good."

"You shouldn't have been trying to lose me," Milek admonished him.

"I didn't know for certain it was you." Not at first, anyway.

Milek sighed. "You know how this works."

"This?"

"Payne Protection," Milek said. "We have each other's backs. No man—or woman—is left alone in danger." Milek would know that. His family had protected him even when he hadn't wanted their protection.

Now Nick could understand Milek's irritation with his fellow bodyguards. "It's *my* job to protect Annalise."

"And it's my job to protect you," Milek said.

"I don't need any protection," Nick said.

Milek pointed toward his wounded shoulder. "You've already been shot. Of course you need protection."

"I've been taking care of myself for thirty-one years," he reminded Milek.

Milek pointed toward the SUV Nick had left idling. "Now you have someone else to worry about."

He couldn't deny that he was worried. "I'll protect her, too."

"How?" Milek asked. "By going off alone without letting anyone know you were leaving?"

Nick wasn't used to having to answer to anyone. For the past year, he'd been the boss. His bureau chief in Chicago had given him full autonomy. Chief Lynch trusted him; the Paynes should, too.

"Where were you going?" Milek asked.

"Chicago."

Milek shook his head. "No. It's too dangerous."

Nick had tried to tell Annalise that. But she'd been determined to go to her closing, to check in on the property management business she ran. And it was Annalise.

He'd always struggled to tell her no. But he had, until that night six months ago.

That night had changed so much.

"Logan won't approve it," Milek said. "And you agreed you're working for him."

Nick sighed and holstered his weapon. "Fine. I'll bring her back to my place."

But that was dangerous, too. Not because of someone finding them there. It was dangerous for Nick to be alone with her. He wanted her too much....

Something was going on with Nick—something that Milek recognized. The internal struggle.

It was more painful than a physical one. He wanted to help. But Nick had to conquer his inner demons on his own. Milek could help him fight only the outer ones. So he followed him again—back to his place.

He had trusted that Nick would go back to his rental house in River City. The FBI special agent had realized it was too dangerous to go to Chicago. So why had he been going? Had he been seeking out his contacts there—the agents he'd worked with out of the Chicago Bureau?

Milek had met most of them, had worked protection duty at a couple of their weddings. They were good guys. But they weren't Payne Protection bodyguards. No one would guard Nick more faithfully than family.

And to Milek, Nick was family. They didn't share blood like Nick did with the Paynes. But Milek owed Nick his life and, more important, the lives of his family. Nick had protected the woman Milek loved and their son. He would do the same for Nick now.

He pulled to the curb behind the black SUV as he had in the alley. But Nick didn't jump right out like he had back there. Instead, he idled at the curb for a while. Long enough that Milek exited his vehicle and hurried up to Nick's side.

The window was already down, Nick's weapon already drawn. Milek drew his as he glanced toward the house. Then he saw what Nick had; the front door stood open. They hadn't left that long ago—less than an hour. It was possible that whoever had broken in was still inside. If they had broken in to get to Nick and Annalise, it was probable they were still inside—waiting for their return.

"I'll check it out," he said.

Nick shook his head. "I will."

"We can't leave her out here alone," Milek said as he glanced around. Other vehicles were parked along the street. Someone could have been ducked down low in one of them, waiting for the opportunity to get Annalise.

"No, we can't," Nick readily agreed. "That's why you're staying with her."

"But I'm assigned to protect *you*," Milek reminded him.

Nick snorted. "Like you never disregarded Logan's orders before."

He had. But it had nearly cost him his life.

"It's too dangerous for you to go in alone," Milek said. He reached for the transmitter on his collar. Thanks to Nikki's computer savvy, they had the same high-tech gadgets the FBI had. "Let me call in backup."

Nick opened the door. "I already waited too long," he said. "If we wait any longer, they'll be gone."

Annalise leaned across the console, her hand extended toward Nick. "Don't go," she implored him. "It's too dangerous."

Milek heartily agreed. But he knew it was pointless to argue with Nicholas Rus. He'd never known a more determined or stubborn or fearless man.

Until Nick turned back to him.

There was fear in his eyes. But it wasn't for himself. Flinching as he lifted his right hand, he clasped Milek's shoulder. Despite the wound to his own shoulder, his grasp was tight—like that of his left hand on his gun. "Protect her," he ordered Milek.

It was an order he couldn't disobey. He nodded. Then he watched as Nick hurried off toward the house and that open door. It was all he could do not to follow him, simply to watch as he disappeared inside.

He lifted his hand and flipped the transmitter on his collar. "Nick's house has been broken into," he reported.

"Are he and the subject inside?" a voice asked. It wasn't Nikki. It was whoever Logan had hired to replace her as the computer guru for his division of Payne Protection.

"Annalise is with him. Nick went inside alone."

"What the hell is Nick doing?" Logan's voice emanated from the radio now.

"He's evaluating the threat," Milek said. But that was his job—the job Nick had refused to let him do.

"He's going to get himself killed," Logan said.

Milek hoped like hell that the boss wasn't right.

Annalise didn't know the man who now sat in Nick's place in the driver's seat. But she reached across the console and grasped his arm. "Please," she said. "Go in and help him!"

He shook his head. "I can't."

Because he thought he had to protect her. She was the subject, according to the first voice that had come through the radio on his collar. She was the client even though she had yet to pay anyone. In her business, the client was always right.

"You have to help him," she said as she stared through the windshield at the house.

Nick had left the door open, like he'd found it. Or maybe because it was broken. It swung strangely from the hinges as a breeze kicked up.

Despite that it was spring, that breeze blew through the open window and chilled her. She shivered.

Milek moved his hand toward the power button to roll it up. But she clutched his arm harder. "No," she said. "Leave it open."

Not that they could hear anything. The house sat back far enough from the street that they could hear no sounds emanating from it. The blinds were drawn, too, so they could see no movement inside.

"Logan's right." At least, she assumed it had been Logan whose voice had come second through the radio. "Nick's going to get himself killed."

He had already been shot. He was in no condition to take on—alone—whoever had broken into his house. There could have been one man or two or more.

She shivered again.

"He's armed," the blond bodyguard said. "And he's a damn good shot."

And just as he made that pronouncement, a shot rang

out. But they didn't know whether Nick had fired it. Instead it could have been fired at him.

She screamed and reached for the passenger door. But the man held her back.

"It's too dangerous."

That hadn't stopped Nick from going inside alone. And it wouldn't stop her. Tugging free of the man's grasp, she pushed open the door and ran for the house.

Ran for Nick...

Chapter 9

So much for the reinforced locks he'd bought. The door had been nearly ripped from the hinges. As he'd pushed past it, Nick had glanced around, but with all the blinds drawn inside, the house was dark.

So much for the bars on the windows and the stockade fence, too. They hadn't kept out his intruder. Who kept breaking in? And was he still there?

Grasping the Glock tightly, Nick moved through the house. Closets and cupboards stood open like the front door. Furniture had been tossed.

Too much destruction had been done for the intruder to be gone already. It would have taken too long to do all this and get away in the short time Nick and Annalise had been gone. The perpetrator had to be inside yet. And Nick heard the telltale thump of something moving.

Maybe it was only the back door. Maybe it had been

broken from the hinges like the front. But as he moved toward it, he located the noise—in the bedroom at the back. Gage had been staying in it, except for last night.

Last night Annalise had slept there while Nick had sat up tensely on the couch, his body aching for hers. She was outside now, safe with Milek. He had to believe that. Or he would be tempted to go back to check on her.

There could have been more men outside, waiting for him to leave her unprotected. But he hadn't left her unprotected. Milek might disobey Logan, but he wouldn't disobey Nick. He wouldn't endanger Annalise or the baby's safety.

So Nick reached for the door of that back bedroom. It wasn't closed tightly, so he only had to push it open slightly to see a dark clothed figure moving around in the shadows. Annalise's few things, the clothes Candace had gone inside the department store and purchased for her, had been thrown around the room. They lay across the hardwood floor and the unmade bed. It looked as if she hadn't slept any more than he had. But then, she was probably too afraid to rest.

And she had every reason to be.

He swung his gun barrel toward the figure and shouted, "Put your hands up! You're under arrest!"

He'd told Logan he was quitting the Bureau, but he hadn't given notice yet. So he still had his badge—his authority. His weapon…

And as the man catapulted toward him, he fired it. If a bullet struck the intruder, it didn't stop the huge guy. He kept coming at Nick and knocked him back against the hallway wall. His breath left his lungs at the force of the assault. And as his head struck the wall, black spots obscured his vision. He peered into the man's face, trying to get a good look so he could identify him.

Nick didn't think it was the guy from the parking garage. But it could have been. A big hand locked around his, fighting for the gun. He fired it again.

And finally the man loosened his grasp. Nick slid down the wall at his back. But he kept his weapon in his hand—waiting for the guy to come at him again. Instead the intruder turned and ran for the back door. Nick needed to get up—needed to chase him. To stop him.

To find out what the hell he wanted.

But he couldn't catch his breath, couldn't completely clear his vision yet. Then another shadow rushed toward him. He should have known the guy probably wasn't alone. There had been two in the parking garage. The one who'd died had probably been replaced with the man who'd just attacked him. This would be the second guy.

So Nick raised his gun. Just as his finger was about to squeeze the trigger, his vision cleared. He noticed the slight figure but for her belly. And the blond hair flowing behind her as she ran toward him.

"Annalise!" He shook in reaction—not from the fight but from the fact that he had pointed his weapon at the woman who carried his baby.

A shadow loomed behind her. He raised his gun higher and met Milek's gaze. "I'm sorry," his friend said. "She got away from me."

She hadn't been in danger outside. She'd been in danger with him. He could have shot her and their baby.

"Are you okay?" she asked. "We heard a shot!"

"No," he said as he finally regained his feet. "I'm not

okay." He was mad as hell. "What were you thinking to come running in here?"

The color drained from her face, leaving her pale but for the bright sheen of her green eyes. Her voice quavering, she murmured, "Nick..."

"Obviously you don't care about your life, or you wouldn't have tried to stop them from stealing your car yesterday, and you wouldn't have run toward the sound of a gunshot," he said. "At least care about the life of our baby!"

She flinched, and tears shimmered in her eyes. "I—I'm sorry."

He was the sorry one. He shouldn't have lashed out at her. He'd been scared. Scared that he'd nearly hurt her. And then he had.

Emotionally.

She was probably in more danger from him than from whoever had broken into his place. He was the one who kept hurting her. And he hated himself for it—probably as much as she was beginning to hate him.

She loved Nick. That was why she'd run toward the sound of the gunshot—because she had been scared that he was hurt. Or worse...

But he was right. She should have thought about their child—about the danger she was putting their baby in when she reacted without thinking. She would be more careful from now on. She wouldn't take any chances with her safety.

Or with her heart.

"You'll be safe here," Milek Kozminski assured her as he showed her into the master bedroom of the warehouse that had been converted into living space. It was all exposed brick and corrugated metal. "My brother and I installed the best security system we could find when I bought the place five years ago. We were barely able to crack it ourselves, so no one else will be able to."

"Is that part of your job?" she asked. "To make sure security systems are secure?"

His mouth curved into a slight grin. "It is now."

Apparently it hadn't always been his job. Was this his home or a property he rented out?

She glanced around. It was furnished yet somehow looked deserted, too, as if nobody had lived there for a while. "Are you going to stay here, too?" she asked.

He shook his head. "My wife and I moved out last month—when we got possession of the house we bought."

"Oh."

"We needed a yard for our son." He glanced down at her belly.

She didn't have to worry about a yard for a while. If Nick was right and she kept putting herself in danger, she wouldn't ever have to worry about a yard. She blinked back the sting of tears. She wouldn't cry. She hadn't back at Nick's place. And she wouldn't here. She was tougher than that.

But then Milek opened the bedroom door, and she heard Nick's deep voice, heard him telling Logan Payne, "You should give this assignment to someone else."

"You don't want to protect Annalise?" Logan asked him.

"I can't."

Milek whirled around as if his body could shield her from what she'd just heard. "You should lie down for a while," he said. "Rest."

She nodded although she knew she wouldn't be able to sleep. But she wanted him to leave her alone. She needed to be alone.

Actually, she needed her life back. She needed to be back at her job in Chicago—buying and selling houses, managing property. She knew what she was doing there. She didn't know what she was doing when people were trying to abduct her or shoot her.

She didn't know how to react—how to protect herself. It didn't even seem like it was really happening, like it was real at all. Why was *she* in danger?

Nick, she could understand. This was his life, the one she had been upset that he'd chosen when he joined the Marines and then the Bureau.

Milek had been gone only a few minutes when the doorknob rattled again. She quickly lay down on the king-size bed to pretend, at least, that she was resting. But she turned away from the door so he wouldn't see her face—her open eyes.

The mattress dipped as someone settled next to her. Surprised, she rolled over and discovered it was Nick who'd joined her. He was lying beside her as if they routinely shared a bed. They'd had only one night.

Her hand rubbed over her belly. One night had been enough, though.

"I thought you were leaving," she said.

"Why would you think that?"

"I heard you telling Logan to give this assignment to someone else," she said. To him, she would always be the pest he wanted to get rid of it. "You don't want to protect me."

He reached out, and his fingertips skimmed across her cheek, brushing back a lock of hair. "I can't."

"I'm sorry," she said. "It was stupid of me to run toward them when they were taking my car. And it was stupid of me to run into the house after we heard the shot."

His hand moved, his thumb sliding over her lower lip. "I'm sorry," he said. "I was too harsh with you."

"You were right, though," she acknowledged. "And I'll be more careful now. You won't have to worry about the baby."

"I'm worried about you," he said. "I almost shot you today." He shuddered, and the bed shook beneath his body.

She slid toward him until they touched. Her arm against his, her hip, her thigh.

Her breath caught as her pulse quickened. She hadn't been this close to him since that night. But that night, they had been even closer. No clothes had separated them. Nothing had as he'd filled her.

"That's why I don't think I can protect you," he said. "I'm so worried about you that I can't focus." He blinked as if he were struggling now. His lashes were so long and thick, so black like his hair. He kept that short, but it was soft. She remembered how soft it had felt that night beneath her fingers, against her breast and her thigh.

She shivered.

And as if he thought she was cold, he pulled her closer, wrapping his arm around her. Her body pressed tightly against his now. But they weren't close enough.

Not as close as she knew they could be.

"You're not just trying to get rid of me?" she asked. "Like you used to?"

He chuckled. "If I wanted to get rid of you, I would have pulled that trigger." But there was no amusement in his blue eyes—only something that looked like despair. "I came too close to doing that, to hurting you."

He had hurt her.

And as if he knew it, his arm tightened. "I'm sorry, Annalise."

"It was my fault," she said. "You were right. I keep putting myself and the baby in danger." Like now...

She should have been protecting herself—protecting her heart as it swelled in her chest, filling again with love for Nick. Love that he didn't want, just like he didn't want her.

"I think it's my fault you're in danger," he said. "Someone's after me, and they're using you to hurt me."

She must have been more tired than she'd realized. "How?"

"Hurting you would hurt me."

"Why?" she asked. "I don't mean anything to you."

His blue eyes widened in surprise. "You really believe that?"

She nodded. "I'm just a pest—"

Before she could say any more, his mouth covered hers. He kissed her gently at first, his lips just brushing across her lips. But then she gasped for the breath that had escaped her lungs. And he deepened the kiss.

What the hell was wrong with him?

Logan had no idea why he had refused Nick's resignation. Sure, he wanted the FBI special agent working for him. Nicholas Rus was one of the most brilliant men Logan had ever met; he was also strong, fearless and intense. And more intuitive than any other person Logan had met besides his mother. If Nick didn't think he could protect Annalise Huxton, Logan should have taken him at his word and removed him from the assignment.

"The condo is safe," Milek assured him.

Logan hadn't realized he'd been staring at it through the windshield of the SUV. From the passenger seat next to him, Milek studied it, too. Made of brick and metal and concrete, the place really was a fortress.

"Nobody can get in there unless Nick or Annalise lets him inside," Milek said, but it was as if he was trying to assure himself now.

The security system wasn't infallible. Logan's wife had breached it once. Sure, she'd set off the alarm, but she had made it inside. Stacy was a Kozminski, though.

"Well, nobody but Garek or I," Milek amended himself before adding, "And Stacy…"

Logan chuckled.

"And none of us poses a threat to Nick." The Kozminskis had once mistrusted lawmen and with good reason. A cop had framed their father for the murder of Logan's father. But they all trusted Nick. Because he was Nick.

None of them had met a more honest man. And Nick had said that he couldn't protect her.

Logan suspected his brother wasn't talking about physically. Even with a shoulder wound, Nick could take care of himself. It was in other ways that Nick thought he couldn't protect Annalise Huxton. The baby she carried had to be his.

He'd wanted to ask, but he worried that Nick would think he was prying. And he would shut them all out when he'd finally let them into his life.

Logan shook his head and focused on the real issue.

"Who does pose a threat to Nick?" he wondered

aloud. "Garek talked to Chekov. He doesn't think it's him."

"And Amber talked to Evelyn Reynolds," Milek said, his voice taking on the usual pride he had in his wife.

Nick had recently jailed the former district attorney for corruption. Evelyn Reynolds had every reason to want revenge against him.

"And?"

Milek shrugged. "Amber doesn't think Evelyn has the ability or resources anymore to go after anyone." He uttered a ragged sigh. "If she did, I think she'd go after Amber instead of Nick." Because Amber now had the job her former colleague had coveted.

Logan nodded. "So who is it?"

Milek shrugged again. "Nick made a lot of enemies in River City."

A lot of dangerous enemies.

"And who knows what he did in the FBI before he came here," Milek continued.

It must have been big to be given the assignment of cleaning up an entire police force. Finding who was after him could take a while.

Maybe even forever.

"I'll talk to his former colleagues," Milek offered.

"I already have a call in to Chief Lynch," Logan said. The Bureau boss would help—if he could.

Could anyone help Nick?

Maybe Nick was right. Maybe he couldn't protect Annalise. He was going to have his hands full protecting himself.

Chapter 10

Her lips were so soft, so silky beneath his. And her mouth…

He slipped his tongue into the heat and tasted the sweetness. Her tongue met his, shyly at first. And then she kissed him back. Her lips moved beneath his, and her teeth nipped, lightly grazing his tongue and his bottom lip.

Given her sweetness, her passion was a surprise. It had caught him off guard that night six months ago. It had severed his always tenuous hold on his control around her. And he'd forgotten who she was and who he was.

He'd acted only on the desire. That desire coursed through him now, heating his blood, making his heart pound furiously.

Making his body tense as need overwhelmed him. He slid his hands down her body, down the length of her back to the curve of her butt and hips. He wanted to bury himself inside her body—like he had that night. He had never felt anything as incredible as being inside Annalise.

Her hands were moving, too, from his hair down the nape of his neck to his shoulders. He flinched as she grazed over his wounded one.

She must have felt that flinch. "I'm sorry," she murmured. "I didn't mean to hurt you."

He knew that. Annalise would never deliberately hurt anyone. Or at least, he hadn't thought so. But she hadn't told him about the pregnancy. And that hurt.

It also worried him.

Could he trust her?

Or was she more like his mother than he ever would have guessed? He pulled back.

"Are you okay?" she asked anxiously. Her fingers touched the bandage on his shoulder. "Do you need to go to the hospital?"

He shook his head.

"The stitches might have gotten torn open when you fought with that man in your house," she said.

It hadn't been much of a fight. He hoped he had, at least, hit the son of a bitch with a bullet. He had his officers at the River City PD checking hospitals and clinics. When his cell vibrated, he hoped it was one of them. He pulled it from his pocket and glanced at the screen.

He didn't recognize the number, but he answered it anyway. It gave him an excuse to roll away from Annalise, to put some much needed distance between them. He sat up on the edge of the bed, his back to her.

"Special Agent Rus here," he murmured into the phone.

"Agent?" his sister remarked. He hadn't realized she'd had his number. But there wasn't anything Nikki Payne couldn't find out on her own. She was an expert computer hacker, probably because Logan had always kept her chained to a desk. "I didn't think you'd really quit."

He hadn't. Not yet. "I haven't had time to give my notice yet," he pointed out.

She actually chuckled. "And you don't want to give up the resources yet, either."

"No," he admitted. She was smart. Logan had probably lost his most valuable employee when she'd switched over to Cooper's team.

"Send your resources over to the alley behind Chekov's nightclub."

He cursed. "What will they find?" He hoped not another damn body. Even though the place had been shut down months ago, bad things continued to happen there. It continued to be a beacon for crime.

"Annalise's car," Nikki replied.

"How'd you find it?" Had she thought to look there, or had she been tipped off?

"Traffic cams."

"You hacked into them?"

She snorted. "What? You going to arrest me for hacking into River City PD?"

"I would have given you access if you'd asked," he said. "Thanks for finding the car."

"It's empty," she said with a weary-sounding sigh. "They must have taken her overnight bag. It's probably been wiped clean, too."

"I'll send over the crime lab to check," he said. "Just

in case." Ideally the men had missed something, like the seat lever or rearview mirror.

"Maybe the techs will find something," she said doubtfully.

She'd probably already checked those places for prints. She was resourceful. She was also stubborn.

"Does Logan know you're working the case?" he asked.

"I don't work for Logan anymore," she reminded him.

"He's still your brother," Nick said. "And he's not going to be happy if you put yourself in danger." Neither would Nick, especially if she was doing it for him. But why would she do that? She resented the hell out of him.

"I shouldn't have let them get away," she murmured.

He knew that feeling of guilt and responsibility. He deserved to feel like that, though. She didn't. "Nikki—"

"Call your crime lab," she said. And she clicked off before he could offer her any reassurances.

It wasn't as if she would listen to what he said, anyway—not when she never listened to Logan. And she actually loved that brother.

"She found my car?" Annalise asked.

He nodded but cautioned her, "It's probably a total loss. It got shot up in the hospital parking garage."

Her fingertips skimmed over his shoulder again. "So did you."

"Maybe I'm a total loss, too," he murmured.

"You weren't supposed to leave the hospital yet, not with all the blood you lost. And you could have been reinjured when that man attacked you in your house," she said. "You should go to the hospital to have them check your stitches."

"I can't leave you."

"The other bodyguards are here."

He shook his head. "They left." But knowing how Payne Protection worked, he doubted they had gone very far. He wasn't accustomed to or entirely comfortable with having all this support. Growing up an only child, he'd thought he would always be a loner. Sure, Gage had followed him around. And Annalise.

But he'd always known they weren't family, only neighbors who had pitied him. They'd had a loving, supportive family—unlike him.

But that was then. Everything had changed when his mother died and left him the letter telling who his father was. Everything but him.

He was still a loner. He still didn't know how to let people in. Not even Annalise.

Except for that one night. That night she had gotten closer than anyone else ever had to him. She'd touched something Nick hadn't even realized he had: a heart.

He was a total loss. Annalise knew it. Like her car, she needed to write off Nick and finally let go of her hope that they would ever be together.

Again.

They'd had that one night. And in a few months, they would have a child. Did Nick want to be a part of their baby's life? He had never wanted to be a part of hers.

Moments after his sister's phone call, he had slipped out of the bed and walked into the other room. She'd heard the rumble of his deep voice as he made calls. Probably to the crime lab. Maybe to his brothers.

He was keeping them apprised. She was the one who

felt in the dark. Not just about why someone was after her but also about Nick.

Despite knowing him almost her entire life, she doubted she would ever understand him. So she focused on her life again. She had calls of her own to make—apologizing to the client whose closing she'd missed. Checking in with her subcontractors for the property management business.

She had so many responsibilities. Movement fluttered inside her belly, reminding her of the greatest responsibility of them all. Her baby.

Nick's baby.

She had to delegate. Her career wasn't as important as her child. She handed out some assignments to her employees. Then she turned off her phone. She wouldn't worry about what was happening in Chicago. But without work to focus on, her mind went back to Nick. Her lips tingled yet from his kisses. She'd thought he'd wanted her again. And maybe he had, until she'd touched his wounded shoulder.

She glanced at her phone again. If she had Logan's number or Nikki's or Milek's, she would have called them—would have convinced them to get medical help for Nick. But she didn't know how to reach them.

She didn't know how to reach Nick, either. Doubting he would return to the bedroom, she opened the door and ran into his chest.

His hands gripped her shoulders, steadying her. "Are you okay?"

She nodded. "I'm fine. I just didn't expect you to be standing outside the door. Is that what a bodyguard does?"

He shrugged. "I wouldn't know. I haven't been a bodyguard very long."

She remembered what she'd overheard of his conversation with Logan and his sister. "You're really going to quit the Bureau?"

He nodded.

Shock gripped her. He loved his job. His enthusiasm for it had been the reason Gage had decided to become an FBI agent, too. "Why would you do that?"

"To keep you safe."

"I won't be in danger forever," she said. At least, she hoped she wouldn't be. "What will you do when I'm safe again?"

"I'll keep working for Logan," he said.

She doubted that. "I know why you're doing this," she said. "You feel responsible, that you put me in danger."

"I'm sure I did."

She didn't believe that. But she couldn't imagine what she would have done to put herself in danger, either. Despite his doubts the night before, she had no crazy exes. No one obsessed with her or wanting vengeance.

"It's not your fault," she said.

"It is if they're after me and they're using you to get to me."

"Why would they use me?" she asked. "Why would they think you cared about what might happen to me?"

He reached out, and his fingers skimmed over her belly. "They must have followed me that night I went to Chicago."

She shivered as she realized what they had observed—him going inside a house with her and not leaving until morning, after they'd made love for hours and hours.

"Why?" she asked, wondering why he hadn't pushed her away that night like he had every other time she'd hugged him.

He shrugged. "I wish I knew."

She suspected he didn't know what she'd really asked when he continued, "I've put away a lot of people. Someone must be after revenge."

And they were using her to get it. Or so he believed. She wasn't convinced.

But she wanted her real question—the one that had bothered her for the past six months—answered. "Why did you make love to me that night?"

He sucked in an audible breath. "Annalise…"

"You've pushed me away for years," she reminded him. "You didn't want me following you, touching you."

"You were a kid," he said.

"I haven't been a kid for seven years…" An adult was considered eighteen. That was how old he and Gage had been when they'd joined the Marines. "You have acted more annoyed with me as we've gotten older, more insistent that you don't want me hugging you."

He caught her hand in his and brought it down to the front of his pants. "This is why," he said as he rubbed her knuckles down the erection pushing against his fly. "Because every time you touch me, I react like this."

Hope swelled in her heart. His hand dropped away from hers, but she kept rubbing her fingers along his fly. Until he groaned.

"You're killing me."

She wasn't trying to—someone else was doing that.

She didn't want to hurt him. She wanted the same thing she'd always wanted from Nick—his love.

That was probably the lost cause. But even if she couldn't have his love, maybe she could have his desire.

She stepped back, through the open door of the master bedroom. Then she reached for him. Linking their hands, she tried to tug him inside with her.

He hesitated at the threshold, his gaze skimming down her face to her belly. "I can't."

"Nobody will get in the condo," she reminded him of what Milek had told her. "The security system is too high-tech. You don't have to worry about keeping me safe."

"Yes," he said. "But I worry about more than just you now." He touched her belly again. "I don't want to hurt the baby."

"You won't." Her doctor had assured her it was safe to have sex. Annalise had nearly laughed when the obstetrician had told her that. She hadn't thought she would get this close to Nick again. But she wasn't close enough.

Not yet…

She had felt the effect she had on Nick. Knowledge was power. She remembered what had driven him crazy that night—how he'd reacted to things she'd done, the sounds she'd made.

She stepped back again, closer to the bed. And she lifted her shirt. Pulling it over her head, she dropped it onto the floor. Her breasts were fuller than they'd been six months ago. They nearly spilled out of her lacy bra.

Nick's gaze was focused on them—so focused that her nipples tightened and pushed against the lace. She needed his touch. She needed him.

She pushed her pants down her hips and stepped out of them. She wore lace panties that matched the bra. They were her regular size. Her hips hadn't spread yet. Only her belly had swelled. She wasn't huge yet—not like the women she'd seen in her OB's office.

Nerves fluttered in her stomach, along with the baby's kicks. She wasn't looking forward to getting that big, to being that uncomfortable.

Maybe she was already too big, though. Maybe Nick didn't find her attractive anymore. Heat rushed to her face. And she leaned over to pick up her shirt from the floor. But before she could tug it on, it was pulled from her hand.

Nick tossed it aside as he reached for her. "You are so damn beautiful," he murmured as if the words were wrenched from him.

He wasn't staring at her body, though. He was staring into her eyes. His hands cupped her face, and he leaned down to kiss her. His mouth covered hers, and he kissed her deeply, passionately. His tongue slipped between her lips.

She gasped at the sensations racing through her. She wanted him even more than she had the last time—because now she knew how incredible it could be between them. Her girlish fantasies hadn't even come close to the reality. To how incredible they were together.

He kept kissing her. But he touched her, too. One fingertip traced down her spine before his hands cupped her hips. He dragged her closer to him. And she could feel the hardness of his erection.

She reached between them for the button on his pants. But she fumbled with it. So he moved her hand aside and pulled the button free. Then he lowered his zipper. He kicked off his pants. Stepping back, he removed his holster and put it and the gun on the bedside table. He pulled his shirt up over his head.

Heat flushed her body at the sight of his chest and arms—all bare skin and rippling muscles. Her gaze lowered, tracing his washboard abs. His erection had pushed up out of the waistband of his boxers. The tip of it begged for her touch.

She obliged.

He groaned as her fingers closed around him. She pushed his shorts down and slid her hand up and down his shaft.

"Annalise…" That muscle twitched in his cheek again.

He pulled her hand from him and lifted her. He carried her to the bed as easily as if she didn't have extra weight now. As if he didn't have a wounded shoulder.

She reached for it but was careful not to touch his injury again. "Nick, you're going to tear your stitches open for certain."

"Don't worry about me," he said.

But she did. She always had. She'd worried about him living alone with that woman who had cared more about her next high than she had about her son. She'd worried about him when he'd joined the Marines and when he'd been recruited into the FBI. She had spent her life worrying about Nick.

And given their current situation, she wasn't about to stop anytime soon. Unless they could stop whoever was after them.

He kissed her forehead, where furrows of concern had formed for him. Then he kissed her nose and her lips and the end of her chin. His lips kept moving, down her throat, over her collarbone.

Finally he pushed her bra down, and his lips closed over the tip of one breast. She arched up as pleasure spiraled through her body. He tugged gently with his lips and then his teeth. A tension began to build inside her.

She squirmed on the bed. His hand was there, moving between her legs. He pushed aside her panties and stroked his fingers over her.

"Nick…"

The tension eased as pleasure coursed through her. But it wasn't enough. It wasn't nearly what she knew he could give her, what they could give each other.

She reached for him, stroking her hands over his back and butt. She pulled him toward her as she lifted her hips. She needed him inside her—needed to feel one with him as she'd felt that night.

He pulled off her panties and dropped his boxers. Then he was there—his erection nudging against her. She parted her legs as he pushed gently inside her. She arched her hips, taking him deeper, and locked her legs around his waist.

"Careful," he murmured, moving slowly as if he still feared he would hurt the baby.

But the baby was safe. Annalise was the one in danger—of falling even more deeply in love with Nick. "It's okay," she assured him.

He tensed. "Just okay?"

A smile tugged at her lips. "Well…"

He withdrew.

She clutched at him. "Nick!"

He pushed back inside her.

She gripped him with her inner muscles, holding him

deep inside her. But he pulled back again. And, teasing her, he stroked in and out.

The sensation built the tension, winding it so tightly that she couldn't get enough of him. She raked her nails lightly down his back and sank them into his butt.

And she rose up and nipped at his chin and his neck.

"Annalise…" He growled her name like a warning.

She didn't heed it. She couldn't listen to reason; she'd completely shut off the voice inside her head that had told her to be careful with Nick. She couldn't deny herself what she had always wanted: Nick.

As he continued to move inside her, the tension finally broke. Her body shuddered as she came. His name left her lips in a scream of pleasure.

He tensed, and then his body shuddered as he filled her. He rolled so that she sprawled across his chest. Her head settled between his neck and uninjured shoulder. Feeling at home and safe in his arms, her eyes immediately drifted closed.

She didn't know how long she slept. When she awakened, her head was on a pillow. Blankets had been pulled over her body, but she still felt cold without the heat of Nick's body. He was gone.

She tensed as she remembered how she had felt the last time she'd awakened alone after making love with him. Then, as now, she wondered if it had really happened at all or if she'd only dreamed it. But their baby shifted inside her, and she knew it had happened.

And when, like last time, she'd accepted that it had happened and he'd left before she awakened, humiliation washed over her. Why did she keep throwing herself at Nick only to have him run away?

He might have wanted her. One night. Now two...

But he didn't love her. And he probably never would.

Tears stung her eyes, but she blinked them back. She had to learn to protect herself. Not from the men trying to abduct her. She had to learn to protect herself from Nick. He was the one who would hurt her the most. Who already had.

But then she felt real pain. It shot through her stomach like a bullet or a knife—so sudden and sharp that she lost her breath at the intensity of it.

What was happening? What was wrong?

Her stomach tightened. As she placed her palms over it, she felt the hardness of it. Something was wrong—with her baby.

The pain came back—radiating throughout her. And she screamed. "Nick!"

There was no movement inside the condo. Where was he? Where had he gone?

She needed his help—needed him to help her save the baby before it was too late. Before they lost him or her...

Penny jerked awake as if someone had called her name. She'd done that when the kids were little. Even before they'd called out for her, she'd known they needed her. Somebody needed her now.

She flipped on the lamp beside the bed. It illuminated the darkness in a circle. On the pedestal table she'd painted a pale blue was her cell phone. She picked it up and stared at it. But the screen stayed dark.

No one was calling her. The kids were older now. They tried to handle things on their own. But ultimately they would reach out to her. They would call her.

Unless it was Nick who needed her. He hadn't yet learned to reach out, to trust that he would get assistance when he needed it. She could only hope that he would learn…before it was too late for anyone to help him.

Chapter 11

Nick had thought he'd heard something. Or at least, that was the excuse he'd given himself to leave Annalise lying alone in the bed in which they'd just made love. Like last time, their intimacy had humbled him and scared the hell out of him.

He'd never felt like that—as if he'd belonged anywhere—until he'd been inside her, their bodies joined. Her heart had beaten in sync with his until she'd fallen asleep. While hers had slowed, his had continued to beat fast.

And despite the release he'd found buried deep inside her, the tension hadn't left his body. So maybe he'd only imagined that he had heard something. But he'd eased her onto the pillow and covered her up.

Then he'd dressed quickly and grabbed up his weapon. He hadn't found anything amiss inside the condo. The open living room, dining and kitchen area had been undisturbed. The bedrooms off the other side of the condo had been empty. So maybe the noise had come from the other side of the back door. It didn't open onto an alley. It opened onto the unconverted part of the warehouse. Security back there wasn't as high-tech as inside the condo.

When he stepped inside, he didn't understand why it wasn't wired with alarms, too. If someone was going to break in, they probably would have wanted to get inside Milek's studio. Penny had mentioned that the younger Kozminski brother painted. She had even pointed out the portrait he'd done years ago, which hung on the wall of her office at the White Wedding Chapel.

But Nick didn't realize how talented or prolific Milek was until he saw all the canvases. They leaned against the walls, stacked upon each other. So many canvases. Only one stood by itself. The canvas too big for an easel, it leaned against a couple of metal barrels in the middle of the room. Paint spattered the cement floor all around it.

Intrigued, Nick walked up to it. And his breath caught at the realism of it. It wasn't just the vibrancy of the paint. It was the vibrancy of the people in the portrait. Milek had caught all of them as they were. Penny sat in the middle like the matriarch she was. She ruled her family with love, though, and it radiated from her— from the warmth in her brown eyes.

The whole portrait radiated warmth and love. Love among mother and sons and daughter. Love between spouses like Logan and Stacy. Even Stacy's brothers had been included in the portrait with their wives. And Nick was there.

Why had she had Milek include him?

He had no doubt that the portrait was being painted at Penny's request. She would have wanted it because her family had expanded. Nick could understand her wanting her daughters-in-law and grandchildren in the portrait. He could even understand her including the Kozminskis; they had been part of her life for a long time—ever since their father had gone to prison for murdering his.

But him...

Nikki wouldn't be happy about his inclusion. Like him, she was alone in the portrait—at the other end of the family from where he was. Keeping them apart had been no accident. Despite being surrounded by all that family, Nick looked alone.

He looked like something was missing. Love.

And Annalise. She should have been in the portrait, too. And Gage. They were his family. They always had been. And now, with the baby she carried, Annalise and he were starting their own family.

Then he heard a noise. This time he had no doubt it was real. And he had no mistake about what it was: Annalise's scream.

He had left her alone in the condo and vulnerable to whoever might have broken in while he'd been distracted. He should have known—no place was impenetrable. And nowhere was safe enough for Annalise. Her scream chilled his blood. She sounded more terrified than he'd ever heard her.

In Afghanistan, Gage had learned to rely on his instincts. If he hadn't, he wouldn't have survived even the first time he'd been deployed. And he certainly wouldn't have survived the last.

His instincts had told him that something wasn't right with Nick and Annalise. He hadn't realized how serious the situation was until he learned she was at the hospital. Would Nick have even told him if Gage hadn't called him?

And the only damn reason Gage had called was that he'd come back to Nick's place and found it had been broken into—again. The door had hung from its damaged hinges. And it had looked as if there had been a struggle in the hallway. There was a body-sized dent in the drywall and droplets of blood on the floor.

Gage had called because he'd been worried.

And Nick had made him even more worried when he replied, "We're at River City Memorial…"

That had been just minutes ago. But those minutes had felt like hours while Gage had driven over to the hospital and parked in the underground garage. It hadn't helped that security had stopped him at the door. They'd frisked him like he would have searched a perp. Apparently, there'd been some trouble there recently and River City PD had advised the security staff to be extra vigilant.

Fortunately Gage had left his gun in his glove box, or they might not have let him into the ER waiting room. The minute he stepped inside, he looked for Nick. But he was probably hurt, too.

Because he wouldn't have let anyone get to Annalise without one hell of a fight. As much as he'd complained about her pestering him, Nick had always had a soft spot for her, something most people probably didn't even realize he had. He always acted so damn tough.

The waiting room overflowed with Paynes—all tall guys with black hair and blue eyes. He walked up to the one who looked the least surprised to see him and asked Logan, "Where are they?"

"I'm here," Nick said as he stepped away from the others.

Hell, even as long as he'd known him, Gage had still mistaken him for one of the others—for one of his half brothers. Nick looked that much like the others.

"Are you okay?" he asked.

Nick nodded. But he didn't look okay. He looked like hell, his jaw shadowed with stubble and what looked to be the beginning of a bruise. The corner of a ragged-looking bandage stuck out of the collar of his T-shirt.

But knowing Nick as well as he did, he understood those injuries were nothing to him.

"What about Annalise?" he asked.

"The doctor's checking her out," Nick replied.

"What the hell's going on?" Gage asked. "Your place has been ransacked again. Everything's all broken up. Was she hurt there?"

And if so, it was Gage's fault—because she had come to River City looking for him. The minute he'd gotten back to the US, he should have gone to see her, should have assured her that he was all right. Sure, he hadn't been, not totally. But at least he'd been alive.

And she wouldn't be in danger now.

Nick shook his head. "She wasn't hurt there."

"But she was hurt."

"Someone carjacked her yesterday," Cooper said. With his close-cropped hair, the former Marine looked the most like Nick. They were even about the same age. Their dad must have been some son of a bitch to get two women pregnant at nearly the same time.

Of course, they didn't talk about him like that. At

least, the Paynes didn't. They acted like the dead cop had been a saint. But that was how people acted after someone died; they remembered only the good things.

Was that how everyone had acted when they'd thought he was dead? Had they remembered only his good qualities? Had *she*? Not his sister but that other woman, the one who'd ripped out his heart before he'd reenlisted?

But at the moment, as anger coursed through him, he couldn't recall any of his good qualities.

"Yesterday?" Clenching his fists, he stepped closer to Nick. "She was hurt yesterday and you didn't tell me?"

"I didn't."

He slapped his palm against Nick's chest and pushed him back. "You answered her phone and told me she was in the kitchen cooking. And she was here—in the emergency room. You lied to me!"

"She wasn't in the hospital yesterday," Nick said. "At least, not when you called."

But she had been.

Gage's stomach churned. He felt sick, so sick at the thought of his sweet sister injured. "What's wrong with her?"

Cooper was the one who stepped up to answer again. "She got a concussion during the carjacking."

Gage's head pounded as he thought of it—of the dangers of a head injury. "She shouldn't have left the hospital, then." He pushed Nick back again. "You shouldn't have let her leave!"

"You know Annalise."

Yes, he knew his sister. She was as stubborn as she was sweet. And she was far stronger than he or Nick had ever given her credit for being. So, yeah, she would have put up a fight to leave. But if he'd been there, he would have made sure that she stayed—that she wasn't put in any danger.

"I want to see her!" Gage said. "I need to see her. Now!" He had to make certain his baby sister was all right. "Where is she?" He didn't wait for any of them to reply, though. He headed toward the doors marked No Admittance.

Before he could push open the doors, a strong hand caught his arm and yanked him back. "No, Gage."

He turned back to Nick, and his anger bubbled, threatening to boil over as his skin and even his blood heated from the intensity of it. He couldn't remember feeling like this—actually *feeling*—in a long time. "No?"

"You need to calm down," Nick said. "You're only going to upset her if you go in acting like this."

He wasn't acting. He was pissed. More pissed than he could remember being in a good long while.

"She's in the hospital," Gage said. "She must already be upset."

"Yes," Nick agreed. "And she can't get any more upset. It won't be good for her or for…"

There it was again in Nick's voice—that caution, that evasiveness. Gage narrowed his eyes and studied his old friend's face. "For *what*, Nick?"

That telltale muscle twitched in Nick's cheek. And it looked as if he made an effort to unclench his jaw before he finally replied, "For the baby."

Shock gripped Gage. He had seen and done things he'd never imagined he would see or do. But he had never been as shocked as he was now. "What baby?" he asked, his voice cracking with the emotions pummeling him. "What the hell are you talking about?"

"Your sister's pregnant," Nick said. "That's why she's here. She thought she was going into early labor."

"How early?" Gage asked. Then he added the better question. "How far along is she?"

"Twenty-four weeks," Nick replied with an almost ominous certainty. Maybe he knew because Annalise had told him or he'd overheard the doctor.

Or maybe…

He shook his head. No. Not Nick.

He wouldn't have crossed that line, not with Annalise.

No, some other guy had to have gotten her pregnant. Gage wasn't naive enough to think his sister was a total innocent. Once she'd hit her teens, she'd started dating. Yet she'd never gotten serious about anyone before— because of her stupid, stubborn crush on Nick.

But Gage had been gone a long time. She must have met someone while he was missing. He glanced around the waiting room. He still saw only Paynes. So where the hell was the baby's father? He had damn well better be next to her bed, holding her hand.

His gaze returned to Nick. And that sick feeling churned his stomach again.

The answer was on Nick's face: the guilt, the regret.

Gage shook his head. "No."

"It's my fault," Nick said. "It's all my fault…"

Since Gage heard she was in the hospital, he hadn't had much of a hold on his temper, but whatever control he had totally snapped. And he swung. His fist slammed right into Nick's clenched jaw. Pain coursed through Gage's hand from his knuckles to his wrist.

Nick—who had killer reflexes—hadn't even ducked. He barely stumbled back.

After shaking off the stinging in his hand, Gage clenched his fist again and wound up to swing once more. But before he could connect with Nick—who stood straight again and ready for another blow—someone stepped between them. Strong hands shoved Gage back.

"You want to fight?" a deep voice asked.

Gage blinked to clear his vision, but he was so angry he was literally seeing red. The man looked like Nick—enough like Nick that he swung. But his fist didn't connect. It was blocked. And he took a blow—to his stomach. He doubled over as pain radiated throughout his body. The pain wasn't from the blow itself but from the old injuries it aggravated: the broken ribs, the bruised organs.

He coughed and choked but came up swinging—for Nick. A hand caught his fist and held it. Again it wasn't Nick but Cooper, who'd stepped between them, who was trying to fight Nick's battle.

"What the hell are you doing?" Gage asked.

"Nick took a bullet to his shoulder yesterday," Cooper said. "He's in no shape to fight. You want to fight? You fight with me."

"I don't have a beef with you."

"Sometimes a soldier doesn't need a beef," Cooper said. "Sometimes he just needs to fight."

Was that Gage's issue? Had he just been itching for a fight?

No. His sister was in the hospital—pregnant and injured—and Nick had willingly taken the blame for her being in that situation.

No. He didn't want to fight just anyone; he wanted to fight Nick until his old friend was as hurt as Annalise was.

Annalise hurt, but it was only her pride. She had made such a fool of herself—with the screaming, with the hysteria—over Braxton Hicks contractions. Most pregnant women experienced them. They weren't even real contractions, just a dress rehearsal for the real thing.

"The baby is fine," the doctor assured her. He pointed toward the monitor showing her baby was curled up, sleeping. Annalise should have been, too. But she'd awoken in such a panic. That had had more to do with Nick being gone than the contractions, though.

Maybe she wouldn't have panicked so badly if he'd been with her. But she couldn't count on Nick being there for her. He would never stop running away from her.

The doctor reached for the belt to remove the monitor for her belly. But she caught his hand. "Can you leave it on?" she asked hopefully. "For just a little while longer."

She couldn't move her gaze from the monitor. She couldn't stop watching her baby—to make sure she or he was really all right. The baby wasn't doing anything now but sleeping. But the screen pulsed with every steady heartbeat. Annalise needed that reassurance—visually and audibly—that her baby was fine.

The doctor nodded. "Sure, I'll give you a few more minutes." He pulled the ER curtain aside and closed it behind him. But just seconds later, the curtain swept open again.

"No…" she murmured, her eyes filling with tears. She needed more time—more reassurance.

"It's all right, honey," a soft voice said.

She glanced up, expecting a nurse. But this woman wasn't dressed in scrubs. She wore jeans and a short-sleeve sweater. Her curls tumbled around her face, and her brown eyes radiated warmth.

"Nikki?"

The woman smiled, and lines crinkled her eyes and creased the skin around her mouth. She was older than Nikki.

"I'm Penny Payne," the woman introduced herself.

"You're Nikki's mom?"

She smiled. "The boys', too."

"Of course." But that didn't explain why she was here—why she'd come to see Annalise.

The woman's gaze moved to the screen. She reached out and touched the baby on the monitor, her finger tracing over the image. As if the child could feel that touch, he moved inside Annalise—stretching and sprawling.

Annalise gasped as she realized what she'd just seen.

Penny chuckled. "Another boy—of course."

"Another?"

"Boys are prevalent in the Payne family."

Maybe Annalise really did have a concussion, because confusion muddled her mind. Nick didn't consider himself a Payne. But that wasn't even the issue. "How do you know my baby is Nick's?" she asked.

Penny's lips curved into a smile—an all-knowing smile. "I know."

Nick hadn't even been certain the first time he'd seen her in the ER.

"I don't think there has ever been anyone else for you," Penny added.

Annalise chuckled now. She hadn't been a virgin when she'd made love with Nick. "I think you have the wrong impression—"

"You don't love him?" Penny arched a reddish-brown brow.

"I love him," Annalise admitted. Tears stung her eyes, but she blinked them back to clear her vision. She couldn't stop staring at that screen—at her son. "Growing up next door to him, I can't remember a time that I didn't love Nick."

"I'm glad he had you," Penny said. Her hand touched Annalise's now with a comforting squeeze. "I have worried that Nick had no one who cared about him growing up."

Why would she care? What kind of person was Penny Payne that she had so much concern for her husband's child with another woman?

Loving. Amazing.

"Nick had me, too," a deep voice said. And the curtain was pushed aside again.

She hadn't seen him in so long that it took Annalise long seconds to recognize her brother. His hair was a darker blond than she remembered and cut so short she could see scars on his skull. Or were those just shadows? He was thinner, too, his jeans and shirt hanging on his long frame.

He was staring at her as if he didn't recognize her, either. And maybe he didn't. His gaze skimmed over her body—over her belly. Then he finally stepped forward and his arms closed around her, pulling her away from the pillow and against his chest.

She couldn't blink away the tears that stung her eyes now. They were too persistent—too numerous. They spilled over and trailed down her face. She had never lost hope—totally—that he was alive. But it had slipped sometimes.

She had wondered...

And she'd worried.

But he was alive. He was really alive.

The baby kicked, as if rejoicing in their reunion, too.

The only person who wasn't rejoicing was Penny. Annalise could see her face over Gage's shoulder. Her brow puckered with confusion and faint disapproval, she asked, "Who are you?"

She didn't just care about Nick's past. She cared about his present, too. She obviously worried that Annalise had another man.

Gage released Annalise and stepped back. His gaze went from one woman to the other. He had no idea who Penny was, either. He must not have met his boss's mother yet.

"This is Penny Payne," Annalise introduced them.

He held out his hand to the other woman. His knuckles were cracked and swollen, blood oozing from fresh wounds on them.

"I'm Annalise's brother—Gage."

"You're Gage Huxton?" Penny Payne asked. And she looked as if she'd seen a ghost. But then, Gage had been presumed dead for months—by everyone but Annalise. Despite the couple of doubts she'd let herself have in dark moments, she had known her brother was too tough to give up without one hell of a fight. He looked as if he'd just been in another one.

And she realized why. He hadn't been surprised to

see her pregnant. He'd known. Nick must have told him. And knowing Nick, he had admitted to being the father.

How badly had Gage hurt him?

Chapter 12

Pain radiated throughout Nick's jaw. He cupped his chin and turned it from side to side. It wasn't broken. He was surprised, though not that Gage had hit him. He'd had that coming. He was surprised that Gage hadn't broken his jaw.

Gage wasn't as strong as he'd been before he'd gone missing. He hadn't yet recovered completely from all those months he'd been gone. At least, not physically.

Personality-wise, he was Gage again. He was the act-first, think-second hothead he had always been. A smile tugged at Nick's mouth, but he flinched as pain radiated through his jaw at the movement.

Something cold pressed against the side of his face. What the hell had happened to his reflexes? Usually he would have seen that coming—like Gage's fist. He had seen that, and he'd purposely resisted the urge to duck.

He'd deserved that punch and whatever other ones Gage might have landed.

Cooper shouldn't have stepped in. Nick glanced up, expecting that was who'd brought him the ice. But his gaze met Penny Payne's warm one.

"I didn't know you were here," he remarked. He hadn't called her. He wasn't sure if anyone had. She had probably just known she was needed.

Not that Nick needed her.

Nick had never needed anyone. But an image flickered through his mind, of Annalise lying naked beneath him.

And need gripped him, overwhelming him with its intensity. He'd needed her last night. And six months ago.

He needed to see her now. The doctor had already spoken to him, had assured him that she and the baby were fine. But he needed to see her for himself, needed to know that she wasn't screaming in pain like she'd been earlier at the condo. Panic clutched his heart as he remembered how terrified she'd sounded.

He needed to make sure that she wasn't afraid any longer.

But Gage had gone back with her. Brother and sister deserved some time alone—after all the months they had been apart.

"I met Annalise," Penny said.

Nick groaned, and it wasn't because of the pain in his jaw. It was because of the humiliation that washed over him. He didn't deserve to be included in the Payne family portrait. On the other hand, he probably fit in more now than he ever had. He was a chip off the old block.

"You must think I'm like my father now," Nick said, "getting a woman pregnant and walking away."

"You're not walking," Penny said as she settled onto the waiting room chair next to him. She patted his hand. Like Annalise, Penny couldn't *not* touch people. She overflowed with warmth and affection. "You just didn't know."

Would she have told him? She had gone six months without telling him. Of course, she might not have realized right away that she was pregnant. But it didn't matter when she'd found out. She should have told him the minute she had. He had a right to know.

Now he didn't know if he would ever be able to trust her. She was like Penny Payne in some ways. But not all ways.

"Your father didn't know about you, either," Penny reminded Nick. "He wouldn't have let your mother leave if he'd known she was pregnant."

The police officer who'd gone undercover to take down a drug kingpin wouldn't have had a choice in whether or not his mother had left. After she'd agreed to testify against that kingpin, she'd been put in witness protection. But even if Nicholas Payne had known...

Nick snorted. "He wouldn't have chosen her over you." No man in his right mind would have. He'd often wondered if his mother had drugged the undercover cop. How else could she have gotten him to cheat on his amazing wife?

But before the drugs had ravaged her, his mother had been attractive. She'd kept an album of old photos—even though she should have left them behind after testifying. Maybe she'd kept the pictures to remind her that she'd once been young and beautiful.

And happy...

He had never seen her happy except in those old photos.

"Your father would have chosen you," Penny said, and she squeezed the hand she held. "He would have chosen to be a part of your life—or he would have tried to talk her into giving up custody to us."

"Us?" He turned fully toward her—shocked at what she was insinuating. "You would have wanted to raise another woman's baby?"

Could anyone be as selfless as she seemed?

Because he was watching closely, he noticed the flicker of pain and resentment. She was careful to hide her true emotions from her family. She was used to being strong for them—ever since she'd become a single parent after Nicholas Payne had been killed in the line of duty.

Nick was glad he'd caught that glimpse of the real Penny. She was human. She hadn't entirely forgiven the man who'd cheated on her.

Her family thought she'd never remarried or even seriously dated because she had loved her husband so much and mourned his loss yet. Nick realized now that it was because her husband had betrayed her. He'd destroyed her trust. And she struggled to trust again— even all these years later.

He squeezed her hand back and murmured, "I'm sorry."

"It wasn't *your* fault," she said.

"That wasn't," he agreed—even though he still felt guilty over the pain Penny had suffered because of him. "But Annalise—that is my fault."

She lifted her free hand to his swollen jaw. "Is that why you let Gage hit you?"

"I deserved more." Cooper should have let Gage pound the hell out of him.

"You deserve happiness, Nick," she said. "You deserve Annalise."

Annalise was happiness—or she had been before he'd put her in danger. Now she was scared. And she must have been angry with him for making love with her six months ago and walking away. That had to be why she hadn't told him she was pregnant—because he'd hurt her. She hadn't even called him or texted him like she used to before he'd slept with her.

If only he hadn't been such a fool.

Penny lowered her hand from his face and glanced toward those no-admittance doors to the ER. "I thought Gage Huxton was dead."

"I didn't realize you knew anything about him and Annalise." It shouldn't have surprised him that she did, though. Penny always knew more than anyone else— even him. And he was the guy who knew more than anyone else, or so he'd thought. For the past six months, he'd been completely unaware that Annalise was pregnant and in danger because of him.

She turned back to Nick and released a weary-sounding sigh. "I'm planning the wedding for FBI Chief Lynch's daughter," she explained.

Nick knew Woodrow Lynch well. After his wife had died, he'd spoiled his daughters to make up for the pain of their loss. "Is she a bridezilla?"

"Megan?" Penny adamantly shook her head. "No."

"Then what's the issue?" He could tell there was one.

Penny replied, "She thinks Gage is dead."

Nick had been so busy, he couldn't remember if he'd mentioned Gage's survival to his boss and Gage's former boss. Maybe he hadn't. Gage hadn't exactly left the Bureau on the best of terms—not after he'd acted like a hothead. "She hasn't heard he's alive?"

Penny shook her head. "I don't think she would be getting married if she knew."

"She would," a gruff voice said as Gage joined them.

Penny jumped and pressed her hand against her heart. "You keep sneaking up on me." And she obviously wasn't used to that.

Gage had gotten good at that, at the silent approach. He hadn't gotten good at hiding his emotions, though. Bitterness emanated from him. "Megan Lynch and I were done a long time ago."

Even if Penny wasn't almost clairvoyant, she couldn't have missed his pain. It was palpable. "I'm sorry," she said. "I didn't mean to interfere."

Of course she did. It was what she always did. But Gage didn't know that. He didn't know Penny.

She stood up as if getting ready to give up her chair to Gage. Nick wasn't certain his old friend would want to sit next to him, though. Or if he even considered him a friend any longer.

Gage caught Penny's arm. "Don't leave," he told her. "I need your help."

"My help?" Her face brightened with hope. "With Megan?"

He snorted. "Hell, no."

Penny cocked her head. "Then what?"

"I need you to plan another wedding," Gage said, "for him and my sister." He nearly shoved his finger into Nick's chest. "Nick and Annalise are going to get married as soon as possible."

Nick should have been horrified, or at least afraid. But he felt none of that. He felt like he did when he made love with Annalise.

Like it was right.

Like it was home...

"Nick and Annalise are going to get married as soon as possible." The words hung in the suddenly silent waiting room. Annalise wished she could grab them from the air and shove them back in her big brother's big mouth.

She had pulled off the baby monitor and dressed as quickly as she could because she'd been afraid of what Gage would do. She'd worried he might have already hurt Nick and that he'd gone back to hurt him some more.

She hadn't realized he was going to embarrass the hell out of her. Her face heated with embarrassment as everyone stared at her. Were they waiting to see if she would agree?

Maybe they thought it was her idea, that she'd gotten pregnant to trap Nick. She'd worried that was what he would think. That was partially why she hadn't told him when she'd found out she was pregnant a few months ago. She'd worried that he would think she'd done it on purpose.

The other reason she hadn't told him was that when she'd found out three months had already passed—in which he hadn't contacted her. No phone call. No email. No text. It was as if he'd forgotten about her completely, while he had never left her mind. Or her heart.

But as much as she loved him—or maybe because she loved him so much—Annalise didn't want to marry Nick because he'd been pushed to the altar at the end of a shotgun.

She forced herself to laugh, but it rang hollowly in the crowded but weirdly silent room. "Don't be ridiculous, Gage."

He turned back to her as if he was surprised she would protest. But then, after all the years he'd watched her chase Nick, he had to be surprised that she wouldn't take advantage of the situation to catch him.

Annalise knew that even though she'd caught Nick, she couldn't hold him. He would run away again. At the moment, she wanted to run first. Her overreaction to the Braxton Hicks contractions had been embarrassing enough, but Gage had mortified her.

"I'm being realistic," Gage said. "You two need to get married."

"Why?" she asked. "This is the twenty-first century. It's almost more common to be a single parent than to be a co-parent."

Nick hadn't had a father. After his father had died, his brothers and sister hadn't had one, either. Penny Payne had managed on her own; Annalise could, too.

As if disgusted with her denseness, Gage shook his head and turned back to Nick. "Tell her you're going to marry her."

Nick's face flushed now. He was apparently as embarrassed as she was. "Gage…"

"Do you want my nephew to be a bastard like you are?" Gage asked.

Annalise's gasp escaped into the silence left after Gage's obnoxious remark. Nick gasped, too. And now the color drained from his handsome face, leaving him pale and shaken. But he wasn't offended. He was in awe.

"Nephew?" he repeated. Then he turned toward her. His blue eyes intense and curiously bright, he asked, "Are we having a son?"

She couldn't speak. Too much emotion welled up, choking her. She could only nod.

Then one emotion overpowered her others: anger. She struck out at her brother, pushing him back. Gage, who was usually so solid and immovable, stumbled away from her. "The only bastard here," she told him, "is you! How dare you call my son that."

Or the man whom she loved.

As he finally came to his senses, Gage shook his head with regret and murmured, "I'm sorry. I shouldn't have said that."

"No, you shouldn't have." Penny Payne was the one who admonished him in that maternally disapproving way that made every child, no matter how old, squirm.

"He's right," Nick defended his oldest friend. He was still staring at Annalise with that strange look of hope and awe and shock.

From the fresh bruise on his jaw, she could tell he'd fought with Gage. Had he struck his head, as well? Did he have a concussion that had addled his brain? Because he couldn't seriously be proposing what she thought he was proposing.

To her.

Confirming it, he uttered the phrase she'd longed for most of her life to hear him say. "We should get married."

Nick didn't love her. And because he didn't love her,

there was no way Annalise could marry him. But she was too overwhelmed to speak again.

Everyone else was talking, offering congratulations and suggesting plans, as if her wedding was a foregone conclusion. She could only stand on the sidelines, watching the action of her own life, and shake her head.

No matter how much she wanted it—how much she'd always wanted it—there was no way she would ever be Nicholas Rus's bride.

Guns weren't allowed in the hospital—which was probably lucky for Nick. Cooper didn't believe Gage would have actually shot his friend and former idol. But he suspected he would have threatened him with it.

Threatened him in order to get Nick to marry his sister...

Not that Nick had put up much of a fight.

Annalise was the one who looked as if she wanted to fight. But no words of protest emanated from her mouth, either. She was probably exhausted. And so was Nick.

Payne Protection needed to get them safely back to the security of Milek's condo. Still talking about a wedding, the group moved through the hospital lobby.

Cooper's marriage had started as one of convenience. Because the real groom had disappeared, Cooper had stepped into his place. He hadn't given up that role—he was still Tanya's husband—because he was the one she'd really wanted to marry.

Did Annalise want to marry Nick? Sure, she carried his baby, but that didn't mean she loved him. The way she'd defended him to her own brother showed that she did.

But sometimes love wasn't enough.

His own parents had proved that to Cooper. Even as much as they had loved each other, his father had still betrayed his mother. He'd broken their vows.

So would it matter if Nick and Annalise married?

Cooper doubted either of them would get the chance, not with someone determined to take them out.

Gage wasn't the only one who posed a threat to Nick. Someone had shot at him. If the bullet had gone six inches or so lower and to the left, it could have killed him.

Nobody could get into the hospital with a weapon. So they were waiting outside. Since it was night yet, the glass doors of the lobby just reflected back the interior. Cooper couldn't see them.

But he knew they were out there—just as he'd known when insurgents were lying in wait for the convoy. He hadn't been wrong in Afghanistan, and he wasn't wrong now.

The minute Nick and Annalise—with Penny and Gage—stepped outside, gunfire erupted. The glass in the lobby doors shattered and sprayed inward, across the terrazzo floor and Cooper's face. He'd known they were out there, but he still hadn't been prepared.

Neither had Nick.

Chapter 13

Nick's head buzzed with the rapid retort of gunfire. Cooper had warned him, had shared his suspicion that someone might stage another attack outside the hospital. He hadn't needed the warning. His instincts had told him the same thing.

They could have tried to sneak out another way. Before they'd left the waiting room, they had studied the alternative exits. But walking into the parking garage or the back alley would have been more dangerous. They could have been trapped. The lobby entrance was along a four-lane street with plenty of room for escape.

The only trick was not to get hit. Ducking low and using his body as a shield to protect Annalise, as Gage used his as a shield to protect Penny, they ushered the women into the open door of the Payne Protection vehicle parked directly outside the lobby doors.

The vehicle—this one with bulletproof glass and metal—withstood the onslaught of bullets.

"Hurry up," Garek ordered from the driver's seat. But he didn't wait for Gage to pull the door closed behind them before he careened away from the curb and into the street. Gage struggled but managed to slam the door closed.

Outside the darkened glass, Nick watched the flashes of gunfire. How many shooters had lain in wait for them?

There had to be more than the one man who'd escaped him in the parking garage and the second man who'd escaped him in his ransacked house.

With all that gunfire, there were definitely more than two shooters. More than two people after him and Annalise. The threat kept increasing. Why?

Who the hell wanted him dead that badly?

Even though the doors were closed, and the distance between them and the shooters grew as Garek sped away from the hospital, Nick kept his arms wrapped protectively around Annalise. His head was even still bowed over hers, her face in his chest.

She trembled against him.

"Are you okay?" he asked her.

He felt her move but couldn't tell if she nodded or shook her head. He eased back slightly. She peered up at him, her green eyes wide with fear and her face pale. But she nodded and assured him, "I'm okay."

He leaned across Annalise to ask Penny. "Are you okay?"

She smiled and, reaching across Annalise, patted his hand and said, "Of course I am."

They hadn't wanted to put her in danger. But she

already was, as much as she looked like her daughter. If she'd gone out another door alone, a gunman might have mistaken her for Nikki and shot her.

Gage seemed okay. He was trying to twist his long body to ease over the console and into the passenger seat. But Garek turned the vehicle, and Gage struck his head on the roof and cursed.

He might have a concussion, but he wasn't shot. So he was safer in the SUV than he would have been in the lobby with the others.

Annalise turned around and peered toward the hospital disappearing in the distance. "Is everyone else okay?" she asked.

"Yes," Garek replied from the front seat as he tapped his radio earpiece. "Nobody got hit." He made a sharp turn, and Gage, settling into the passenger seat, hit his head on the bulletproof side window.

He cursed again.

"Drive it like you stole it," Garek remarked.

Instead of getting mad, Gage chuckled and said, "You'll need to teach me how."

Unlike some of the kids in their neighborhood, Nick and Gage had avoided joining gangs. But Nick hadn't resisted because he hadn't wanted to steal cars. He had resisted because the gangs around them had mostly sold drugs. And he hadn't been about to support his mother's addiction.

"Pay attention," Garek advised his passenger. "I'll show you how to make sure nobody's tailing us."

Garek's lesson took a while because he wanted to make extra certain that none of the gunmen had followed them from the hospital. He wanted to protect not

just Penny, whom they all adored, but Nick and Annalise, as well.

Before he moved to River City, Nick would never
have believed he would become friends with an ex-
convict like Garek Kozminski. A man who'd served
time for manslaughter and was rumored to be as re-
nowned a thief as his infamous father. But Nick wasn't
just friends with the man; he was family, too.

And when he married Annalise, she and Gage would
also become family. Over Annalise's blond head, he met
Penny's gaze and nodded.

He didn't need to say it aloud for her to understand
his intentions. She would plan his wedding. And knowing Penny, she would have Milek add Annalise and
Gage to that family portrait, as well.

The only thing Nick had to worry about was keeping Annalise and himself alive for their wedding day.

Annalise couldn't stop shaking, and it wasn't just
because the spring night was unseasonably cold. Heat
blasted from the vents in the condo, but her skin and
her blood wouldn't warm. She had gotten so cold when
those shots had been fired at the hospital, shattering
the lobby doors and windows. It was a miracle no one
had been hit.

She shivered.

"You need to get back in bed," Nick said as he led her
toward the master bedroom. His arms had been around
her from the moment they'd started across the hospital
lobby. But for once, his closeness hadn't warmed her.

"It's almost dawn," she murmured as she noticed
light beginning to filter through the skylights in the
living room. They passed through it quickly, though,

into the darkness of the bedroom where there were no skylights. Not even a lamp had been left burning.

She shivered again as she imagined men hiding in the darkness, like they had hidden outside the hospital. She turned back toward the light of the living room.

But Nick propelled her gently toward the bed and pushed her down onto the edge of the mattress. "You need your rest," he said. "You're exhausted and probably in shock."

As if she were a child, he undressed her, taking off her shoes and pulling down her pants. He left her in her shirt and panties, gently pushed her onto her back and covered her with blankets. The sheets were cold against her back, and she couldn't stop shivering.

Concern furrowed Nick's brow. "Maybe you should go back to the hospital."

"No!" she sharply protested. She wished she had never gone, that she hadn't overreacted to what nearly every other pregnant woman experienced. "I'm fine."

Calling her out on the lie, he said, "You're not fine." But instead of insisting she go back to the hospital, he kicked off his shoes, took off his holster and weapon and crawled under the blankets with her. He wrapped his arms around her as he had in the hospital lobby. Tucking her head beneath his chin, he held her closely.

She felt his heart beating against hers. It was pounding quickly. He hadn't been unaffected by the gunfire, either. Only one person really had seemed unaffected.

"I'm not Penny Payne," she said resentfully.

"What?"

"She was so calm," Annalise remarked. "Like getting shot at was no big deal."

Nick chuckled at her petulance. "She's had more experience with that than you have."

"She's been shot at before?"

He nodded, his chin bumping against her head. "She has, just like every other member of her family. They've been through a lot together. That's why she's so strong."

Annalise's brief flash of resentment gave way to admiration and envy. Like the rest of her family, Nick obviously thought very highly of the woman. "I wish I could be like her."

"You *are* like her," Nick said.

Annalise laughed. "Now you're just patronizing me."

He eased her away from him and tipped up her chin. Light filtered in from the living room and fell across his handsome face, highlighting his every chiseled feature and the seriousness in his blue eyes. "I thought that the first time I met her."

"What?"

"That she was like you."

Annalise smiled. If only…

She wished she had that kind of strength, that kind of composure under pressure. "Why did you think that?"

"Because she is so friendly and warm," he said. His mouth curved into a slight grimace. "And so affectionate. She radiates—" his grimace grew as he struggled to express himself "—like you radiate."

"I radiate?" she asked. "What do I radiate?"

"Love."

So he was aware that she loved him. Maybe that was why he had agreed to Gage's crazy idea. Because he felt sorry for her.

"You're so sweet and loving to everyone you meet," Nick continued.

So maybe he didn't take how she acted around him personally. Maybe he didn't know how she really felt about him.

"That's why it has to be my fault," he said. "That's why whoever has been terrorizing you with the break-ins and thefts must be doing it because of me."

She stroked her fingers along his swollen jaw. "It's not your fault."

"I am responsible."

"Why?" she asked. "Because you've taken criminals off the street? That's a good thing. You're doing good things, Nick." She had never doubted that he would. He had always been her hero.

His hand moved lower, over the swell of her belly. "This will be a good thing," he said. "Our son…"

Tears stung her eyes. "Of course."

"I should have protected you that night."

They'd gotten carried away with passion. Protection had been the last thing on both their minds.

"I will protect you from now on," he promised.

She shook her head.

"I will—"

That wasn't what she was protesting. "You don't need to marry me to protect me."

He needed to marry her only if he loved her. And she doubted that he did.

But he wanted her. She felt it in the tenseness of his body, in the erection straining against his fly to press against her hip. She wanted him, too. Making love with him would finally warm her up, would stop her shivering. Even now her blood was beginning to heat and pump faster in her veins.

He touched her, his hands moving over her bare

thighs to her hips. He slid his fingers beneath her panties and teased her. He stroked his thumb over her most sensitive spot until she squirmed and moaned.

So she teased him back. She stroked her fingers over the ridge of his erection until finally he undid his pants and pushed them down his legs. He pulled off his shirt, too, and hers. Within seconds nothing separated them. They were skin to skin.

He kissed her everywhere but her lips. He kissed her shoulder and her elbow. And the curve of her hip. Then he moved his mouth lower and made love to her with his lips and his tongue.

Her hands in his hair, she clasped him against her as she arched her hips and came. But it wasn't enough. He touched the tightened tips of her nipples, and the pressure wound inside her again. Only he could give her the release she needed, when he buried himself inside her. But he didn't lift her legs. He didn't push inside her.

Instead he flopped onto his back, his chest rising and falling as he breathed heavily, fighting for control. She wanted him out of control. So she leaned over and teased him as he had teased her. She licked her tongue down the pulsing length of him.

He groaned her name and tangled his fingers in her hair. She slid her lips around him and took him deep in her mouth. But it wasn't enough.

He bucked beneath her. But he didn't come like she had. So she eased back. Then she straddled him. Rising up, she guided him inside her. She was still wet and ready for him. He edged slowly inside until he filled her. But she wasn't able to take all of him.

She moved up and down, clutching at him with her inner muscles as he gripped her hips in his hands. He helped her move, helped her find the rhythm that drove them both to madness. He bucked beneath her as she rode him. Then he slid one hand between them and stroked her with a fingertip.

Her body tensed, then shuddered as an orgasm overwhelmed her. She screamed his name and collapsed on his chest. He gripped her hips and shoved up, driving deep, as he shouted his release.

He didn't pull out, just pressed her against him and pulled the blankets over them. And he held her as if he never intended to let her go.

But Annalise knew better now than to get her hopes up. She understood that when she awakened, he would probably be gone again. There was no way he would ever marry her because there was no way he would ever stop running away from her.

She wasn't the one he needed to outrun, though. He needed to outrun whoever was after them. Or getting married would be the least of their concerns.

The River City Psychiatric Facility for the Criminally Insane was every bit as scary as Candace Baker-Kozminski had imagined it would be. But she had convinced her husband, Garek, that she was the one who needed to pay this visit.

But even as tough as she was, she was unnerved. Patients yelled. They flailed. They beat themselves with their fists until men in white suits restrained them.

But far scarier than any of that behavior was the eerie stare of the woman sitting across from her. Tori Chekov studied her as she might study a cat she was about to torture cruelly. A small smile played around her mouth, and a gleam of insanity twinkled in her dark eyes.

"I have dreamed of seeing you again," Tori admitted.

Candace had, too: nightmares. Nightmares of this woman killing Garek. But she always awakened in the comfort of his embrace, his strong arms locked around her.

"Really?" she asked, as if she cared.

"I have imagined all the things I would do to you," Tori said, and her dark eyes hardened with hatred.

Candace forced a laugh. "Nice to see that expensive psychiatrist your dad hired has done you so much good."

Tori's smile widened. "Oh, you'd be surprised what she's done for me."

A chill chased over Candace's skin. This woman might be locked up, but she was still dangerous. And maybe she was using her psychiatrist to cause problems on the outside. Problems with Nick?

"You've done a lot for me, as well," Tori said.

"I have?" She sure as hell hoped not.

"Those self-defense moves you taught me when you were my bodyguard."

Candace felt a twinge of regret and embarrassment. Tori had used those moves against her. "Yes?"

"They've protected me in here—" she pitched her voice to a creepy whisper "—with all these crazies."

"I think you should be in prison," Candace honestly remarked. "It was your father and Special Agent Nicholas Rus's idea to commit you here."

For life. That was the only reason, as one of her victim's, that Candace had agreed to the sentence Nick had hammered out in exchange for Viktor Chekov's confession. He had owned up to all his crimes. So if he was going after Nick, he probably would have admitted it.

Would Tori?

"My father is a weak old man," Tori replied with disgust and hatred.

"And Agent Rus?"

Tori's lips curved, and that crazy glint sparkled in her dark eyes. "He is one beautiful man. I dream about him, too."

Candace didn't have to wait long before Tori added, "I dream of all the things I would do to him—" she uttered a wistful sigh of resignation "—if I wasn't in here."

Fortunately she was in there. But Candace wasn't certain that meant she and Nick were actually safe. If Tori really wanted to get to them, Candace suspected that she could. And she would.

Chapter 14

Nick understood where Milek had found the inspiration for his family portrait as he gazed around the condo living room at everyone gathered for the Payne Protection Agency meeting. Nikki wasn't there, but since he was, that wasn't unusual. And Logan usually excluded her from the bodyguard business meetings, anyway.

It wasn't a family meeting because the spouses weren't there, at least not the ones who weren't bodyguards. The children weren't there, either—just his baby, his *son*—inside Annalise's belly.

She had insisted on being included in the powwow. And since she was stuck in the condo, too, it would have been hard to exclude her, even though she had no real reason to be there. The attempts on their lives had nothing to do with her.

But Logan, who was always thorough, interrogated

her, anyway. "No disgruntled clients?" the former River City PD detective asked.

She shook her head.

"No jealous ex-boyfriends?"

She laughed—as she had when Nick had asked. She glanced at him before shaking her head.

Logan looked at him, too, as if considering that he was a jealous ex. When it came to Annalise, Nick was jealous and possessive. But he wasn't an ex, not yet.

He would marry her so his son's parents would be married when he was born. But Nick doubted Annalise would want to stay married to him. She deserved more. She deserved someone who could love her as she loved—freely and affectionately.

"This is stupid," Gage said. Since returning from his last bodyguard assignment, he had been sticking close to Annalise. And of course he had insisted on being included in the Payne Protection meeting. "You're wasting your time questioning my sister."

"He's right," Nick said.

Instead of looking grateful for the confirmation, Gage glared at him. He had not forgiven him for crossing the line with Annalise. Ignoring his remark, Gage continued, "She has no enemies—unlike Nick."

"They've only been going after Annalise to get to me," Nick agreed. Gage had no doubts about that, just as he didn't. The others had been more hesitant because they didn't know Annalise. They didn't understand how she was like Penny and could have no enemies.

"You have too many enemies," Garek said.

"We're narrowing it down," Nick reminded him. Garek had ruled out Chekov. And while Candace wasn't certain his daughter had nothing to do with it, Nick was.

The break-ins at his places and at Annalise's had started before he'd taken down the Chekovs. Until he had, they'd had no reason to want vengeance on him. They hadn't even been aware they had been in his sights.

He trusted few people. Only Garek Kozminski had been aware of that plan, and Nick had brought him in only because he'd needed his help. He needed all of their help now—for Annalise.

"We're narrowing it down to people you've pissed off more than six months ago," Gage said. "That's still a hell of a lot of people."

Nick couldn't agree more. He had compiled a list. And even to him, it was overwhelming. He had passed out copies to the others, and they riffled through the pages.

"Seriously?" Garek Kozminski asked. "You've pissed off more people than I have."

"And that's saying something," his brother Milek added.

"Are these all professional enemies?" Parker asked.

When someone had been trying to take him out, everyone had thought it was personal. That he had pissed off a lover's husband or something.

Nick had never been the playboy his half brother had been rumored to be. He nodded. "Of course."

"Why?" Logan asked. "You could have a jealous ex-lover, too."

Like Annalise had, he laughed at the far-fetched notion. "That's ridiculous."

"It makes sense," Candace said. "A jealous woman is more likely to go after a man's girlfriend than a professional enemy would."

"I'm not his girlfriend," Annalise said quickly, defensively.

She wasn't his girlfriend. What was she? Lover. Mother of his unborn child? Fiancée? He hadn't put a ring on her finger. Not yet.

But he had no doubt Penny was planning their wedding. The professional wedding planner had probably started planning it the moment she'd heard about Annalise showing up in River City. Pregnant with his child.

Hell, Penny had probably known before he had.

Would he know if Annalise hadn't been in danger? Would she have told him? That was why he'd trusted few people—because few people had proved worthy of his trust. Gage.

And as a reward, he had betrayed that trust when he'd crossed the line with Gage's sister. Why should he expect trust when he'd done nothing to earn it himself?

"We need a list of ex-girlfriends," Logan prodded him as he waved those pages around. "So this is complete."

"You don't think the list is long enough as it is?" Garek asked with a weary-sounding sigh. "There are already too many to check them all out."

"You need Nikki's help," Parker said.

"She doesn't work for me anymore," Logan reminded them.

And from their faces Nick could tell, they all doubted she would help. They didn't know how much she'd already assisted him. Not that the crime lab had found any prints in Annalise's stolen car. As Nikki had surmised, it had been wiped clean.

Cooper said, "I'll put her on the case."

Nick had already emailed her a copy of the list. He

suspected she was working on it—checking alibis, known associates, everything Nikki checked.

But even as good as Nikki was, he doubted they would be able to whittle down that list to the right suspect anytime soon. He could only hope that they stopped the person before it was too late, before he lost Annalise.

Annalise was lost. And it wasn't because they all spoke at once that she couldn't understand what they were saying. It was their reasoning she couldn't follow. They were brilliant bodyguards. Every one of them had been something else before creating or joining the Payne Protection Agency.

They'd been police officers or detectives, soldiers or FBI agents. Or thieves.

And all of these brilliant people believed someone was using her for revenge against Nick. Even Nick thought so.

But it made no sense to her. Why?

Nick would have to have feelings for her—beyond responsibility—for her situation to really affect him. And he didn't have feelings for her. He didn't love her.

He hadn't even made love to her again since that dawn they'd escaped the shoot-out at the hospital. As she'd suspected, she had awakened later that day alone. And he hadn't shared her bed since.

For the past couple of nights, he'd planted himself on the couch, as if anyone could bypass Milek Kozminski's security system. Nick was just running, as far away as he could while still being close enough to protect her.

And since that dawn, he hadn't mentioned marrying her again. He obviously had no intention of following through on a wedding despite her brother's proverbial shotgun threat.

So how would hurting her cause Nick any pain?

She was the one suffering. She was the one living with a man she loved but knew she could never really have. She was the one who'd put her career on hold while she lived in relative captivity. With a twinge of regret, she glanced at her brother.

He'd been through far worse than what she was going through. So she had no right to feel sorry for herself. No reason to sulk. Because she couldn't stand inaction, she moved to the kitchen. She would cook or bake, depending on the ingredients available. She would do anything but pine for Nicholas Rus. She'd spent too much of her life doing that.

Gage had spent most of his missing six months in pain. And it hadn't all had to do with his captivity. It had had to do with the kind of pain he saw on his sister's face.

Heartache.

It was worse by far than anything anyone could physically suffer. It left a gaping hole where a heart should be. And there was no filling that hole with anything but love.

So when that love wasn't returned, the hole just remained open and gaping and sore like an untreated wound.

He'd seen that pain on her face in a vulnerable moment. But she was doing her best to hide it now. She bustled around the room, offering food to everyone present. The house was warm from the heat of the oven and her personality. It was fragrant from the smells of the feast she had thrown together.

"She's so much like Mom," he heard Parker Payne murmur.

Logan nodded in agreement. "Nick's right. This is about him. Not her."

Gage had been telling them that, but they'd had to see for themselves the magic that was Annalise.

Nick had seen it. He'd tried turning a blind eye to it for years. He'd tried to ignore her. But she had been persistent. And if she had a flaw, Annalise's only one would be her stubbornness. She'd wanted Nick for so long.

Gage shouldn't have been surprised that she'd finally worn him down. But he was disappointed. Nick had always been his hero—the man he had hoped to become someday. Strong. Smart. Honorable.

This time, he'd crossed a line with Annalise that he would never be able to uncross. Marrying her wouldn't make him honorable. It would probably only put her in more danger.

All the Paynes looked alike, but he knew it was Nick who settled onto the couch next to him. "I was wrong," he said.

"No, you weren't," Nick said. "It's all my fault. You should have hit me harder."

Gage grunted. "Yeah, I should have."

"So you're not talking about hitting me?" Nick touched his jaw as if it still hurt.

But Gage knew he wasn't as strong as he'd once been. Before he'd gone missing, he would have broken Nick's jaw had he hit him like he had. But before he'd gone missing, he had never wanted to hit Nick.

"You know what I'm talking about," Gage murmured.

Because he was Nick, he always knew everything. That was why he had come to Nick when he'd gotten back to the States. Because he hadn't wanted to talk. He'd just wanted someone to know—without his having to say a word. But now he wanted to make sure Nick understood, so he said, "You can't marry her. It would put her in more danger. Then whoever's after you will know she's important to you."

Nick grunted his agreement. "You're right." He understood. He knew what he had to do—or actually *not* do.

He couldn't make Annalise his bride. Marrying her wouldn't just put her in more danger physically, though.

She would also be in more danger emotionally—because while she would have Nick's name, Gage doubted she would ever have his heart.

He suspected Nick had had that gaping hole in his chest for a long time.

Maybe he'd never even had a heart to lose.

Chapter 15

Annalise was safe in the condo, Nick assured himself. It was okay that he'd left her. Her brother was there. Gage would willingly give up his life for hers.

So would Nick.

But Annalise didn't want his life. She wanted something else from him. Something he had never been able to give her or anyone else.

Gage wasn't the only one protecting Annalise. Candace and Garek had stayed, as well. Nick wasn't sure who was following him; he just knew that someone was.

Since he hadn't picked up the tail, he guessed it was Milek. It would have been a point of pride with the younger Kozminski brother to go undetected this time. Nick probably could have made him—had he cared. But since Annalise wasn't with him, he didn't care. Her safety was his only concern.

Not his own.

He didn't want to endanger this woman, either, so he had been careful when he'd left the condo. He'd taken a circuitous route to the White Wedding Chapel. The only person who might have been able to follow—given the way he'd been driving—was Milek. Milek would protect Mrs. Payne, too, if Nick had brought danger to her like he had Annalise.

Before he could even reach for the door, though, someone burst through and slammed into his chest, nearly knocking him down the stairs he'd climbed. He gripped her shoulders to steady her.

And Megan Lynch glanced up at him through tear-filled eyes. "Nick? Nicholas Rus?"

He nodded.

Her face flushed bright red. "I'm sorry. I wasn't looking where I was going."

She was obviously upset and in a hurry.

He held her shoulders a little longer and asked, "Are you okay?"

She jerked her head in a sharp nod, and a few wisps of brown hair escaped the bun at the nape of her neck. By her father's own admission, he had doted on her and her sister after their mother died. But few other men had ever paid Megan Lynch attention. She was almost painfully shy, and maybe because her mother had died so young, she'd never learned how to wear makeup or flattering clothes. So she wasn't just shy. She was awkward, too.

For some reason, Gage had found that endearing. Everyone else, including Megan, had thought he was just doing the boss's daughter in order to get ahead in the Bureau. But Nick knew Gage better than that.

Unfortunately, Megan had not.

"I'm fine," she said. And because she'd been raised to be polite, she added, "And how are you?"

He touched his swollen jaw. "Could be better."

She sighed. "Me, too."

He squeezed her shoulders. "Is there anything I can do?"

She shrugged, and his hands fell away. "It'll be over soon."

She acted as if she was talking about a root canal or winter. Not her wedding.

He opened his mouth. He needed to tell her about Gage, if she didn't already know. But first he said, "I'll be talking to your dad soon." He would make sure that Chief Lynch knew Gage was alive and let him decide what to do with that information. The Marines had determined to keep his escape secret. Nick wasn't certain if that was to protect Gage from unwanted media attention or if there was a concern about the insurgents who'd held him somehow getting to him again.

She nodded. "Of course. He talks about you often, Nicholas. You're one of his favorites." The tears shimmered in her eyes.

Lynch had had another favorite: Gage. Until he'd left.

"Congratulations," he offered belatedly. "Penny will make sure you have a beautiful wedding."

She nodded, and the tears brimmed over and trailed down her face. Her voice quavering with emotion, she murmured, "I'm sure she will." Then she broke free of him and ran down the steps to her car parked at the curb in front of his SUV.

He continued up the steps and pushed open the door. He passed quickly through the foyer and descended the interior stairwell to Penny's office in the basement. Despite it having only one small window, the space was sunny and bright. And it wasn't because of the yellow paint or lighting. It was because of the woman who radiated sunshine and warmth.

"Good afternoon, Nicholas," she greeted him with a smile as she glanced up from her desk.

"Penny…"

"Did you run into Megan Lynch?" she asked.

He nodded. "Literally. She ran into me. I don't think she could see me through her tears."

Penny sighed. "She's the unhappiest bride for whom I've ever planned a wedding."

"Did you tell her Gage is alive?" Maybe that was why she'd been crying. But wouldn't those have been happy tears? Unless Gage was right, and she didn't care if he was alive. Or maybe she didn't want him alive.

Penny shook her head. "No. I didn't." She studied his face for a moment. "You didn't, either."

"No," he said. "Gage is already angry enough with me. I didn't want to make it worse."

"Marry his sister," she said. "That'll make it better."

Nick shook his head. "Gage has changed his mind about that. He knows what I know—being around me puts Annalise in more danger."

"That's a load of bull and you know it," Penny accused him.

He drew back in surprise. Penny had never said a sharp word to him before—even though she'd had every reason to be upset when he had turned up in River City looking exactly like her sons, like her dead husband. He must not have heard her correctly. "Excuse me?"

"I'm talking to you like I would talk to Logan or

Parker or Cooper," she said. "I call them on their non-
sense, too. I never thought I would have to do that with
you."

"Because I'm not your son?"

"Because you're usually smarter than they are," she
said. "And you *are* my son."

"Penny—"

"I don't care that another woman gave birth to you,"
she said. "You're *my* son now."

"I saw the family portrait Milek is painting for you,"
he admitted.

"Then you know how I feel," she said.

"You may feel that way, but the rest of the family…"

"Feel the same way."

Logan had made it clear that he did. And Nick had
never picked up on any animosity from Parker or Cooper. But…

"Not Nikki," he said.

"She's coming around," Penny said.

He shook his head. "No, she's not."

Sure, she had called him about finding Annalise's
stolen car. And he'd emailed her the list of his enemies.
But he hadn't actually seen her since that horrible day
in the parking garage. She hadn't attended any of the
Payne Protection Agency meetings. Of course, Logan
never included her in anything he perceived as dangerous, and she had been in more danger that day than
any other in her life. But because of that, Nick had
expected her to insist on being involved. While she'd
found the car, she hadn't called him again. She hadn't
even emailed him back that she'd received his list. She
probably didn't want to help because she didn't care
that he was in danger.

Unfortunately, Annalise was in danger, too. So Nick needed his sister's help. He would have to call her, see if she'd checked out the list or added her own name to it.

"The portrait is missing someone," Penny said.

Nick tensed. "Did my father have another—"

Her glance as sharp as her tone had been earlier, Penny stopped him from saying the rest. *Bastard.* That was what he was—just like Gage had called him. And if he didn't marry Annalise, his child would be a bastard, too.

Of course she was right. It was the twenty-first century now. And there were probably more single-parent households than two-parent households. But he wanted his son to have his name, to know who he was.

Until his mother had died, Nick had never known who he was.

"The portrait is missing Annalise," Penny said.

He had thought the same thing when he'd seen it, that he looked so alone. Like Nikki on the other side of the portrait. But as much as he would have liked to, he couldn't bring Annalise into the family. He had already put her in enough danger.

"I can't marry her," Nick said.

"Now that's ridiculous," Penny said. "She was in danger in Chicago. She is in more danger alone than she is with you. No one will protect her like you will— because you love her."

Since the first moment Nick had met her, he had felt a connection with Penny Payne. He had more of a kinship with her than with the family with whom he actually shared DNA. So he admitted to her what he never had to anyone else. "I don't know what love is."

She flinched as if he'd slapped her. "Oh, Nick."

He shook his head. "I don't want your pity." But he had it; he could feel it even before he noticed the tears shimmering in her eyes.

"You don't have my pity," she insisted. "You have my love."

"Why?" Because he looked like the man she had loved and lost, the man who had betrayed her love?

"For the same reason that Annalise Huxton loves you. Because you're you."

Maybe they loved him. But he couldn't return that love. He didn't know how. So he only reiterated, "I can't marry Annalise because I can't give her what she deserves. I can't love her."

Annalise glanced across the SUV console at the man who looked the most like Nick of all the Paynes. Nick was gone, though. He'd been gone for a while. He was running again.

She knew why Nick was gone. She wasn't as certain about why her brother was gone. He'd been here when Nick had left, but he hadn't stayed long. So it was Cooper Payne who had to drive her to the Payne Protection Agency. She had put her career on hold as much as she could. But there were things she needed to handle. For one, she needed to use the office equipment at Payne Protection.

She asked the former Marine, "Why isn't Gage protecting me?"

Cooper glanced across the console at her and replied, "He doesn't trust himself yet."

A twinge of concern squeezed her heart. "He was on assignment when I arrived in River City," she said. "Is he worse now than he was?"

He looked bad, like he'd aged years instead of months since she'd seen him last. And he was so thin and haggard-looking.

Cooper shook his head. "No. He's actually doing quite a bit better."

"Then why wouldn't he trust himself?"

Cooper offered her a quick smile. "Because your safety is too important to him. He wants to make sure you have the best protection." But as he said it, his brow furrowed, and his focus turned to the rearview mirror.

"I hate that I need protection," she said.

Nick blamed himself, but she wasn't entirely convinced the men coming after her had anything to do with him. How could they think that she mattered that much to him when she didn't believe it herself?

"You do," Cooper said.

And she realized why his focus had turned to the rearview. "Someone's following us."

Dread knotted her stomach. She was so sick of the attacks, of the vehicle chases and the gunshots. She wanted her life back, her boring, unendangered life. But all of that had changed after the night she'd spent with Nick. Nothing had been boring since then.

Cooper cursed, then apologized.

"I grew up with Gage," she reminded him. She was used to swearing. She actually felt like swearing herself now. If not for her baby, she might have. But she didn't know how much her son could hear in her womb.

Or feel. She had to make sure he stayed safe. She slid her palms over her belly, but she couldn't protect him—if whoever was following them caught them.

Unless...

"Isn't it one of you?" she asked hopefully. "Another Payne Protection bodyguard?"

Like when Milek Kozminski had been following Nick.

But she could tell from the grim look on Cooper's face that it wasn't. He had no idea who was following them.

So if it wasn't a friend, wasn't it a foe?

One of the men who'd attacked her was dead. Nikki had seen him that day, lying on a gurney in the ER hallway. And she had been so relieved it wasn't Nick.

She had to make sure that it didn't wind up being Nick yet. The list he'd emailed was too long even for her to work and eliminate suspects before someone eliminated Nick. But besides that, she couldn't help but think that they were all missing something.

Nick assumed someone was after him and Annalise out of a quest for vengeance. While Nikki owed her half brother for saving her life in the parking garage, she still wasn't entirely ready to let go of her resentment of him. She would actually find it pretty sweet if she could prove Nick—who was usually right—wrong.

So she'd gotten out from behind the desk where Logan had always tried to put her. And she was doing fieldwork. Even though all of River City PD had been searching for it, she was the one who'd found Annalise's stolen car.

She might find something no one else had at Nick's place. Boards had been nailed across the front door to keep out intruders. And her.

The bars on the windows offered her no entrance, either. Using her skills as a former gymnast, she leapt onto the stockade fence and pulled herself up and over it so she could get into the backyard. That door hadn't been boarded up, and there were no bars on the windows in the rear of the house.

With a surge of excitement, she reached for the lock pick tools the Kozminskis had given her. She could finally test her newly learned tricks. But when she reached for the door handle, it turned easily.

It hadn't been locked.

With a sigh, she slipped the tools back into her pocket. She would be able to use them eventually now that she was working for Cooper. He wouldn't treat her as Logan always had. He would respect that she could take care of herself.

Like Nick did.

How was it that the brother who'd known her the least amount of time knew her the best?

Because he was Nick.

He had that same uncanny ability her mother had, which was so weird and gave Nikki another reason to resent him. She didn't care that he knew her so well. She cared that he had the gift of her mother's that she'd always wanted.

She always felt as if she were in the dark, like now. With all the blinds drawn, the house was pitch-black, as if it was night already. She stumbled over things that had been strewn across the floor.

She expelled a ragged breath. The place must have been trashed. She doubted Nick, who was always so controlled, was this much of a slob. Now, Parker...

She would believe that of Logan's twin. Not Nick.

The place had been destroyed, but it had also been

searched. Every closet and cupboard had been inspected, the contents of every drawer tossed out.

This wasn't about vengeance.

Triumph surged through her. Nick was wrong.

A sharp noise drew her attention to the front door. A board cracked. Wood splintered. Someone was breaking in.

Her hand trembling, she reached for her weapon. She could fire it. She had proved that in the hospital parking garage. It might have been her bullet that had killed the man.

She shuddered as she remembered him lying on that gurney. She had never killed anyone before. She'd felt no triumph in having done it. She'd felt only horror.

But if it came down to it again—her life or someone else's—she would pull the trigger. She moved her finger toward it as she pointed the gun barrel at the front door.

Chapter 16

The boards were flimsy. Nick broke them easily with his foot as he kicked in the door. It bounced back against the interior wall as light from outside streamed in. Like the beam of a flashlight, it illuminated a dark-clothed shadow standing in the hall. That light bounced off the metal of a gun.

He silently cursed himself for losing Milek. As he'd suspected earlier, Kozminski had been his bodyguard. He'd been testing himself when he'd lost him, and he seriously hadn't thought he would need protection.

He'd been wrong.

Just as the shot rang out, Nick ducked. Wood splintered the jamb near his head. He rushed forward, toward the shadow. He could have fired back, but he couldn't get answers from a dead man. He tackled his intruder instead, knocking him to the ground as he grabbed for the gun. He snapped it easily from the person's grasp.

Breath whooshed out of the suspect, followed by a very unladylike curse.

"Nikki?" He quickly rolled off his intruder.

She choked and gasped for the air he'd knocked out of her.

"Are you okay?" he asked anxiously as he helped her sit up. He hadn't expected to find her inside his house, shooting at him.

She leaned against the wall of the hallway where he'd been knocked down a few days before. She drew in a deep, unsteady breath. "And everybody wonders why I don't like you."

He chuckled as he held her gun aloft. "I'd better not hand this back to you yet. You almost hit me once."

"I didn't know it was you," she said.

"Or you would have hit me?"

She laughed now. "I wasn't aiming to kill," she said. "Or I would have hit you."

He didn't doubt that. She was a good shot. Logan had no idea the caliber of bodyguard he could have had if he'd given Nikki a chance.

"That was just a warning shot," she said.

"Warning shot?" he repeated.

"You were breaking down the door."

"I live here."

She laughed again. "So it's okay for you to break down your own door?"

"Seems like everybody else has done it whether they live here or not."

"I went over the fence," she said. "And the back door was unlocked."

She sounded almost disappointed. Then he noticed the tools that had fallen from her pocket when he'd knocked her down. He handed her the set. "Might not be a good idea to let a lawman see these."

"You're not a lawman anymore," she said. "You're a bodyguard."

When he said nothing, she narrowed her brown eyes and studied his face. "You haven't given your notice yet?"

He groaned. "I've been having my detectives keep me apprised of what's going on at the station while I take some time off."

"Have you changed your mind?"

It wasn't that he didn't want to be a bodyguard. But he didn't want to be Annalise's bodyguard. Being around her only seemed to put her in more danger. "Not about the job. I still intend to talk to the chief." Just like he'd told Megan. He needed to give his notice.

"Have you changed your mind about the assignment?"

He nodded.

"I think you're wrong about someone using Annalise to get back at you."

His heart swelled. He hoped he wasn't the reason she was in danger. "What did you figure out?"

She stood up and gestured around them. "Somebody was looking for something."

"Or just trashing the place."

She shook her head. "No. It's a search. Drawers. Closets. Cupboards."

"There were holes in the drywall at other places." He turned toward the living room. "Cushions ripped open."

"You thought it was vandalism."

"A message. Like the gunshots," he said. "That's not

someone looking for something. You were there in the parking garage—"

"I caught them around your SUV," she said. "They could have been trying to steal it—like they'd stolen Annalise's car. That had been searched, too."

He nodded. "But the gunfire outside the hospital the other night…" Nobody had been looking for anything that night but blood.

She shrugged. "You're probably pissing them off."

"You know the feeling," he teased.

A smile tugged up her lips, seemingly against her will. "Yeah, you piss me off all the time."

He held out her gun to her, but when she reached for it, he pulled it back. "Sure you're not going to shoot me with it?"

"I would have done that a long time ago if I wanted you dead."

And what she'd said finally clicked with him. "If someone wanted Annalise dead before now, she would already be dead." She had been on her own for the past six months.

Nikki nodded. "This isn't about killing her or you. It's about getting something from you."

"So the gunfire could have been warning shots."

She shrugged. "Or a distraction."

He glanced around his place. "What are they looking for?"

"You tell me," Nikki said.

He sighed. "I have no idea."

Nikki's dark eyes had narrowed with suspicion, the warmth and amusement all gone. "Really? No idea?"

"No."

"Somebody thinks you have something."

She did, too.

But he wasn't like the people he'd arrested for corruption. He had never confiscated a drug dealer's money or assets for himself instead of putting them into evidence. And he was offended that Nikki thought he could have. Hell, he was offended that anyone thought he could have.

"I don't have anything," he murmured.

"That's too bad," Nikki said.

"Why?"

"Because if you had something and gave it back, this could all be over," she explained. "You and Annalise would no longer be in danger."

Since he had nothing to return to whoever thought they were the rightful owner, he had no idea how to make sure that Annalise would be safe again.

Annalise didn't feel safe.

She knew that Cooper was a good bodyguard—good enough to head up his own franchise of the security business. But she didn't understand why he'd driven right past the Payne Protection Agency.

"You told me someone is following us," she said with a nervous glance in the side mirror. "Shouldn't we stop for help?" She would have felt safer in the security offices with the other bodyguards.

She would have felt safer with Nick. Why had he left the condo? He hadn't said. The others had assumed he was working the list of enemies he'd given them. And Milek had followed him, which had reassured her. He wouldn't be able to lose Milek.

Was Cooper as good?

He snorted. "You think I need help losing a tail?"

She was not reassured—until he reached up to the device on his collar. He touched a button and spoke into it. "Hey, guys, I picked up a shadow."

"I see him." Another voice emanated from the small radio on Cooper's collar.

Annalise looked in the side mirror again, but she noticed nothing out of the ordinary. "Someone else is behind us?" It was a Payne. All of their voices sounded so alike.

"Of course," Cooper replied. "When family is in danger, we work as a family." So he hadn't been protecting her alone.

She released a slight breath. She was safer than she'd realized. But still...

Remembering the barrage of bullets the other night, she pressed her palms over her belly. She wasn't worried about just her safety. She was worried about her baby.

"And because we aren't alone, maybe we should try trapping him," Cooper suggested.

"No!" The shout crackled through the radio. Since it was closer to his ear, Cooper flinched.

But Annalise heard it clearly, too. And she recognized the voice. Nick.

"Don't listen to him," Annalise said. She wanted this to be over. She wanted her life back. "You need to catch him. You need to find out what he wants with me."

Because she didn't believe it was vengeance over something Nick had done. Sure, she didn't think she'd made any enemies, but maybe she had. Maybe someone resented something she'd done. Maybe it wasn't Nick who had put her in danger but she who had put Nick in danger.

Because if the person knew her, he would know how she felt about Nick—how she had always felt about Nick. She loved him.

* * *

He was probably making a huge mistake. And if the plan failed, Nick would kill him. But Cooper understood Annalise's frustration over not knowing who was after her or why.

And the only way to make certain she stayed safe was to find out. The risk wasn't as great as Nick probably thought it was.

The entire Payne Protection Agency force—all the newly divided franchises reunited—was working this assignment. For Nick.

They wouldn't let anything happen to Annalise and the baby she carried. They wouldn't let the tail get close to her. They'd only let him think that he could.

So Cooper slowed down as he headed toward the part of the city that had yet to recover from the economic downturn. He headed toward the area that was all abandoned warehouses and factories. If whoever was following him intended to a make a move on the vehicle—on Annalise—he would do it here.

"Is everyone in place?" he asked, and he heard the telltale nervous break in his own voice. The plan was risky. But with everyone working together, there was no way someone could get hurt.

"No," Nick protested again. "It's too dangerous."

"We've got this." It was Logan who spoke—Logan who was the boss on this assignment. But they all knew who was really the boss: Nick. And he hadn't approved this plan.

"The vehicle is coming up too fast," Nick said. "It's going to ram you."

Cooper glanced in the rearview mirror and realized that Nick was right. The truck that had been following them had shot forward—past Parker's SUV. The former vice cop was a good driver, but he wasn't as good as he needed to be now.

Cooper pressed on the accelerator, trying to get farther ahead of the truck. If it rammed them at the speed it was coming...

Annalise would be hurt. So would the baby.

He cursed. An intersection was coming up, the light changing to red. This area wasn't as populated, so he could take the chance of blowing through it without being hit. So he did.

The vehicle behind him wasn't as lucky. As the truck hit the intersection, an SUV hit it, coming at it full force. Metal crunched. Tires squealed. And both vehicles spun around.

Annalise reached over the console and grasped Cooper's arm. "Who was that? Who hit the truck?"

She must have recognized the black SUV like he had. It was a Payne Protection company vehicle. He cranked the wheel to turn around, to head back toward the crash.

From the curious silence on the radio, he knew who'd been driving that SUV. And from the way Annalise's hand clutched his arm harder, it was obvious that she knew, too.

"Nick," he murmured.

Nick had been driving the SUV that took out their tail. But through the spider-webbed glass of the front window, Cooper could see that his half brother wasn't alone. The person slumped in the passenger seat had brown curls. Nikki was with him.

He braked and glanced over at his own passenger. Annalise's face was pale with fear, but not for herself. She was afraid for the others like he was.

Cooper saw no movement inside either crumpled vehicle. He saw nothing but smoke curling out from beneath the hoods. Then sparks ignited.

"Go!" Annalise shouted at him.

He flung open the driver's door and ran toward the crash. He had to get to Nick and Nikki before their vehicle blew.

Chapter 17

Gasoline fumes burned his nose, the scent heavy in the front seat of the SUV. Nick blinked and tried to focus. With the air bags pushed against the cracked windshield, it was hard to see. But the sparks were an unmistakable warning. He glanced toward the passenger seat. Nikki was slumped against the side window, blood trickling from her head onto the glass. Since they'd hit the other vehicle head-on, the side air bag hadn't deployed.

"Damn it!"

What if she was seriously hurt? Her head? Her neck? Dared he move her?

The sparks ignited with a hiss, and flames shot up from the engine. Heat instantly filled the front seat. He had no choice. He kicked open his crumpled door. Then he reached for Nikki. He couldn't wait. He had to get her out now. So he dragged her limp body over the console and out the driver's side. Despite her slight weight, his wounded shoulder ached in protest. But Nick ignored the pain. He clutched Nikki close as he ran from the SUV.

He'd only made it a few yards when the flames hissed again. A whoosh knocked him to the ground and the vehicles exploded. As he fell, he rolled so that he didn't crush Nikki. But he lost his grasp on her. She fell to the ground next to him.

Her face was so pale but for the blood trickling from the wound on her forehead. His gut twisted with guilt. He shouldn't have put her in danger. "Nikki?"

"Nikki!" another voice echoed his. "Nick!"

There were more voices shouting over the noise of the burning vehicles. Glass shattered. Flames hissed.

Suddenly, strong hands reached for him, helping him to his feet. They didn't touch Nikki, though. Her brothers stood over her, staring down in horror at her.

"Is she…" Logan asked, his face growing pale as his voice cracked with fear.

It had to seem like his worst nightmare come to fruition. He had tried so hard to keep her safe.

"Dead?" Nikki was the one who finished the question for him. Her eyes fluttered open and she stared up at them. "I sure as hell hope not. There's a lot I want to do with my life before that happens."

What? Nick wanted to ask her. But there was a more important question. "Are you all right?"

She sighed and reached out her hand. "I will be once you help me up."

Before he could close his hand around hers, someone shoved him back. "What the hell were you thinking?"

Logan shouted at him. "You could have killed her. You could have killed both of you!"

"I had to stop that truck."

He'd been thinking about Annalise and the baby. And with the speed with which that truck had been bearing down on them, they would have been hurt. Or worse.

He turned to Cooper. "Are they all right?"

He nodded. And he looked as guilty as Nick felt. They'd both taken chances they shouldn't have taken.

"You compromised the whole operation," Logan said. "And nearly got Nikki killed."

Nick had never seen the oldest Payne so angry. He stepped toward Nick, yelling in his face until small hands wedged between them, pushing Logan back.

"Shut up," Nikki yelled at Logan. Then she turned toward Nick and threw her arms around him, hugging him. "Thank you!"

"Saving you from the crash he caused is the least he could do," Logan said.

"No," she said with a glare at her oldest brother. He'd beat Parker from the womb by just a few minutes, but he'd never let anyone forget. "That's the least any of you could do. Nick did the most. He treated me as an equal. Now and that day in the parking garage. He trusts that I can take care of myself, unlike the rest of you."

Logan opened his mouth, probably to argue. And there was plenty to argue about in that statement since Nick had wound up saving her both times. But for once, the oldest Payne didn't have to have the last word. He closed his lips and just nodded.

Nikki was okay—that was all that mattered now. But Nick turned with frustration toward the burning vehicles. The other driver hadn't made it out of the crash. And as badly as his body was burning, they might never learn who he was.

Annalise had never been so afraid as she'd watched the vehicles explode. She would have pushed open the passenger door—would have run toward the wreckage as everyone else had. But the SUV must have been equipped with some special security system, and Cooper had locked her inside. She hadn't been able to open her door. And she hadn't been able to see anything but the flames rising from the blackened metal.

She'd thought for certain that Nick was dead...until, long moments later, she'd seen him and his family walk around the burning vehicles. He and Nikki had survived. The driver of the truck hadn't been as lucky.

She grimaced as she remembered what she'd seen, what she'd wished she had never witnessed.

"Are you having more of those contractions?" Nick asked with concern.

Everyone else had left an hour ago. But he sat up— as he had the past few nights—on the couch.

She shook her head. "No. I'm fine."

"It's late," Nick said. "You should get some sleep."

She was afraid that if she closed her eyes, she would see that crash again. But instead of the other man burning, she would see Nick.

"What about you?" she asked. "You must be exhausted." He had spent night after night on the couch— watching the door.

Exhaustion darkened the skin beneath his bright blue eyes, and that muscle twitched again in his cheek, above his tightly clenched jaw. He hadn't changed. He still wore his jeans and a black shirt. Blood stained the shirt. She wasn't certain if it was his—seeping through from his shoulder wound—or if it was Nikki's.

He shrugged off her concern. "I'm fine."

He wasn't. He had been shot. And he'd been in a car accident.

"You should have gone to the hospital with Nikki," she said.

"I didn't need to."

"She said the same thing."

"She'd lost consciousness for a little while," Nick said. And that muscle twitched in his cheek as tension filled him. He must have been reliving the accident, too. "She needed to be checked for a concussion. And she probably needed stitches."

She heard the guilt in his voice, the regret. "I'm sorry," she said. "I shouldn't have left the condo earlier."

"Why did you?" he asked.

"I—I had all this work I needed to do," she said. "I needed a fax machine and a way to telecommute—"

"And Logan offered his office," he surmised.

She nodded. "But I shouldn't have risked it." She ran her palms over the baby. She shouldn't have risked his life for her career.

He sighed. "I'm the one who shouldn't have left."

"Where did you go?" she asked.

"To see Penny."

She suspected it hadn't been to discuss wedding plans. Probably to end them.

"That's fine," she said. She hadn't agreed to marry him, anyway, even though it was what she'd wanted as long as she could remember. "I had plenty of protection."

"But you were still in danger," Nick said.

Tears stung her eyes. "Will I always be?" she wondered aloud. "Will I ever be safe again?"

"Of course," he said. "We'll get to the bottom of this. We'll figure out who's after me."

"That vehicle was tailing me," she reminded him.

"Because of me."

"You don't know that."

He sighed. "No. But Nikki and I have come up with another theory."

So had she. "I think it could have more to do with me than I realized. Maybe another real estate agent wants to eliminate me as competition." It was possible. The Chicago real estate business could be quite cutthroat. "Or maybe I do have a stalker."

He narrowed his eyes. "I thought you didn't have any crazy exes."

"I don't," she said. "But a stalker can be anyone. I could have smiled at someone on the street and given him the wrong impression."

He nodded slowly as if considering it. "You do have a very friendly smile."

She didn't know if he was complimenting or teasing her.

"I really don't think this has anything to do with you," he said.

"You and Nikki talked it over," she prompted him.

He nodded more quickly now. "We would have presented our theory to everyone tonight, but it was more important that Nikki go to the hospital and get checked out."

More important than his getting checked out. Nick had always been such a loner that he'd acted as if he could barely tolerate her and Gage following him around. But it sounded as if he was beginning to care about this family he hadn't known he had until his mother had died.

And if he cared about them, could he someday come to care about her, as well? She'd spent years trying and had never reached his heart. It had taken them only months. She had to accept that it just wasn't meant to be.

"We'll have a meeting about it tomorrow."

"That's good," she said. The danger needed to end. She wanted her life back.

"And in the meantime, you're safe here," Nick said. "Nobody can get inside this place."

"I don't feel safe," she said. That was why she couldn't sleep. She had felt safe only one place—in his arms.

As if he'd read her mind—as he always did—he wrapped his arms around her and pulled her against his chest. His heart beat fast and heavily. Maybe it was residual adrenaline from the crash.

Or maybe it was…

She stared up into his face and saw the way his blue eyes darkened, his pupils dilating. He wanted her, too.

"You need to go to bed," he said. And he lifted her easily in his arms—despite his wounded shoulder and her extra weight—and carried her into the master bedroom.

She locked her arms around his neck so that when he laid her down, she pulled him down with her. "I'm not tired," she said.

"Oh, I didn't say you were going to sleep," he murmured. Then his mouth covered hers. He kissed her passionately, as if he'd been starving for a taste of her lips.

She had been starving for him. Her body ached with desire. She had felt so empty—so hollow—without him. She pulled at his clothes, trying to tug off his shirt, his belt. But she was too anxious—too inept.

He stepped back and pulled off his holster and gun. His shirt followed, and his jeans. He was so damn sexy.

She reached for her clothes. She wanted to be as naked as he was, wanted nothing between them but skin. But she fumbled with the buttons.

He undid them. And as he parted her blouse, he pressed kisses against the skin he exposed—on her throat, then the curve of her breast and her belly. The baby shifted beneath his lips.

And a smile spread across Nick's face. Was he happy about the baby? She hadn't thought so. She'd seen only his shock. Until now…

She wanted to ask him how he felt. But then his mouth was on hers again. He kissed her, his lips sliding over hers. She gasped at the delicious sensation, and his tongue slipped inside her mouth. It stroked back and forth between her lips.

Desire overwhelmed her.

He unclasped her bra and pushed it and her blouse from her shoulders. Then he touched her breasts. Cupping them in his palms, he teased the nipples with his thumbs.

She moaned and pressed against him, wanting more. His erection pushed against her hip, so she wrapped her fingers around it. She stroked him.

He groaned, and his control snapped—like it had that night they'd made love the first time. He lifted her so that she straddled his lap. Then he eased inside her and filled the emptiness.

She felt whole again. Safe.

But she felt so much more than that. As he moved inside her, the tension built. She clutched at his shoulders and his back as she moved frantically. She rocked and bounced and arched, desperate for the release only he could give her.

He clutched her hips in his hands and helped her match his rhythm. They moved together as one. And they came as one, shouting as pleasure overwhelmed them.

He dropped onto his back on the mattress and pulled her down on top of him. He wrapped his arms tightly around her, as if he never intended to let her go.

But Annalise knew better.

She knew he wouldn't stay.

He cursed as he watched the news footage of the crash. Another lackey dead.

He'd lost one man in the hospital parking garage. And now another...

Nicholas Rus was good. Too good. The FBI special agent had made so many enemies that it hadn't been hard to find more men to take him on. The only problem was that they didn't want what *he* wanted. They wanted vengeance. Because Rus had shut down so much crime in River City and Chicago, they wanted him to pay—with his life. They were imbeciles. The shoot-out at the hospital wasn't going to get *him* what he wanted.

What was *his*...

But he had been looking—as discreetly as possible—for months. And his patience had worn out. Where the hell was it? What had Nicholas Rus or that woman done with it?

One of them had it. They had to.

They probably just didn't realize what they had. He had to get it before they did. Or maybe he would make Nicholas Rus bring it to him. He just needed to make sure he had something Nick wanted as desperately as he wanted his property.

The woman was the key. Annalise Huxton was the key to him reclaiming what was rightfully his.

Chapter 18

Nikki looked like death. She'd already had the bruise on her left cheek. Now she had another on the right side of her face along with a short line of stitches near her temple.

Nick's heart contracted with regret that she'd been hurt—because of him. "I'm sorry," he murmured as she stepped inside the condo.

Her brown eyes twinkled. "Sorry? You're the first one to make sure I'm included in a Payne Protection meeting."

Nick was sympathetic. He knew what it was like to be on the outside looking in on a family. He had felt like that with the Huxtons. He'd understood he wasn't one of them, but at least Gage and Annalise had tried to include him. Nikki had known she was a Payne, but her brothers had never included her like they should have.

Until now…

Everyone else fell silent as she walked into the condo. They were probably staring at the bruises. Nikki tensed as if she thought they were going to throw her out.

Nick said, "Now that Nikki is here, she's going to run the meeting."

Predictably, Logan bristled. "She's not up to speed on this assignment."

"She's more up to speed than you think," Nick said. "She's been working this assignment all along. She found Annalise's stolen car for me when the whole River City Police Department couldn't find it."

"You had no right to put her on this assignment," Logan said.

It wasn't the first time Nick had heard that. He'd put Garek Kozminski on assignment for the FBI and had nearly gotten him and Candace killed. He'd made mistakes. So he wasn't going to argue with his half brother, especially now that Logan was his boss.

Logan's face flushed with anger as he continued, "You've put her in danger over and over again."

And Nick didn't feel good about it. But he felt compelled to point out, in Nikki's defense more than his own, "And she survived it. She is tougher than you all have given her credit for being."

Nikki didn't just smile. She beamed.

And Nick's heart swelled with pride in her. He finally understood Gage's connection with Annalise. He glanced over to his friend sitting next to Annalise. Right now, Gage looked better than Nikki did. Whatever physical injuries he had sustained while he'd been missing were healing. Nick hoped his other injuries were healing, too.

"Suck-up," Parker called him.

Unabashed, Nick grinned. Maybe he should have sucked up to his sister a while ago. "She's smart, too."

"We never disputed that," Logan said. "That's why she's best behind a desk."

Nikki snorted derisively.

"She figured out what no one else has," Nick said. "This isn't about revenge."

"What is it about?" Annalise asked the question. She'd been worried that it was about her, that she had made someone jealous or obsessed. She could have. Her smiles were powerful enough to make a stranger on the street fall in love with her. But Nick doubted it had anything to do with her.

Everybody looked at Nick, but he turned toward his sister.

Nikki shrugged.

"I thought you figured it out," Logan said, frustration joining his earlier irritation.

"We don't know *what* it's about," she said. Her suspicion from the day before was gone.

The tightness in Nick's chest eased. Nikki didn't think the worst of him anymore. She didn't think he was corrupt, like all the cops and public officials he had busted in River City. Maybe she was even beginning to trust him.

Logan's brow furrowed with confusion, and he began, "I thought—"

"It's about *something*," Nikki said. "But we don't know what."

Nick could see the others were still confused, so he explained, "People think either Annalise or I have something they want."

A ragged sigh of relief slipped from Annalise's lips. "Of course."

"The break-ins," Gage said. "I thought it looked like someone was searching for something."

Nikki nodded. "That's what I thought when I checked out the scene of the last break-in."

The scene where she'd nearly shot him. But he kept that to himself. He didn't need the others to think she'd overreacted. Her quick reflexes were what would keep her alive when she was a true bodyguard.

"And that's probably the reason for the car thefts, too," Nikki continued. "They think Annalise or Nick has something."

"What?" Logan asked.

"I have no idea," Nick said. But he glanced at Annalise, who had fallen curiously silent after her sigh.

"I had some idea," Nikki sheepishly admitted.

Logan groaned.

"What?" Annalise and Gage asked the question together.

Explaining for his sister again, Nick said, "She thought I was dirty. That I stole drug money or something that should have been entered into evidence."

Gage uttered that rusty-sounding laugh of his. "You, dirty? That's hilarious!"

Nick hadn't found it amusing at all.

And realizing that he had been offended, Gage laughed again. Then he turned toward Nikki, whose face had grown red with embarrassment. "You really don't know squeaky-clean Nick. He's the only one Chief Lynch considered sending up to handle the corruption in River City because the chief knows for certain he's beyond corruption."

And that tightness in Nick's chest eased even more. Despite his crossing the line with Annalise, Nick hadn't completely lost Gage's respect.

But the tightness only eased. It didn't disappear entirely. It wouldn't until they figured out what someone wanted so desperately from him that they kept going after Annalise. Maybe they had figured out that if they wanted to work an exchange, the only things Nick cared enough about to barter were Annalise and their unborn baby.

Garek waited until the team had returned to Payne Protection Agency before he spoke. He shut the door behind them and settled into the chair across from his boss's desk. Most of the team—including his beautiful bride—had stayed outside the condo for added security for Nick.

Even if Cooper would have assigned her fieldwork, Nikki was in no condition to work at the moment. So she settled carefully into the chair next to him. She looked like hell, but she was also happier than he'd ever seen her before.

The irony was that the guy who'd made her unhappy—by merely existing—had made her happy again. Or maybe that wasn't ironic but appropriate. Nick had given her the respect her other brothers hadn't.

She'd earned that respect, though. He believed her theory was right. Maybe she'd been right about everything.

He began, "Just playing devil's advocate here."

Logan snorted. "You enjoy that role too much."

"But what if we've been wrong about Nick?" he wondered aloud. "What if he *is* dirty?"

Logan shook his head. "Not possible."

Garek didn't think so, either. But he trusted that
Nikki was right. It made sense that someone had been
breaking into Nick's and Annalise's places and vehicles
because they were looking for something. But Nick had
to have something they actually wanted badly enough
to kill to get.

So how could he not know that he had it? And it had
to belong to someone desperate, someone dangerous.

"I agree," Nikki said, which shocked Garek for a
couple of reasons. First, she was actually concurring
with something Logan had said. Second, she trusted
Nick. Of course, he had saved her life more than once.

But perhaps the fact that Nick had rushed to everyone's rescue multiple times had blinded them to his
true nature. Maybe he wasn't as squeaky-clean as the
Huxtons believed. Actually, Gage had been the only
one to speak up on his behalf. Annalise had remained
curiously silent.

Did she know something the others didn't? She was
obviously closer to Nick than anyone else. Garek suspected that nobody understood him better than she did.

"You've been quiet," Nick said after the others had
left. She was sitting on the couch, and he knelt in front
of her and studied her face. "Are you feeling all right?"

Annalise felt sick. But it had nothing to do with her
pregnancy and everything to do with what she had done.
It was all her fault. It had to be. "No…"

His handsome face tensed with concern. "I'll take
you to the hospital."

She shook her head. "No, I don't need to go to the
hospital." Even if she was having medical issues, she

wouldn't risk it, not after what had happened the last time they had gone.

"Is it the contractions again?" he asked. He put his hands over her stomach as if he could feel them, too. Or as if he could make them stop.

He was so protective. But that was just his nature. She couldn't read more into it than that. She couldn't convince herself that he actually cared about her.

"No," she replied. "It's not the baby."

He leaned closer, his blue gaze intense as he studied her face. "But I can tell you're not feeling well."

Tears stung her eyes—tears of regret. "That's because of what I've done," she admitted.

He tensed and eased away from her. "Annalise…"

"It's my fault." It had to be.

"What did you do?"

She'd realized it when Nikki had been talking. She'd realized then what a huge mistake she'd made. "You're going to be furious with me."

Chapter 19

Dread settled heavily on Nick, pulling his shoulders down. He flinched at the pain. His gunshot wound had barely begun to heal. But his physical pain was milder than what he was feeling emotionally.

He got back to his feet and paced the length of the living room before turning back to her to ask, "What did you do?"

What could Annalise have done that had put them in danger? Gage had called him squeaky-clean, but Annalise was more honest than he was. Or so Nick had always believed.

She'd been just a kid when he'd lived next door to her. And he hadn't stayed in touch with her throughout the years like she had tried to stay in touch with him. He had no idea what kind of men she'd dated. She might have fallen for a bad boy who'd gotten her into trouble.

"I know what you told me to do."

He'd told her a lot of things over the years. To stop following him around.

To stop hugging him.

He hadn't really meant those things.

"What did I tell you?" he asked for clarification.

"You asked me to get rid of your mom's house."

"You said you rented it." He wished she'd burned it down instead. Or sold it.

She nodded. "The tenant paid the whole year's rent in cash."

A chill raced down his spine. "Someone paid for the year up front? Is that normal?"

She shrugged. "I've had it happen before, when someone has sold a house and wants to rent."

"Had this guy sold a house?"

"Maybe," she said. "But I didn't handle the sale. I probably wouldn't have rented to him if he hadn't been able to pay the cash up front."

The short hairs lifted on Nick's nape. "Why not?"

"He had no credit history. No job history."

"But he had a year's rent money?"

"In cash."

Criminals had cash. Who the hell had she rented to? "Annalise…"

"I'm sorry," she said.

"There's more?" he asked.

She nodded. "You told me to get rid of all of her possessions, too."

"And you didn't."

She had never believed he'd meant the other things he'd told her—or she would have stayed away. She would have stopped hugging him. But she hadn't. So she must not have thought he'd meant what he'd told her about his mother's estate, either.

"Did you rent the place furnished?" he asked. That would have made sense and explained why she hadn't gotten rid of anything.

She shook her head. "The tenant wanted me to," she said. "He even offered to pay me extra. But I didn't want to leave her possessions there."

"She had nothing of value," he said. "You could have left everything. Or given it all away."

"I kept her belongings," Annalise admitted.

"But I told you to get rid of everything."

"I thought you might change your mind," she said. "I didn't want you to have any regrets."

"I regret that you didn't get rid of her crap," he said. Especially if having it had put her in danger. "Did you bring it home with you?"

She shook her head. "I have a few storage units. I either put stuff in them when I'm staging houses or store the stuff I use for staging in them."

"I don't think my…" He hated calling her Mom. In the short time he'd known her, Penny Payne had already been more of a mother to him than the woman who'd given birth to him had ever been. "… I don't think Carla had anything you could use to stage a house."

"No," Annalise admitted. "But I thought you might want something of hers, something to remember her by. And I didn't want to have given it all away."

He had something to remember her by: the letter she'd left telling him who his father really was. She had given him the family he'd never thought he would have. She had given him a real mother. And she had allayed the fear he'd always had that his father was some drug dealer.

What else had she given him? Had she left him something that had put his—and worse, Annalise's—lives in danger? She had given him one family. But if he lost Annalise and their unborn baby, he'd lost the family he could have made for himself.

"What do you think you're doing?"

Annalise dropped her sweater into her open suitcase, turned around and found Nick leaning against the doorjamb. "I'm packing."

"Why?"

After she'd admitted to ignoring his command to get rid of all of his mother's things, she'd thought he would be happy to get rid of her.

"Because we're going back to Chicago," she said.

"Why would we do that?" he asked.

How could he not know? He was the lawman. She was just a real estate agent. "Because we need to go through the storage units and find what they're looking for."

"Did you see a wad of money?"

She shook her head.

"Of course not," Nick said. "Because anytime Carla got her hands on money, she used it to buy drugs."

She ached for Nick, for the sad little boy who'd grown up too quickly next door to her family.

"So it must be something else," she agreed.

He shook his head. "What? If it was anything of value, she would have pawned it for money for drugs. There's nothing."

"Then why did someone break into her house and

mine and yours?" she asked. "Just hours ago you said somebody thinks you have something they want."

"Thinks," Nick said. "We don't actually have it."

He was probably right. But that only increased her frustration. "How do we convince whoever is after us that we don't have it?"

She wanted her life back. She'd worked hard to build her career. And as a single mom-to-be, she needed it more than ever.

"We find him."

"How do we do that?" she asked.

He shook his head. "Not you. You've already been in too much danger because of this."

And she heard the anger again. He was mad that she hadn't done as he'd asked, that she hadn't gotten rid of everything. Hell, he was right. If she'd known what was going to happen to her life, she would have burned down his mother's house herself. But she'd done what she'd thought would be best for him, like she always had.

She'd thought *she* would be best for him. That was why she'd been so persistent in loving him. She'd thought she could make him happy. But all she had done was create more problems for him.

He would be better off without her. She tossed another sweater in the suitcase. Candace had been sweet to buy her more things. But now she had too much.

"Why are you still packing?" he asked.

"I have a job, too," she said. "I have a life that I can't stay away from any longer."

"You still want to go back to Chicago?"

She nodded. She needed to go back, needed to get away from him before she fell any deeper in love with him. Before she began to imagine that they could actually have a life together. It was clear that Nick didn't want that. She wasn't even certain that he wanted to have a baby together. Or if she really would be raising their child alone.

"Give us more time," he implored her.

"Us?" Her heart swelled with hope.

"The Payne Protection Agency," he said. "Give us more time to figure out what you and I might have that someone wants. We'll check out the renter in Carla's house. We'll find out if he's involved in all of this."

"Of course."

He was talking about his family. They were the *us*. Not her and him. They had never been an *us*. And maybe it was time that she accepted that they never would be.

"Annalise?" he called her name as if he'd said it more than once.

She raised her gaze from the suitcase to his handsome face. "Will you give us time?" he asked.

She'd already given Nick her whole life. She couldn't give him any more time.

Penny had a wedding to plan. But it wasn't the one she wanted to plan. She wanted to plan Nick's to Annalise. As if thinking about him had summoned him, he appeared in the doorway to her office.

She caught a glimpse of what he must have been like as a boy, longing for love. She'd worried that he hadn't had any in his life. But after meeting Annalise Huxton, she knew he had. The girl next door had loved him her whole life.

Before she could even greet him, he said, "She's leaving." And his voice was full of frustration and pain.

Penny pressed a hand to her heart as it leaped with fear—for the young woman and her unborn baby. "But she's in danger."

"She's not leaving right now," he said. "I talked her out of that. But she'll leave soon."

"Not if you stop her."

"I can't," he said. "She has a great career in Chicago. She has to go back."

Penny shook her head. "Give her a reason to stay."

"What reason can I give her?"

"You know what reason, Nick," she said. The most important reason. "Give her your love."

His handsome face—so like her sons' faces—twisted into a grimace. "I don't know how."

Her heart ached for him, for the love he'd never known. "Nick…"

He shook his head, brushing off her sympathy. "I don't know how to love someone," he said. "You can't give what you've never received."

"Hasn't that changed?" she asked. "Haven't we changed that for you?"

He sighed. "I think it's too late."

"It's never too late to love someone," she insisted.

He looked at her, his blue eyes steely, his gaze intense.

"What?" she asked uneasily. Nick could see through her like no one else ever had. Even his father had never understood her like this son of his.

"You talk about love," he said, "but I don't think you're an expert, either. I don't think you know how to love any more than I do."

"I know how to love," she insisted. "I love my kids. I love you."

"What about a man?"

"Nicholas died so many years ago."

"Exactly," he said. "He died years ago. You should have moved on. You should have had another relationship."

She shivered at the thought. "I didn't need another one. I had my great love."

"I don't think so," he said.

"Because he cheated on me?"

"Exactly. He didn't deserve you, Penny. He betrayed your love and your trust, and I think you never had another relationship because you're afraid you'd get hurt again. You're afraid to trust again." He stepped closer, and for once he took her hand instead of the other way around. He squeezed it gently. "I think you're afraid to love."

She couldn't argue with him. She couldn't even stop him as he walked out of her office. But she followed him and watched as he pulled away from the chapel. She wasn't the only one. Another vehicle pulled away from the curb and trailed after his.

Was it someone from Payne Protection? She shivered and knew that it wasn't. Someone else followed Nick. He wasn't in danger of losing just his heart. He was in danger of losing his life, too.

Chapter 20

Nick was being followed. But he was alone, so he didn't care. He wasn't putting Annalise or Nikki in danger. His life was the only one at risk.

He couldn't give Annalise his heart. He didn't have one to offer her. But he could give her back her life— the one she'd worked so hard to build for herself. That was the least he could do for her, for all she had endured because she'd thought she was helping him.

She didn't realize he'd made peace with his mother long ago, before she'd died. He'd realized she had a disease, an addiction she couldn't beat. He hadn't been able to help her because she hadn't wanted help.

So he'd dedicated his life to the people he could help. He could help Annalise.

He could stop the person who was after them. He spoke into his phone. But he wasn't talking to anyone at the Payne Protection Agency. He asked for directions to the nearest storage facility. Whoever was following him thought he was going to get whatever the hell he thought he had.

Maybe he could lure him out in the open. Maybe he could end this now. He turned in the direction the phone had told him. He was sure whoever was following him wasn't alone. There had to be someone else back there.

A Payne Protection bodyguard...

Milek. Garek.

The only person he was certain it wasn't was Nikki. Her brothers weren't going to let her anywhere near him until this was over. And maybe not even after that.

As he thought of her, his phone lit up with her number. He touched the speaker button. "That was quick," he said. He'd called her on his way to the White Wedding Chapel.

"It was easy," she replied. "He gave Annalise a fake name on the rental application."

"That was why she couldn't find any credit or work history for him," he surmised. "But if all you have is a fake name..."

"Fake name," she said. "Real person. Ralph Adams died over thirty years ago."

"Ralph Adams..." The name sounded vaguely familiar.

"Your mom testified in his murder trial," she said. "Her testimony helped put away the drug dealer who killed Ralph. Darren Snow. His nickname was—"

"The Iceman," Nick said. After her death—after he'd found that letter—Nick had checked out everything his mother had claimed in it. He'd learned about the Iceman.

"Who was just paroled," Nikki said, "six months ago."

Nick glanced into his rearview mirror, trying to catch a glimpse of the driver in the vehicle tailing him. "It has to be him."

"But what does he want?" Nikki asked. "What could your mom have that he thinks is his?"

The car was bearing down on him quickly. The driver was not even trying to hide the fact that he was following Nick.

"We'll have to talk about that later," Nick said. "I have to go now."

He clicked off the phone and returned to his directions to that storage facility. It had to be close—the facility and the end of the danger in which he and Annalise had been living.

Annalise shivered. And it wasn't just because of the conversation she'd overheard Nikki having with Nick about a killer drug dealer named the Iceman. It was because of the abrupt way that conversation had ended.

"What's going on with him?" she asked.

Nikki's face had paled beneath the bruises, and she shook her head. "I don't know. He seemed like he was in a hurry."

"To get back here?" Annalise asked and hoped.

Instead of answering her, Nikki clicked another button on her cell phone. "Hey? Who's on Nick?"

She hadn't put the call on speaker, so Annalise couldn't hear the name that Nikki heard. But from the look of doubt and concern on her face, she suspected she knew.

Gage. And apparently Nikki didn't think Annalise's

brother was ready for the assignment. Unfortunately, neither did Annalise.

"Does he know where Nick is going?" Nikki asked whomever she'd called—probably her brother Logan. She grunted. "Of course not."

Nikki turned her focus back to the computer she'd brought to investigate the person to whom Annalise had rented Nick's mother's house. Because Annalise had been giving her information, she'd been sitting next to Nikki and could easily see the screen. After tapping the keyboard a few seconds, Nikki pulled up Nick's phone record.

"Yeah, I'm hacking," she told her brother—with no shame. "Last thing Nick did was get directions to the nearest storage facility." She gave Logan the name and address.

Even though he wasn't on speaker, Annalise could hear Logan's curse. He knew what Nick was doing.

"Is anyone else close enough?" Nikki asked. She really didn't trust Gage as Nick's only backup. And she cursed at Logan's reply.

Annalise's stomach churned with concern and with the baby's restless kicks. It was as if he knew, too, that his father was in danger. She waited until Nikki clicked off the phone before she said, "He's risking his life."

Nikki shrugged. "Just leaving the condo puts his life in danger."

Hers, too. Annalise had learned that the hard way. But she wanted to leave now. She wanted to be with Nick—to make certain that he was all right.

"What's going on?" Annalise asked.

"He picked up a tail after he left Mom's chapel." There was more unsaid in Nikki's tone.

"And…?" Annalise prodded her.

"He's leading the tail to that storage facility."

"He's using himself as bait," Annalise realized. "To catch whoever's after us." And he was out there with only her brother as backup—a man who hadn't trusted himself to protect her. Why had he trusted himself to protect Nick?

He obviously wasn't ready. And if Nick died, would Gage ever be able to forgive himself? Would she?

It was Annalise's fault that Nick was in danger in the first place. She should have sold the place the way he'd told her to—totally furnished. Then his mother's possessions would all have been gone. Nobody would be looking for something he was so desperate to retrieve that he was willing to kill.

But then, according to what Nikki had said, the Iceman had killed before. He would have no compunction about killing again.

Gage had heard the doubt in everyone else's voices. They'd thought him ready to protect an elderly woman from her own paranoia. They hadn't thought he was ready to protect Nick. Just a couple of days ago, he wouldn't have thought he was ready, either. He hadn't trusted himself to protect Annalise. But he'd been feeling better—stronger.

He hadn't been having the nightmares like he had before. He hadn't been sleeping much, so the nightmares weren't really an issue.

Maybe what he'd been through wasn't the reason the others hadn't trusted him to protect Nick. Maybe it was because of what Nick had done to Annalise.

He'd gotten her pregnant.

Gage waited for the betrayal and anger to rush over him again. But instead, he felt an odd surge of happiness. He was going to have a nephew, a child that would be equal parts of the two people Gage loved most in the world. Now.

He had loved someone else more before. But that seemed like a lifetime ago. He wasn't the man he'd been back then. That man was still missing.

Gage doubted he would ever be found. That was fine, though. Maybe it would make it easier for him to move on—at last.

What about Nick?

When they caught whoever was after him and Annalise, would Nick move on? Or would he want to be part of his son's life? Part of Annalise's?

She loved him. She had always loved him.

But what about Nick?

He touched the radio on his collar and asked, "What the hell are you doing?"

"Gage?"

"Yeah."

"You're my tail?"

"I don't know who the hell your tail is," Gage said. But he'd been following him since Nick had left the chapel. "He's driving a rental. And all I can see through the back window is a bald head."

"So there's just one of them?" Nick asked.

"As far as I can tell…" Inside that vehicle. But there could have been other ones—ones that had stayed farther back so neither he nor Nick had made them.

Nick's sigh of relief rattled the phone. "That's good. We've got him outnumbered. We can catch him."

Gage worried that Nick was giving him too much

credit. "This is risky," he said. "We haven't had time to plan. We need more backup."

"They're on their way." Nick was certain, probably because the Paynes seemed to travel in a pack. There would be other bodyguards close.

But Gage didn't think they would make it in time. The gate to the storage facility came into view. Nick must have broken the lock and jimmied open the gate, because that rental vehicle passed easily through. Not wanting to tip the man off, Gage hesitated a moment before driving through the broken gate himself.

The storage units were tall and deep enough for motor homes and boats. There were also—so many rows that he had no idea which alley Nick had driven down. Or the man who'd been following him.

"Nick?" he called into the radio. "Where the hell are you?"

Nick must have shut off the radio so he wouldn't give away his location to other man. But Gage needed to know where he was in order to protect him.

As he passed another row, he noticed a car parked far down the alley, its taillights burning holes in the gathering darkness. The sun was just beginning to set, but here between the tall buildings, it looked like night already.

Gage stopped his vehicle and called out his location into the radio. Nick might not be able to hear him, but the others hadn't shut off their radios. And they were on their way. But as Gage opened his car door, he heard the gunshots.

And he knew no one else would get there in time to help. It was up to him. He was Nick's only backup. His heart pounding frantically, he drew his weapon from his holster and headed around the front of his SUV. He'd parked it to block off that alley—to trap the car inside it with no escape.

The taillights turned to backup lights. Tires squealing, the car reversed—heading right toward him. Now he was the one trapped between his vehicle and the one bearing down on him. He lifted his weapon and squeezed the trigger. He had no idea if his shots struck anything but metal and glass.

He heard the metal ping. The glass shatter. But the car kept coming. Feeling the whoosh of air as it neared, he jumped, launching himself at the side of the one of the units. Metal crunched, and he waited for the pain.

But the car missed him. It didn't miss the SUV. It struck it hard, hard enough to push it back. But it didn't leave a space big enough for the car to get through. Brakes squealed again as the car lurched to a stop.

The driver's door opened. The man was just a shadow. The only thing Gage saw was the gun he held, the barrel pointed directly at him. He lifted his own weapon and flinched as shots rang out.

The sound of gunfire had memories rushing over him—of other firefights. Of losing friends…

Where was Nick?

What had happened to him?

Would Gage find him as he had the others? His body bloodied, staring up at him through lifeless eyes…

Chapter 21

Nick cursed. He'd fired shot after shot. But from how easily the man ran away—around his wrecked vehicle and Gage's—he doubted he'd hit him.

At the moment, he was the least of Nick's concerns, though. "Gage!"

If anyone had been hit, it was Gage. The man had struck him either with his vehicle or with his bullets. Nick's stomach lurched as he relived seeing Gage trapped between his SUV and the car bearing down on him.

Gage couldn't have survived hell only to die at home—because of Nick. Nick would never forgive himself. And neither would Annalise.

He rushed over to where Gage's body was slumped against the metal door of one of the storage units. Dropping to his knees, he leaned over him. He couldn't see any blood but Gage's jeans were torn and so was the sleeve of his shirt. His short golden hair was mussed, too. "Are you okay?"

Since night had begun to fall, the light above the door of the unit kicked on and shone down on his friend like a spotlight.

Gage's eyes—the same clear green as Annalise's—were open but unfocused, as if he couldn't see. Or as if he could see something Nick couldn't, something only inside Gage's mind.

"I'm sorry," he murmured. "Sorry I didn't save you."

"I'm fine," Nick said.

Gage just shook his head as if he didn't believe him. But Nick wasn't sure he'd even heard him.

"Are you hit?" Nick asked. Maybe he just couldn't see the blood. He didn't want to move Gage, didn't want to risk injuring him more like he could have Nikki had she been hurt more seriously. Nothing was going to blow up here. The only risk was the gunman returning to shoot at them again.

He kept his weapon in his hand, ready to fire if he needed to. He could check Gage for injuries only with one hand. His wounded shoulder ached in protest, but he moved his arm, running his hand along Gage's ribs.

The other man flinched. He was hurt. But Nick didn't know if the injuries were new or old ones that had been aggravated. What the hell had Gage gone through all those months he'd been missing?

Nick touched the radio on his collar, turning it back on. "I need an ambulance."

"You're hurt?" Logan asked.

"Not me," Nick said.

"Gage?"

A strong hand clasped his. "No," Gage murmured. "I'm fine."

He wasn't fine. His eyes were still unfocused. And he kept flinching even though Nick wasn't touching him. He was reliving the nightmare he'd endured.

Then Nick's nightmare returned as he heard footsteps moving across the concrete behind him. He had his gun, but he wouldn't be able to fire it fast enough to save both him and Gage.

Had she lost one of them? Or both?

Candace and Nikki claimed everyone was fine. But they drove her to the hospital, both their usually beautiful faces grim with worry. If everyone was fine, they wouldn't have brought her here. Annalise was frantic.

She had nearly lost both men before. Gage all those months he had been missing in Afghanistan...

And Nick in the very hospital garage in which Candace parked the Payne Protection SUV. He'd been shot. He could have been killed then. It could have been his body she and Nikki had seen on that gurney.

Nikki reached for her hand and squeezed it. "He's fine."

Which *he*?

They wouldn't have brought her to the hospital if at least one of the men she loved hadn't been hurt. More Payne Protection bodyguards joined them. Garek and Milek helped escort her to the elevator and up to the emergency room.

The doors slid open to Logan and Parker pacing the lobby. They looked as grim as Candace and Nikki. "What's wrong?" she asked. "Who's hurt?"

She turned toward those doors marked No Admittance and thought about forcing her way through them—just as someone stepped out.

Nick glanced at her before looking at the others. "You shouldn't have brought her here."

"Why not?" she asked. "What's wrong?"

Oh, God, it was Gage.

"It's too dangerous," Nick said. "You remember what happened last time."

The gunfire in the lobby. She would never forget. But that didn't matter now.

"What's wrong with Gage?" She reached out and clasped Nick's forearms, gripping them for support.

"He's fine," he replied, too quickly.

"He wouldn't be here if he was fine," she pointed out. "Why did you bring him here if he wasn't physically hurt?"

Nick's face was as grim as everyone else's had been. And that muscle twitched in his cheek, his telltale sign of stress. "I don't think he was physically injured."

"What happened?" she asked.

"There was gunfire—"

She gasped as panic overwhelmed her, stealing her breath away. She gripped Nick more tightly and ran her gaze over him. He didn't look as if he had been hit. "But you would know if he'd been shot…" He would know for certain whether or not her brother was physically injured.

"A car nearly hit him, though."

"Nearly?"

"It missed him. But he'd had to move quickly to get out of the way."

He'd gotten out of the way, and he hadn't been shot.

"Why did you bring him here?" she asked.

Nick released a ragged sigh. "He wasn't…he wasn't… right. Something was wrong."

Cooper walked up. "He was probably having flash-backs," he said. "The gunfire probably triggered it."

"He kept thinking I was hurt," Nick said. "That I'd been hit." He shuddered.

And Annalise's heart ached for what both men she loved had endured. "Will he be okay?" she asked.

Nick nodded. "We brought in a doctor who gets it, who's been there and knows how to help him."

Annalise wished she could help her brother. But he hadn't come to her when he'd finally come home. He had come to Nick. And Nick had gotten him help.

"Can I see him?" She wanted to make certain he was all right. That he was still the Gage she had known and loved their whole lives.

Nick didn't argue with her like he had when she'd first arrived. He slid his arm around her and brought her back to the emergency room. For once, Annalise wasn't the one being treated. But she felt no relief.

Nick paused outside a curtain and warned her, "He's sleeping."

He announced it as if it was monumental that her brother was asleep. She didn't understand, but she had no intention of disturbing him. She only wanted to make certain he was all right.

Nick pulled back the curtain. Gage lay on a gurney, his eyes closed. There was no tension in his body. He looked completely relaxed. He looked like Gage again.

She stepped closer and slid her hand over her brother's.

"In all the nights he spent at my place," Nick said, "he hadn't slept."

Now she understood why it was so monumental that he was sleeping at last.

"I'm sorry," Nick said.

She glanced back at him, confused. "Why?"

"If I'd known it was Gage on my protection duty…" He moved forward, too, so that he stood behind her, the heat of his body warming the chill from hers.

"You shouldn't have risked your life, either," she admonished him. In a few months, he was going to be a father—unless he had no intention of being involved in his son's life.

"I had to try to end this."

"Did you catch him?" she asked. She doubted that they had, though, or everyone wouldn't have looked so grim.

He sighed, and this time the breath was ragged with frustration. "No."

Her shoulders sagged. It felt like her burden grew. A burden of guilt and regret. She should have done what Nick had asked. He'd wanted nothing of his mother's. If she'd gotten rid of it all like he'd wanted, nobody would think he had something he didn't.

His hands covered her shoulders and squeezed. "We're getting closer," he said. "We'll get him."

But the Iceman was getting closer, too. He'd nearly run down Gage tonight—nearly shot him and probably Nick, too, although he hadn't admitted it.

Two men had already died. She worried that more men would before it was all over. She worried that the men she loved would die.

Darren had almost had him, could have killed him. A dead man couldn't lead him to what was his. But once he'd recovered his property, Nicholas Rus was a dead man.

The FBI special agent had tried to trick him, leading him to that storage facility. If what he wanted was in storage, it was probably in Chicago. Near the place the US Marshals had relocated Carla to after she'd testified against him in River City.

But it was small enough that it could have easily been transported to River City. Nicholas Rus could have found it the last time he'd been at his mother's six months ago. He could have brought it back with him then. Or even before.

When she had died…

Too bad her death had been of natural causes—or as natural as years of drug abuse could be on a body. If Darren had known where she was, if he'd had a clue…

But he hadn't known where she was or that she was even still alive until after she'd died. Then the bitch had had some lawyer send him a letter taunting him. He'd gotten it before he'd been granted parole.

He'd been damn lucky that whoever read prison mail hadn't realized what she'd been talking about, about the evidence she would have used against him had he ever found her.

She was damn lucky that he'd never been able to find her. Evidence be damned, she would have died a long time ago—that traitorous whore. And it would not have been as painless as an overdose. He would have made her suffer for all the years he'd spent behind bars because of her.

While he couldn't make her suffer anymore, he could make her son suffer. But he wasn't sure if what would hurt Nicholas Rus the most was killing him or killing the woman and the baby she carried.

It had to be Rus's kid. In all the months Darren had followed her around, he hadn't seen her with any other man.

Annalise Huxton was a good woman.

Too bad she would wind up dying because of her love and devotion to Nicholas Rus. Yes, she was the key, the way to get back his property and to get back at the man who'd kept him from it.

Chapter 22

Nick had worked hard so he would never make the mistakes his mother had. He had never gotten involved with the wrong people. He'd never tried drugs. Hell, he rarely ever drank, because he hated the thought of losing control.

The only time he had ever lost control had been with Annalise. He'd wanted her so badly that he hadn't thought about how it would complicate their relationship and potentially destroy his friendship with her brother. He hadn't thought about protection, either. And now she was pregnant with his son.

What kind of father would he be when he'd never had one? Hell, he hadn't had a real mother, either. Hadn't had love...

Would he be able to love their son like he deserved to be loved? Like Annalise deserved to be loved?

Penny thought he was capable. But she was like Annalise, always so optimistic and hopeful. Except when it came to her own life. After Nicholas Payne had broken her heart, she hadn't trusted it to anyone else.

She didn't know or trust love much more than Nick did.

"Don't worry about this." Nikki's voice emanated from the cell phone sitting on the coffee table in front of the couch on which Nick had sprawled. "I'm working it."

"You shouldn't be working it alone," he said. "I ordered the transcripts of the Iceman's trial." Maybe they would find a clue in them to what his mother had taken from her former drug dealer and lover.

"And I'll have hacked into the court records before you get them," Nikki said.

He chuckled because she was right. And a little scary…

He was glad she was on his team now. Well, technically she was on Cooper's. But they were all working together now because they were family. His heart swelled at the thought. Despite what he'd said to Penny, he had one. He had a heart; he just had never learned how to use it, how to open it to receive and express love.

"Get some rest, Nick," his sister advised him. "We're getting close."

She was as optimistic as her mother when it came to work. Nick doubted she would ever trust anyone with her heart, either, not after learning the man she had respected most had betrayed her mother.

"You need some rest, too," he said.

"I need some respect," Nikki grumbled.

"You have it." She had his. And she was earning the

respect of her other brothers. They would see her for the capable woman that she'd become.

She said nothing for a long moment. He must have flustered her. Finally she spoke again. "I'll let you know what I find out. Good night."

"Good night." He clicked off the phone. With the light pouring through the skylights, though, it was probably closer to dawn. He'd spent too much of the night at the hospital with Annalise, watching Gage sleep.

He was all right, though. It was Annalise whom Nick worried about more. She was blaming herself for not getting rid of his mother's things. But even if she had, the Iceman might have thought they still had whatever it was.

What the hell was it?

What had his mother done?

Annalise could feel Nick's pain and frustration— just like she'd heard it in his voice when he had talked to his sister. From the bedroom doorway, she watched him. He was lying down, but he wasn't trying to sleep. His eyes were open as he stared up at the skylights.

"You're not going to take your own advice?" she asked.

He tensed as if she'd startled him. Then he sat up and stared at her. "What advice?"

"To get some rest." She'd heard him tell Nikki—after he'd already sent her to bed.

"You didn't take it," he pointed out.

She shrugged. "I can't sleep."

"Don't worry about Gage," he said. "I think he's getting better. Finally getting some sleep should help him a lot."

She suspected Gage had bigger issues than sleep,

maybe even bigger than what had happened when he'd been missing. Because he'd already been hurting before he'd reenlisted. His heart had already been broken.

Like Nick would undoubtedly break Annalise's.

"I'm not worried about Gage," she said. And at the moment, she wasn't.

He stood up then and walked toward her. "Are you worried about the baby?"

"Always," she admitted. "I worry that I won't be able to take care of him."

Nick reached out and skimmed his fingertips along her jaw. "That's ridiculous," he said. "You take care of everyone. You're a natural mother." The fingertips of his other hand skimmed over her belly. "This little guy is very lucky to have *you*."

"What about you?" she asked.

Nick uttered a ragged sigh. "You're more than enough."

A twinge of pain struck her heart. "You don't want to be involved at all?" she asked. She'd known that Nick didn't love her, but she thought he at least *cared*—about her, but also about their baby.

"I don't know how to be involved," he said. "I never had a father."

And he hadn't had much of a mother, either. Annalise had been taking the blame for not getting rid of the woman's things. But it was Carla who'd stolen something from a drug dealer. What had she taken?

"Do you want to be involved?" she asked. That was the important question.

Her belly shifted beneath his hand, which he'd pressed against it. And his blue eyes widened with surprise and wonder as they had every time he'd felt the baby move. He reacted like it was a miracle.

Maybe it was. She had never expected that Nick—who had always griped at her for touching him—would make love to her with such passion that they made a child together.

He was looking at her now—and the surprise and wonder was still in his gaze. Along with something else...

But she was probably only imagining it. Nick didn't love her. As he'd said a million times, he didn't even know how to love.

Nick didn't love her. But he wanted her. His hands moved from her belly to her breasts. She wore only a light nightgown. Her nipples puckered through the thin material. He brushed his thumbs across them.

She bit her bottom lip to hold in the moan that burned the back of her throat. But then his mouth was there, his teeth nipping lightly at her bottom lip, too. She gasped at the delicious sensation, and his tongue stroked soothingly over her bottom lip before sliding inside her mouth.

He kissed her deeply, passionately—so passionately that her knees weakened and she trembled. He swung her up in his arms and carried her to the master bedroom.

"What are you doing?" she asked. He hadn't answered her last question, hadn't told her whether or not he wanted to be involved in their son's life.

Or was this his answer?

"You told me to get some rest," he reminded her. He laid her on the bed, then stripped off his clothes.

Somehow she doubted he was going to get any rest. And neither would she. But she would rather have Nick than sleep any day.

She held out her arms, reaching for him, tugging

him down onto the bed with her. His erection prodded her hip. But he held back, held on to control, and made love to her. He touched her everywhere, his fingertips gliding over her skin. And he kissed everywhere he touched.

He made love to her with his mouth. She squirmed against the mattress, clutching at him as she sought the release she needed from the tension he'd built inside her body. Finally it broke, and she cried out his name.

Nick tensed. She knew he needed it, too. He needed her love. She showed it in her touch, in her kiss.

She made love to him with her mouth. But he pulled back and pulled her down on top of him. He helped her straddle him and take him deep inside her. His hands on her hips guided her, teased her.

Until she felt that unbearable pressure building again. She needed it to break. Needed Nick...

She rocked against him, and her body shuddered as the orgasm overwhelmed her. She'd never felt the pleasure Nick gave her. She'd never felt that soul-deep connection with anyone else.

Only Nick...

Could all of that be only her imagination—like the love she'd thought she'd glimpsed in the depths of his blue eyes? Or was it possible that Nick loved her but didn't know how to express it? Or maybe he didn't think that he could express it right now because he didn't know if either of them would survive the danger they were in.

The ding of an incoming email jerked Nikki awake. Not that she'd been sleeping on purpose. She must have nodded off at her computer. She straightened up from slumping over her desk at the Payne Protection Agency.

She had come back to Logan's offices because it was where she'd worked the longest. She didn't have her desk set up yet at Cooper's—because she didn't want a desk job anymore. She wanted fieldwork, wanted to be a real bodyguard. Not a computer nerd.

But being a computer nerd had its perks, too. She opened her email with a cry of triumph. She'd told Nick she would get the transcript before him, and she had, but probably only because she'd hacked his email and stayed awake until it came in.

She felt a momentary flash of guilt. But it wasn't as if she wasn't going to tell him what she learned. It wasn't as if she didn't trust that he would have told her what he'd found out.

He would have.

Probably.

But then again, he was Nick, and he was used to being a loner. Used to making his own plan and carrying it out like he'd tried to at the storage unit.

Everyone else had been upset with him for going rogue. But Nikki had understood. He'd had an opportunity, and he'd taken it. He would have been a fool if he hadn't at least tried to take down the man who'd been terrorizing Annalise.

He loved her. He looked at her the same besotted way her other brothers looked at their wives. The way the Kozminskis looked at theirs.

Did Nick know it, though?

From what she'd found out about his biological mother, Nikki suspected he'd had very little love in his life. Just Annalise...

She reminded Nikki of her mom. She was that affectionate, that nurturing. So Annalise's love would have been enough.

Why hadn't Penny been enough for Nikki's dad? Why had he betrayed her with a woman like Nick's mom? She flipped through the transcripts that painted a vivid picture of Carla Monelli. Rus had been the last name of the US Marshal who'd relocated her after she'd testified against Darren Snow.

She had probably seduced him, as well. She'd been beautiful with that kind of waiflike vulnerability a lot of men found irresistible. Nikki was petite like her mom, but she had never been vulnerable and never would be. Not physically and sure as hell not emotionally.

Penny was tough, too. She'd had to be or she wouldn't have survived all the pain she had suffered because of a man. Even before he'd been killed in the line of duty, Penny had lost Nicholas Payne.

To Carla...

A woman who would have done anything to feed her addiction. But that addiction might have been men as well as drugs. Nikki's heart ached for the childhood—or lack thereof—that Nick must have had. With a woman like Carla, he would have had to be the responsible one. The adult.

No wonder he was as independent as he was. He was used to having to take care of himself. And her...

But Carla had done something to take care of herself. She'd taken something for insurance. Testifying against the drug dealer had gotten her away from the abusive man as well as setting her up in a new life, in a new city, with a new name and a house and a job.

Maybe she'd thought she would have a man with her,

maybe Nikki's dad. But he had stayed with his wife. She hadn't entered the witness protection program alone, though. She'd been carrying Nick and whatever she had stolen from the Iceman.

Money?

Nick had doubted it. He'd said she would have used it for drugs. He'd said she would have pawned anything of value, as well. So what was it?

She had testified against Darren for witnessing one murder. But he'd been suspected of several others. What if the gun that he'd used was found?

Nikki snapped her fingers. That was what she'd taken. Hell, Nick should have figured that out. Not long ago, he'd sent Garek Kozminski undercover to find a gun to link Viktor Chekov to a murder.

That gun had implicated another killer entirely, though. But Nick had still brought down Chekov. If he found this gun before Darren Snow found it, he could send the recently paroled killer back to prison. No wonder the Iceman was so desperate to get it away from Nick.

As Nikki had learned over the years, desperate men were incredibly dangerous. Nick had to be careful. But he wasn't the only one. Anyone helping Nick was in danger, too. Nikki had already been hurt. She touched the bruises on her face. Her skin was tender and swollen. And the stitches pulled at the cut on her temple. Pulled and itched.

She resisted the urge to scratch them. Barely.

A few bruises and a little cut were no big deal. Annalise had gotten a concussion, and Nick had been shot. The Iceman was definitely dangerous.

To all of them…

She had no more than considered the thought when she heard it—the sound of someone rattling the outside door, trying to get in. It was too early for anyone else to be arriving at work. Even Logan didn't come in this early—at least, not since he'd married Stacy Kozminski.

No. It had to be someone else breaking in.

Maybe someone who had realized that she'd been helping Nick—that she had the answers he wanted. She reached for her weapon. This time her hand shook less than it had before. She was getting used to pointing the barrel at someone, getting used to firing.

Because she knew with a killer like the Iceman, she would get only one chance to protect herself.

Chapter 23

Nick must have been given an old key when he'd hired on to Payne Protection, because it had stuck in the lock. He'd had to wiggle it to get it to turn. He'd thought he had seen Nikki's coupe in the lot, but the door had been locked.

She might have locked it for protection, though. With a killer like the Iceman on the loose again, they were all in danger. Maybe it was that anticipation of danger that had him ducking the second he heard the cock of a gun. But the bullet had already been fired, so he was too late to avoid a hit.

If Nikki hadn't jerked the barrel at the last moment and sent the bullet into the wall above his head, he would have been hit.

"Damn it!" she cursed. "You need to stop sneaking up on me!"

"Agreed," Nick said. "You're too damn trigger-happy."

"I am now," she agreed. "Getting shot at tends to make you that way."

He chuckled. "I can't argue with that."

"What are you doing here?" she asked. "I thought you were going to get some rest."

"Thought you were, too," he said.

He had known she wouldn't rest, though. That was why he was there. He'd figured she wouldn't have been able to stop working the case. And he hadn't wanted her to be alone and vulnerable.

He had left Annalise alone, but only in the bed they'd shared. Parker had taken over the couch in the living room. He would make sure nobody got past him to get to her.

"You knew I'd be here," she said. "You're just like Mom." She snorted. "Which is weird and impossible but totally true."

He wished he was like Penny Payne. She had no problem showing her affection and warmth for others. But that was for her family. She hadn't given her heart to another man.

"I knew you'd be here," he said. "And I figured you hacked my email."

Her face blushed a bright pink, which highlighted the darkness of her bruises. He felt too bad about her injuries to get mad at her for invading his privacy.

"You got the transcript," she said. "I found some other stuff."

"Like…?"

She had two computer monitors. One held the trial transcripts from his email. Another displayed a montage of old photos. She pointed first to the transcripts, to the part she'd highlighted about the missing murder weapon.

He cursed. How had he not realized it?

And of course his mother wouldn't have dared to pawn a murder weapon. She wouldn't have wanted to be implicated in those crimes. It would have blown her new identity and the arrangement she'd had with the River City district attorney.

"Ironic, huh?" Nikki asked. "You were looking for a gun to nail Chekov, and your mother had one this whole time."

"But where?" he wondered. Growing up, he'd never seen a gun in their house. She must have hidden it somewhere and hidden it well.

"We'll figure it out," Nikki said. "The good news is that the Iceman hasn't found it yet or he wouldn't still be looking."

That was good news. But they had to find the murder weapon before he did. If he got to it first, he would destroy it, and if they couldn't tie him to any of the destruction at his or Annalise's homes or to the attempts on their lives...

Then he would remain a free man.

The transcripts had nothing else to reveal, so Nick turned to the photos. Carla had once been beautiful, with huge, vulnerable dark eyes. The other photo could have been Nicholas Payne. It was a mug shot, though. Of course Payne had been undercover when he'd met Carla, when he'd turned her against her lover. How complete had his cover been?

But he leaned closer and read the name on the book-ing. Darren Snow. His breath hissed out. "Damn...he looks like..."

"My dad," Nikki said.

"He looks like I did at that age," Nick admitted. "Maybe your dad didn't cheat on your mom. Maybe Darren Snow is my dad." The thought filled him with dread, but he knew it would make Nikki happy.

She shook her head and dismissed the idea. "You're my dad's son," she said. "After you showed up in town, Mom told me that she'd always known he had cheated on her with your mom. He told her about it right after it happened."

"Why?" Nick wondered. "Did he think it was honorable to tell her the truth?" He could find no honor in a man who'd cheated on a good woman.

Nikki shrugged. "Maybe he couldn't live with what he'd done."

Or he had been looking for an excuse to leave. Maybe he'd thought that Penny would throw him out once she learned the truth. But instead, she'd forgiven him.

"I don't know how she forgave him," he said.

Nikki sighed. "Me neither. I want to think it's because she loved him."

"You don't think she did?"

"Times were different back then," Nikki said. "She was pregnant with Cooper. She already had twin sons less than two years old. Maybe she stayed with him because she didn't know if she could handle raising kids alone."

"She handled it after he died," Nick reminded her. "I think she loved him." Even though he hadn't deserved her or her love—kind of like he didn't deserve Annalise or her love.

But Annalise loved him. He couldn't deny her feelings. She'd always made them blatantly clear, and never more so than when they made love and she gave herself so generously to him. No. He didn't deserve her.

Nikki touched her computer screen and pulled up a picture of their father in his River City police department uniform. His black hair was cut short in the photo, like Nick's and Cooper's, and his eyes were the brilliant blue Nick saw every time he looked in the mirror or met one of his brothers' gazes.

"You're his son," she said. "The same as Logan and Parker and Cooper. He wouldn't have lied to her about cheating. He wouldn't have hurt her like that for no reason."

"But he hurt her."

"*He* did," she said. And she glanced up from the monitor. "Not *you*."

Since he had showed up in River City a year ago, he'd had a heavy pressure on his heart. He had regretted how his appearance had affected the Paynes. Mostly he'd regretted how much he had upset Nikki. And he'd never thought she would get over her resentment of him.

Had she? It felt as if she had finally let it go.

She looked at the picture of their father again. "You're his son. You're my brother." She didn't glance up at him now, and her bruised face had reddened with embarrassment over getting emotional.

Poor Nikki. She always thought she had to be as tough as her brothers, that she couldn't show any of her emotions. She had probably mistaken having emotions for weakness.

Nick thought it was a strength, one he didn't possess

himself. He cut her a break and teased, "Wow. You must really want to go with me to find the gun."

She looked at him then and laughed. But her laughter quickly faded. "Of course I'm going. You wouldn't even have known what you were searching for if it wasn't for me."

Actually, he would have once he'd read the transcript she'd hacked from his email. He didn't point that out, though. He liked this new relationship with his sister. He liked that they finally had one.

"I have a more important assignment for you," he said. "I want you to protect Annalise. She's going to want to go along as badly as you do."

Nikki opened her mouth as if she was about to argue. Then she smiled instead, as if she knew something he didn't. But he knew…

Annalise was sweet and loving, but she was stubborn as hell. She'd had to be, or she would have given up on him years ago. She was going to insist on going.

Annalise had awakened alone hours ago. Maybe that was why she was so angry. Nick would let her close physically but never emotionally. He kept running away from her.

Now he was trying to run even farther.

Back to Chicago.

"I have to go," Annalise insisted.

They were all there in the living room of Milek's condo. There was no mistaking this meeting for a family one. The Payne Protection Agency meant business today. Guns were spread across the coffee table and the granite counter along with surveillance equipment.

Intent on getting their gear ready, they were all pretty much ignoring her, just as Nick always had.

Just as she always had, she pestered him. She clasped her fingers around his forearm and turned him toward her so he had to look at her. So he had to listen.

"I put your mother's stuff wherever I could find room," she said. "It's spread between three storage units along with all kinds of other things I use for staging houses. You're going to waste too much time looking at the wrong things. I can tell you what's mine and what was hers."

That muscle twitching in his cheek, Nick shook his head. "It doesn't matter how much time we waste," he said. "I'm not putting you at risk."

"With all of you there—" she gestured at the room crowded with bodyguards "—I won't be at risk. I'll be safer there than I would be here."

"She's right," Nikki said.

"You're just saying that because you want to go, too," Logan accused her. He glared at Nick. "I told you that you could work for me only as long as you respected that I'm the boss. You can't hand out assignments."

"Nikki works for me," Cooper said. "And I'm fine with Nick giving her a job."

Logan cursed, but they all ignored him. Annalise was glad she wasn't the only one they were ignoring.

Nikki spoke again. "Annalise is right about needing to be there. We can't risk the Iceman finding that gun before we do. We can't waste any time getting to it."

Annalise reached out and grabbed the other woman's hand. From the first moment they'd met, they had bonded. That hadn't been just because they'd fought of armed carjackers together. It was because they understood each other so well.

Nikki smiled and squeezed her hand. And they both turned toward Nick.

Annalise couldn't get through to him, but Nikki had. He released a ragged sigh and nodded. "Okay, but the priority is making sure that Annalise is never in any danger."

She had gotten what she'd wanted. She was being included. But Annalise didn't feel any triumph. Only trepidation.

Had she done the right thing?

Or had she put her life and her baby's at risk?

Cooper spared a glance at Gage, who sat in the passenger seat of the SUV Cooper was driving. They were behind the one carrying Nick, Annalise, Nikki and Candace. Logan and Parker were in the front. Milek and Garek brought up the rear. He wasn't certain which one of them was driving. They'd been arguing about it up until the moment they had all left the condo.

And as heavily as rain had begun to fall, he couldn't see them clearly in his rearview mirror.

The convoy to Chicago brought back memories for Cooper. He could imagine the memories it brought back for the soldier who'd just recently returned from hell. But Gage was back now. Even before the Kozminskis had radioed about the tail, Gage had spotted it.

He glanced over at Cooper now. And there was fear in his eyes. But it was the healthy kind of fear. The kind of fear that was for the present, not for the past that couldn't be changed. Gage was worried about his sister—not about the soldiers he hadn't been able to save.

At the time, it had sounded like a good idea to bring Annalise along to search the storage units. But now...

Now she could wind up a civilian casualty. Cooper felt that worry himself and saw it in her brother's eyes. But Gage was 100 percent again, which was a damn good thing, because they would need every team member fighting at full capacity.

They were being followed from River City to Chicago, but it wasn't just one vehicle. There were several.

They were going into war.

Chapter 24

Nick had spent so much of his life pushing Annalise Huxton away from him. He should have been an expert at it by now. But when it had mattered most, he hadn't pushed her away. Now she was in danger.

"What's the plan?" Logan asked *him*, his voice emanating from the radio. Despite all his bluster about being the boss, he was willingly handing over the responsibility to Nick now.

Her brown eyes wide with shock, Nikki stared at him. Logan had surprised her.

But he hadn't surprised Nick. Logan knew that this was Nick's call. The woman he cared about—the woman who carried his unborn baby—was in danger. It was Nick's responsibility to keep them safe.

If only he hadn't put them at risk.

Now that he had, he needed to figure out how to mitigate that risk and keep them safe.

Annalise sat in the backseat with Candace. The female bodyguard had her weapon out, ready to fire, but Annalise didn't look reassured. She'd heard everything that had come through the radio. She knew they were being followed. She knew she was in danger. Her fear was apparent in how shallowly she breathed, in how pale her face had become.

She should never have experienced the kind of fear she was feeling. She wasn't like him or Gage. She hadn't chosen a life of risk.

But she had chosen him. He wanted to ask her why. It was something he'd never asked her before. Why did she love him? He'd never given her any encouragement—until that night they'd made love. He'd never given her any hope that his feelings would change, that he could actually have feelings.

Why had she persisted?

Why hadn't she given up on him?

He had—long ago. He'd given up the hope of ever having a family, of ever feeling as if he belonged somewhere. Now he had a family. They might not have embraced him at first, but they were there for him now. When it counted…

When it would keep Annalise safe.

"Do we separate and divide them?" Logan asked.

That would divide them, as well. Nick was used to going it alone. Even as an FBI special agent, he hadn't often worked as part of a team. He'd gone undercover on his own to sniff out corruption in police departments across the nation. That was how he'd wound up with the assignment to clean up River City PD—because he'd been doing it for years.

Alone.

That was how he'd lived his life. Or had tried.

But Annalise had always been there. No matter how much he had complained, he hadn't really minded. He'd actually appreciated her attention—her love.

He couldn't lose her now.

"No," Nick replied. "There's safety in our numbers. We stick together."

Nikki smiled her approval. She was in danger, too—just like her other brothers had feared she would be. But there was no fear on Nikki's face. Like Candace, she had her gun out, grasped in a steady hand. She was ready.

Nick wasn't. He didn't want to lose Annalise. He didn't want to lose anyone else, either. And if there were as many men following them as Milek and Garek had warned, there was a very good chance there would be a confrontation.

A shoot-out.

With that much gunfire, there were bound to be casualties—on both sides.

The bulletproof vest weighed heavily on Annalise's shoulders—along with the burden of guilt. If only she had listened to Nick.

If only she had gotten rid of all of his mother's things.

No one would be in danger. Now everyone was—everyone Nick cared about—because of her. She could tell that he cared for them. Maybe he hadn't wanted to. After all, he was Nick, always so determined to be a loner.

But there were no loners in the Payne family. They all stuck together. Like Nick had said, there was safety in their numbers.

Yet Annalise didn't feel safe—even with the bullet-proof vest. It hung low, covering her belly. The baby would be safe from a bullet. But if Annalise took one in the head... The baby might not survive without her. The risks of his being born this early were too great. He moved restlessly inside her as if he felt her fear.

She was scared, not just for herself but also for everyone else. Milek and Garek were posted at the storage unit gate so the vehicles following them couldn't get inside. Logan and Parker were nearby to back them up. Gage and Cooper stayed in front of the storage units Annalise searched with Nick and Nikki and Candace.

The rain was falling even harder now, beating down on the metal roof of the unit. Would they be able to hear if someone snuck up on them?

"There's so much stuff," Nikki murmured.

Annalise felt compelled to apologize again. "I shouldn't have kept everything." But she hadn't known what Nick might want, what could have meant enough to his mother that it would help him remember her.

She'd wanted him to have some fond memories of the woman who'd given birth to him. But she realized now that there were few fond memories to be had of Carla.

"What could she have hidden a gun inside?" Nikki asked the question.

Annalise had no idea. She knew what would stage a house, not what would hide a weapon.

"A book. A statue. A canister," Nick replied. "Something out of character for Carla to own."

"How is owning a book out of character?" Nikki asked.

"The woman never read," Nick replied. "And she

wouldn't have kept anything that could possibly have been of value."

"Are you sure she didn't pawn the gun?" Candace asked. She stood at the door to the unit, staring outside as if looking for any sign of danger.

Maybe that was why no one had been able to find the gun—because it was gone.

"No," Nick and Nikki answered in unison.

"It would have showed up in the system again," Nick said. "The kind of people who buy guns from pawn-shops use them, usually in the commission of a crime."

Nikki snorted. "Yeah. And I checked records. Nothing matching its ballistics has been used in over thirty years."

"So where would she have hidden something for thirty years?" Annalise wondered.

A book. Like Nick said, Carla had never read. But there had been a collection of books. A whole series about famous criminals. Annalise had thought they were Nick's, something he might have had to read when he was in Quantico. But he had never returned home after leaving for the Marines. So she realized now the books wouldn't have been his.

What had she done with them? She'd taken them out of the house shortly after Carla had died because she'd thought they were Nick's and she hadn't wanted them to go into probate in case Carla hadn't had a will.

And yet Carla had had a will. Her lawyer had been holding that letter for Nick to be read after her death. That letter had given him a family.

There had been another letter, too—one they'd learned had been sent to the prison where Darren Snow had been serving out the last of his sentence. Maybe that letter would take away Nick's family since it had sent the Iceman after Nick. And the Paynes had risked their lives for him and her.

She heard the gunfire…

It was even louder than the rain hitting the roof. It sounded as if it was near the gates.

"We have to get out of here," Nick said. He grabbed her arm with one hand. His weapon was out in the other.

But Annalise resisted. "I know where it is," she said. "I can find it."

She'd put those books in the storage unit that contained her personal things. Her condo was so small that she had no place in it to store her holiday decorations and out-of-season clothes. She used one of the units for all that. It had given her a little spark of hope to see what she'd thought were Nick's possessions among hers, as if they would one day be together.

Now she doubted that would ever happen, even if they survived. Nick would never stop running from her. He was trying to run now toward the SUV parked outside the unit. But once they cleared the door, Annalise jerked from his grasp. If it hadn't been raining, she probably wouldn't have been able to slip free of his hold.

She had the keys to all the units in her hand. She had to find the one that opened the unit on the end. Her hand was shaking badly, and the keys were getting wet like her hair and her skin and her clothes. She dropped the keys on the pavement. "I need to open—"

"There's no time," Nick said.

The gunfire grew closer now. The men had made it past Milek and Garek. Beneath the bulletproof vest, her heart pounded wildly with fear.

Nick was right. There was no time.

Then Candace and Nikki began to fire their weapons. Where were Gage and Cooper? Their SUV was still parked at the end of the row. The back door opened.

Nick swung Annalise up in his arms and rushed toward it. "We need to get you out of here." But when he neared the SUV, it wasn't Gage or Cooper who leaned out to grab her.

The man's head was bald, his blue eyes icy with hatred. "Where's the gun?" he asked.

Nick held up his own barrel pointed toward the Iceman.

But the killer laughed and pressed the barrel of his weapon against Annalise's temple. "Try it," he dared Nick. "And she's dead before she and her baby hit the ground."

That muscle twitched in Nick's cheek. "We didn't find it."

The Iceman's gun cocked. The sound echoed inside Annalise's head. "That's too bad."

"I know where it is," Annalise said. She wasn't fighting just for her life. She was fighting for her son's. He deserved a chance.

He deserved a life.

She couldn't fight like she had the day the men had stolen her car. If she tried to claw at this man's face, he would just kill her. He was that cold. She had to reason with him instead. "Let me get it for you."

He didn't loosen his grasp on her. Despite how wet her clothes and hair were, he held her easily. He was strong, so strong that he jerked her fully inside the SUV with him, onto the backseat. Now her body blocked his. He was using her as a shield as more bodyguards closed in behind Nick. Shots continued to ring out—bullets pinging off metal, shattering glass.

"No, he'll get it for you," the Iceman said. "He'll get me the gun in exchange for your life."

"I don't know where it is," Nick said.

"My unit," she told him. "Number fifteen."

"Find the gun," the Iceman said. "And call me once you have it."

"I don't have your phone number," Nick said.

"You have hers." He reached for the passenger door to pull it closed.

"You won't get out of here alive," Nick threatened him.

"Then neither will she," he said.

Tears stung Annalise's eyes. But she refused to shed them. She refused to let either this man or Nick see her fear. She had to send Nick a message about where to find the gun without telling him exactly where it was.

If she blurted out that it was in the books, the Iceman might just kill them all right there and find it himself. He had brought enough men with him to outgun the bodyguards. But if it would take a little longer for him to find it, he wouldn't risk it. Even now she could hear sirens in the distance.

The police were on their way. He wouldn't risk sticking around for them to arrive.

"He's a killer," she told Nick, hoping he'd get the message. That he would look in those books about serial killers for the gun. "He won't hesitate to pull the trigger."

The Iceman chuckled. "Listen to your girlfriend," he advised Nick as he pulled the door shut.

"Drive!" he ordered the man in the front seat.

Where was Cooper? Where was Gage?

Had she gotten her brother back just to lose him here, when he'd been trying to protect her? She closed her eyes as grief threatened to overwhelm her. There had been too many shots fired. Someone had gotten hurt.

Or worse…

Darren clasped her phone in his hand. Why hadn't it rung yet?

"What the hell is taking him so long?" he asked.

"Maybe he couldn't find it," the woman suggested, her voice quavering with fear.

She was smart to be afraid. She probably knew that even if Nicholas Rus brought him the gun, there was no way she was going to live. He couldn't leave a witness like he had before.

He should have killed Carla thirty-two years ago. Then he wouldn't have spent half his life behind bars. He wasn't going back.

There was no way in hell he would return to hell.

"You told him what unit it was in," Darren said. "He should have found it by now." And he probably had. The guy had a reputation for being squeaky-clean. He'd probably turned the damn gun over to the FBI.

Once they ran ballistics and DNA and whatever the hell else they could get off evidence nowadays, they would be able to link him to more murders. A lot of murders…

It wasn't like the old days when all it had taken to convict someone was an eyewitness. A jury wanted solid evidence. The gun was it. "I've got to get out of here," he told the driver. And he wasn't talking about the alley where they'd parked the stolen SUV. He wasn't talking about Chicago.

He needed to get the hell out of the country—to somewhere without extradition.

"What about her?" the driver asked.

He lifted the gun to her head again. She flinched as he pressed the barrel against her temple. "I'm going to kill her."

And once she was dead, he would kill the driver, too. He couldn't leave behind any witnesses anymore.

Chapter 25

Why the hell wasn't the Iceman answering Annalise's phone? She'd had it on her. She always had it on her. While she'd left her purse in the SUV, the phone hadn't been inside. She must have put it in her pocket while they'd been searching the units.

Had Darren Snow given up waiting for him? It had taken Nick too long to get rid of the police, who'd showed up to investigate the gunfire, and find the gun. He should have realized what Annalise was telling him about the killer—about the trigger.

The gun was inside the books he'd found in her storage unit. The series of serial killer books had been out of place among her cheerful assortment of decorations and clothes. But it had taken him a few minutes to realize that was where she'd meant him to look.

Hell, she could have just told him. But she'd probably

been worried that the Iceman would kill him then and just find the gun himself. She would have been more concerned about Nick's life than her own.

She was probably concerned about everyone else, as well. She couldn't know that they had all survived the gunfight. Everyone was okay.

But her…

Panic pressed on his lungs, stealing his breath away as his heart raced. "Answer the damn phone!" he yelled.

Nikki jumped; his outburst had startled her. The others were too shell-shocked to react. If they hadn't been wearing vests…

The shots that had hit them would have killed them. The vests had stopped the bullets but not the impact. Ribs were bruised or broken. But no one had sought medical treatment.

Gage paced the storage unit. "You shouldn't have made us stand down," he said. "You shouldn't have."

"He had his gun pressed to her head," Nick said, his heart aching as he remembered the fear on her face. "He would have killed her." And the damn vest he'd put on her wouldn't have saved her.

Nothing would have.

Maybe nothing had.

He could see the thought on the faces of the others. They thought she was dead. Even Gage…

"She never gave up hope on you," he told him. "Everybody else thought you were dead, but Annalise wouldn't consider it. She knew you were too damn stubborn to give up."

Gage released a shaky breath. "And I've got nothing on her. She's a helluva lot more stubborn than I am."

Or she would have given up on Nick years ago. He

saw that on Gage's face, too. She hadn't given up on him, and he wouldn't give up on her. He hit redial.

And finally someone picked up the call. "Special Agent Rus," Darren Snow greeted him.

"No," Nick replied. "I'm not an FBI agent anymore. I'm a bodyguard." But he had failed to protect the person who mattered most to him.

The Iceman chuckled. "So you haven't brought that gun to the FBI evidence locker yet?"

"I haven't," Nick said. "And I won't. I'm bringing it to you—in exchange for Annalise. Just like we agreed."

"I had heard you're a man of your word," the Iceman replied.

"What about you?" Nick asked. "Are you a man of your word?" He'd read those trial transcripts. Darren Snow was no Viktor Chekov. While Chekov was a killer, he lived by a certain code. The Iceman had no code—no moral compass whatsoever.

"I was beginning to think that you'd turned on me, Nicholas," Darren said, "just like your whore of a mother did."

"I'm nothing like my mother," Nick said. At least, he wasn't like the one who'd given birth to him. He'd rather be like Penny Payne—the woman who wanted to assume the role of his mother.

"I've heard that," Darren said. "I've heard you're all about law and order. It's hard for me to believe that you'd turn over evidence to me."

"We made a deal," Nick said—although he hadn't been given much choice in the matter, not with that gun barrel pressed against Annalise's head. "I'm holding up my end of it. Are you going to hold up yours?"

The Iceman chuckled again. But Nick didn't know what had amused him. His uneasiness grew.

"I want to talk to her." Nick hadn't given up, and yet he needed to be certain that she was all right. He needed to hear her voice.

The Iceman's silence unnerved him and the others. They all glanced at each other, as if wondering…

Worrying. That Nick had taken too long, that he'd called too late.

"Nick?" Annalise's voice emanated from the speaker on his phone and echoed hollowly throughout the storage unit in which they all stood.

He uttered a ragged sigh, and the pressure on his heart eased. She was alive. "Annalise, are you all right? Has he hurt you?"

"You heard her," the Iceman said. "She's alive. For now. But she and your kid she's carrying don't have much longer if I don't get that gun in my hands."

"Where do you want to meet?" Nick asked.

"You're not going to try to lay a trap for me, Nicholas?" the Iceman asked.

"Of course not." He would take no chances with Annalise's life.

"We'll meet out in the open, Nicholas, so I can be certain that you've come alone." And he named a park not far from the storage facility. "Near the basketball courts."

Logan was shaking his head, but Nick ignored him. "Agreed. But you won't see me or the gun until I see Annalise. Alive."

The Iceman chuckled again—like he had a secret joke. Before he clicked off the phone, Nick heard Annalise shouting out a warning, "Don't trust him, Nick!"

Gage cursed. He had probably guessed what her outburst would cost Annalise. Pain.

The Iceman would hurt her. But he wouldn't kill her. He wanted the gun.

"You need to listen to her," Logan said. "You can't trust him. You can't go alone, and you can't bring that gun with you."

Nick shook his head. "I'm going to do exactly what he says."

"That's evidence, Nick," Logan reminded him. "You can't turn it over to a criminal. You know better."

Nick shrugged. He knew the law, probably better than anyone else present. But for the first time in his life, the law didn't matter to him. He didn't care about right or wrong. He cared only about Annalise.

"We could switch the gun," Logan suggested. "Get one that looks like it."

"There's no time," Nick said. "And he would know."

"It's been over thirty years since he saw it last," Logan argued.

"He would know," Nick said because of his face. If the Iceman was going to believe Nick had brought the real gun, he'd need to see the struggle on his face, the guilt he'd feel for handing over evidence. While he'd feel some guilt, it wasn't the moral struggle he'd thought it might be. It was no struggle at all.

It didn't matter what the law said was right or wrong. All that mattered was Annalise.

Had Nick heard her? Had he heeded her warning? Annalise's heart pounded quickly and frantically. She knew Darren Snow had no intention of letting her or

Nick live. He'd called up the men he'd hired, the ones who'd survived the gun battle at the storage unit.

There had been fatalities. She hoped only on the Iceman's side. Her brother had to have survived. He was tough—tough enough to make it through whatever hell he'd endured in Afghanistan. It would take more than a bullet to end his life.

She hoped the same for Nick. Because the Iceman had set up the park. He had shooters positioned on rooftops—ready to take head shots once the gun had exchanged hands. If Nick showed up at the park, he wouldn't leave alive.

And neither would she.

"I'm sorry," Darren told her. But his apology lacked sincerity. "You seem like a sweet girl. But I can't risk going back to prison."

She nodded as if she commiserated with him. But she could never understand a human taking another human's life, unless it was in self-defense or defense of someone else.

"You really should have rented the place to me furnished," he said. "Then we could have avoided all of this nasty business."

"It is my fault," she agreed. And there was no way she could remedy it now. Nick had been right to push her away all these years. If she hadn't been so stubborn…

If she'd given up on him years ago, he wouldn't be in danger now. And neither would she.

The rain continued to fall, beating down on the roof of the stolen SUV—flooding the parking lot near the basketball court. No one played on the courts. Thanks to the rain and the encroaching darkness, it was deserted.

But for the man who stood with his back against one of the buildings near the court. Even through the rain, she could tell it was Nick. His black hair was wet and slicked to his head, but his eyes shone brightly in his handsome face.

The Iceman wasn't as certain, though. He peered at him. "Is it him or one of those bodyguards…?"

The driver shrugged. "Looks like him. And you told him to come alone."

The Paynes wouldn't have allowed that, though. Would they? The family stuck together, protected each other. They had to be out there, ready to protect Nick. But she peered around and could see no one else.

From inside the SUV, she couldn't see the men Darren Snow had positioned on the rooftops, either. She didn't doubt they were there. He'd offered to pay them well.

Would Nick see them? He wasn't looking up. He was staring instead at the SUV.

"There's no one else around," the driver said. "It has to be him."

The Iceman hesitated yet, looking uncertain.

"It is," she said. "It's Nick." She'd loved him too long to mistake him for anyone else.

The Iceman released a breath. He believed her. Finally he opened the back door and pulled her across the seat and out the door with him. She stepped into a puddle, the water rushing over her shoe to soak her foot. Within seconds, her clothes were soaked, too, down to her skin.

The Iceman had taken the bulletproof vest from her. It wouldn't have mattered if she'd worn it, though, not when he'd ordered his snipers to take head shots. He wore it himself under his coat.

He didn't expect Nick to honor their deal any more than he intended to honor it. But he didn't know Nick.

He didn't know that he was a man of his word.

He gestured for Nick to come forward. Nick stepped away from the wall and crossed the basketball court. And Annalise held her breath.

They weren't supposed to shoot yet, though. Not until Nick handed over the gun.

Wait for my signal, the Iceman had told them. *Once I know it's my gun, I'll raise my hand. That's when you open fire.*

"Don't give it to him!" she shouted at Nick. "He's going to kill us."

Nick didn't react. He wasn't surprised by her warning. He'd known. But he'd come alone, anyway.

For her? Or for their baby?

Where was everyone else?

It was just the two of them—against a killer.

The Iceman jerked her arm behind her back until she cried out at the pain. "Stop it!" he told her. "Or you won't die quickly. You'll just die painfully." In his other hand he held a gun, pressed against her face.

"Let her go," Nick said as he rushed forward. "She has nothing to do with this!"

The Iceman chuckled. "She has everything to do with it, Nicholas. You wouldn't have brought the gun if I hadn't taken her." He used the barrel to gesture at Nick. "Did you bring it?"

"Of course."

The Iceman's pale eyes narrowed skeptically. "I find

it hard to believe that a man of your high moral values would have compromised his principles like this."

Nick held up a velvet bag—one in which a fifth of whiskey usually came. His mother had liked to drink, too. "It's in here." He tossed it over.

But with the Iceman's grip on her and his gun, he couldn't grab it before it hit the ground. He let her go so abruptly that she fell to the wet pavement.

Gunfire erupted. And Nick lunged toward her, as if to cover her body with his. But before he reached her, a bullet struck him. She didn't know if it came from above or from Darren Snow.

His gun was pointed at Nick. Nick kept coming.

He fired again.

Annalise screamed and, desperate to help, she grabbed up the bag. Knowing Nick, it could have been a decoy, a fake weapon. But she pulled out a real gun, the metal heavy and cold. It probably wasn't loaded.

Snow had forgotten about her lying on the ground. His focus was on Nick now. He stepped forward and pointed his gun at Nick, who was sprawled on the ground, rain falling on his face. His eyes were closed.

Was he already dead?

Darren must have wanted to make certain, because he cocked his gun and lowered the barrel close to Nick's head. Annalise lurched to her feet and squeezed the trigger of the gun she held—the gun that had already been used to kill.

Her wrist snapped at the recoil, and the weapon fell from her suddenly weak grasp. Pain radiated up her arm.

Darren Snow spun toward her, his eyes open with surprise. Then he dropped to his knees on the pavement and fell forward. She screamed as she saw the wound in the back of his head. Had she done that?

Had she killed a man?

She didn't care at the moment. All she cared about was Nick. She dropped to the ground next to him. "Are you all right? Nick?"

But his eyes—his beautiful eyes, usually so bright—remained closed. She'd killed a man to save him. But she might have been too late.

She had known, as Penny always did, that her children were in danger. This time it had been all of them. Panic constricted her heart, squeezing it painfully. She didn't know how she'd managed the drive to Chicago or how she'd found the hospital where they were.

But she'd managed somehow to get to them. Was she too late, though? Had she lost one of them?

She hurried to the waiting room.

"Mom," Logan gasped as she walked in. Instead of protesting her being there, he hugged her tightly. As if he was a little boy who needed comfort.

Since his father had died, he'd been the one who'd given the comfort—even to her. Tears stung her eyes. It was bad. Even worse than she'd feared...

"Who is it?" she asked. Who had she lost?

She pulled free of Logan's embrace and peered around the crowded room. Other people might have been there, but she saw only her family.

Milek and Garek Kozminski stood close together, almost as if they were holding each other up. "Are you all right?" she asked them.

Milek nodded.

"Gonna take more than an SUV to wipe us out," Garek assured her as he pulled her into a hug.

But as she hugged him back, he flinched. He'd been hurt.

They all looked the worse for wear. Gage Huxton had blood smeared on the side of his face, but she wasn't certain if it was his. He would have done anything to protect his sister. Just like her boys would have Nikki.

Nikki—dear sweet Nikki—had already been bruised and stitched. But she wore those wounds like badges of honor. Stubborn girl.

A smile tugged at Penny's lips. She loved her baby girl so much. And she worried about her nearly as much as she worried about Nick.

"Nick?" she gasped his name as she realized who wasn't present. "Where's Nick?"

"Surgery…" The voice came from behind the others. They stepped aside to let Penny through to the chair where a frail-looking Annalise sat. "They took him back right away…"

They must have been at the hospital a while—long enough for Penny to make the nearly three-hour drive. But Annalise's clothes still looked damp from the rain. Or perhaps it was from the blood that stained them.

Penny dropped to her knees in front of her chair. "Are you okay? Has someone checked you out?" She glanced around at the others. Hadn't anyone helped her?

"She refused," Gage said. And from his tone, it was obvious that he'd given up arguing with his sister.

Penny touched the young woman's hands where they covered her belly. Her skin was as cold as ice. "You need to let someone look at you," she said. "You need to make sure your baby is all right."

Her green eyes brimming with tears, Annalise shook her head.

And panic gripped Penny. Had she lost the child? Was that why she had blood on her clothes?

"Get help," Penny yelled at the others. "She needs a doctor." Penny worried that it was already too late for the baby.

What about Nick? He'd been in surgery such a long time. Was it too late for him, too?

Chapter 26

Nick fought his way to consciousness. He'd been out too long. He knew it. Something bad had happened. He could feel it in the heaviness of his heart, which beat slowly with dread. The last thing he remembered was lunging toward Annalise, but he hadn't reached her before the shot had taken him down.

Had she been hit?

Was she safe?

"Annalise!" He jerked awake with her name on his lips.

"Are you okay?" a soft voice asked.

He struggled to keep his eyes open—to focus on the face above his. Penny Payne stared down at him, her brown eyes warm with concern.

His throat was dry, and he tried to swallow, tried to clear it. But his voice sounded gruff when he said again, "Annalise…"

Penny took his hand in hers. Was she offering comfort? Or was she the one who needed it?

He squeezed her hand and urged her, "Tell me. Was she shot?"

Penny shook her head. "No. She wasn't shot. But you were."

He remembered the flash of pain he'd felt. He didn't feel it now. His body was actually numb. It was his mind that was reeling. And his heart—it hurt, too.

"The surgeon is worried because the bullet was close to the spine," she said, "too close."

Nick tensed, his muscles tightening.

She spoke softly and gently as she must have to her kids when they'd had nightmares or missed their dad. "He's concerned that you could have some paralysis."

Nick squeezed her hand again, and then he kicked at the sheet covering him. "I'm not paralyzed," he said.

Not anymore.

He'd been paralyzed most of his life—afraid to let himself feel love. But not anymore.

"I'm getting out of this bed," he said, "and I'm going to find Annalise."

He needed to make sure she was all right. But more important, he needed to make certain she knew that he loved her. That he had always loved her—he'd just been too scared to admit how much she had meant to him: everything.

Penny pushed him back against the bed. "You need to rest, Nick. You were in surgery for hours."

So where was Annalise? Had she given up on him?

After all these years of loving him, had she finally changed her mind? Had he waited too long to tell her he loved her, too?

"If she wasn't shot," he said, "why isn't she here?" Images flashed through his mind. He remembered the way Darren Snow had shoved her to the ground. Had it been hard enough to hurt her? To hurt the baby?

Dread washed over him. "It's the baby, isn't it?"

Penny squeezed his hand again. "Nick…"

He kicked at the sheet again, and this time he managed to swing his legs out of the bed. "I have to be with her. Have to make sure she's okay."

If she'd lost the baby, she would be devastated. Hell, he would be, too. But he was more worried about her.

"Why, Nick?" Penny asked. "Why do you have to be with her?"

Had the woman lost her touch? Usually she understood what was going on with people before they understood it themselves. How could she not know what he had just realized?

"Because I love her," he said. "I love her!"

"You could sound a little happier about it," a soft voice remarked.

Penny didn't look surprised at the sound of Annalise's voice. She must have known she had come into the room. She smiled and stepped back from the bed. "I'll leave you two alone," she said. "You need to talk."

But Nick couldn't talk. Maybe he *was* paralyzed— because all he could do was stare at the woman he loved. She looked so beautiful, more beautiful than he had ever seen her.

The way he was staring at her made Annalise uneasy. "Are you okay?" she asked. Maybe she needed to call his doctor. He didn't look right, more like dazed. Maybe it was the drugs.

Maybe that was why he'd said what he had. That he loved her.

Dare she believe him?

"Nick?" Instead of going for a doctor, she stepped closer to the bed. She had been so worried that she'd lost him. That he wouldn't survive the shots he'd taken.

He blinked as if snapping out of a trance. And now he looked at her as if he were truly focusing. His gaze ran over her tangled hair and down her bloodied clothes. And he reached out for her, pulling her into his arms.

She tried to hold back. She didn't want to hurt him.

"It's okay, sweetheart," he said, his voice gruff with emotion. "We can have another baby."

Another one? What was he talking about?

"I know you're upset, but we have each other. We'll get married—"

"What?" The doctor had said she was in shock—that was why she'd been so cold, so out of it in the waiting room. It must not have worn off yet. "Why are you talking about getting married?"

He must have known it didn't matter to her what Gage had said. Annalise wouldn't have let her brother force him to marry her.

"I love you," he said.

And she was as shocked as the first time she'd heard him say it. Was she dreaming? Had she fallen asleep in the waiting room and she was only imagining that she was here—in his arms? She slid her arms around his neck. He felt real to her. Warm and strong despite having been shot.

He tightened his arms around her, pulling her close yet. "I want to marry you because I love you. So i doesn't matter that you lost the baby. We'll have an-other—"

Finally realization dawned, and she pressed her fingers over his lips. They were dry beneath her touch. He'd been through so much. No wonder he was confused. "I didn't lose the baby." And as if to prove it, their son kicked.

Amazement and relief brightened Nick's eyes as he felt it. "You didn't." He pulled back and stared down at her clothes. "But the blood."

"It's yours," she said. "From the park…" And it might have been Darren Snow's, too.

"I don't know what happened," he said. "You fell and the gunfire began. Is everyone okay?"

She nodded. "Your family took out the snipers Darren Snow had on the rooftops. He was the one who shot you."

"What happened to him?" he asked.

"He's dead." She shuddered as she remembered how he'd stared up at her with such surprise.

Nick pulled her close again. And he noticed her wrist. The doctor had wrapped the sprain. That—and the shock—had been her only injury. Now his eyes widened with shock as he realized how she'd hurt her wrist—from the recoil from the old gun. "You shot him?"

She shrugged. "I shot that gun. But I don't know if it was my shot that hit him." Gage claimed that he'd done it—from one of the rooftops. But she didn't know if he was telling the truth or only trying to make her feel better. He understood her well enough to know that she would struggle with having killed a man.

But she wasn't sure that she would. Nick was alive.

That was all that mattered. That and the fact that he loved her.

"And now I love you even more," he remarked. "There's something I want to ask you."

He had already said they were getting married. But if he wanted to propose properly, she wasn't going to stop him. Smiling she asked, "Yes?"

"Why do you love me?"

And she laughed.

"I'm serious," he said.

Realizing why he was asking, pain constricted her heart. Now she knew why he had pushed her away, why he had never accepted her love. He hadn't believed anyone could love him.

"You are the most amazing man," she told him. "You were amazing even when you were just a boy. You have such honor and integrity. You always want to do the right thing. You always want to protect everyone else."

And maybe that was why he'd spent so many years pushing her away. He'd wanted to protect her.

"I didn't think I deserved your love," he said. "I didn't think I was worthy of it."

"Nick…"

"My own mother couldn't love me," he said.

"She was an addict," she reminded him.

"She was all I had."

Annalise shook her head. "You had me."

He clasped her closer. "I'm so sorry I didn't realize how I felt sooner. I didn't recognize it."

He didn't recognize love because he'd never felt it before. Her heart ached for all he had missed. "I'm not the only one who loves you, Nick," she assured him.

"You have a family out there who is frantically worrying about you."

He smiled. "I'm sure Penny has assured them that I'm fine. Right now she's probably getting them all fitted for tuxes for the wedding."

"It's too soon to worry about fittings," she said.

"I'm marrying you as soon as I get out of the bed, Annalise." And he tried to stand again.

"I've spent my life waiting to marry you, Nicholas Rus," she told him. "I think I can wait a little longer."

"I can't. I want to marry you right away. I don't want to waste another minute of time that I can be with you."

Tears stung Annalise's eyes. She'd always known she'd loved Nick. But she hadn't known Nick could love like this—as completely as she loved him.

"Shh…" he murmured. "I don't want you to cry."

"I've shed a lot of tears over you," she admitted.

He grimaced. "I don't ever want to make you cry again."

She leaned forward and pressed her lips to his. They kissed softly, tenderly. He lifted his fingers to her face and wiped away her tears.

"You'll make me cry again," she said. "Because these are happy tears. And you've made me so happy…"

She'd thought all she'd wanted was for Nick to survive his gunshot wounds. She hadn't realized how badly she'd wanted him to love her—until finally she had her wish. Her dream was realized.

Nicholas Rus loved her as much as she loved him.

"Make me happy," he said.

She tensed. "You're not?" she asked. Of course, he was probably in pain. He'd just had surgery. She tried to pull back, but he held her tightly.

"I will be," he said, "when you finally agree to become my wife. Marry me, Annalise. Right now."

She laughed. "I guess I'm the one who will need to teach our son patience."

"You have been patient with me," he said. "For so many years. That's why I don't want to wait. I don't want you finally to give up on me."

"Never," she assured him. "I will love you for the rest of our lives, Nicholas Payne."

"And I will spend the rest of our lives loving you."

Nikki smiled with pride. Even though she worked for Cooper, Nick had given her another assignment. She would have thought it would have gone to Gage—who'd known him longest. Or to the FBI agent he'd roomed with in Chicago—Jared Bell. Or even to one of the brothers he'd just recently discovered. But she was the one he'd asked to be his best man.

After all the times she had been a bridesmaid, it felt good finally to wear a tux instead of a damn dress. Her mother had been sad, though.

Not about the marriage. She had been thrilled to throw together Nick and Annalise's wedding. She had even been happy that Nikki was his best man.

But she'd admitted that she wanted for Nikki what Nick had with Annalise. She wanted her daughter to be as happy as all her sons were.

From her place at Nick's side at the altar, Nikki stared out at everyone gathered in the church. It was good to see her brothers so happy—with women they'd made as happy as they were.

But her mother stood alone—as she had for so many years. And Nikki realized that Penny needed to worry about herself instead of her. She was the one who needed to find someone to make her happy, someone who finally and truly deserved her.

Nikki was happy. Her brothers were finally taking her seriously. She wasn't going to be strapped to a desk anymore. She was going to do fieldwork.

Probably.

As soon as she was fully healed.

It had been only a couple of days since the shoot-out at the storage units. She was surprised that Nick could even stand after the surgery on his back.

But he stood tall and proud beside her, staring at the doors of the church. Music began to play, and everyone stood and turned toward the back—to Annalise starting down the aisle, holding on to her brother's arm.

Her parents hadn't been able to get a flight out of Alaska in time for the service. But they would make the reception later.

Annalise wore the same wedding dress so many other Payne brides had worn. Penny's dress.

It was lace and satin, very vintage and graceful. If Nikki ever married—and she doubted that would happen—she wouldn't wear that dress. But Annalise looked beautiful in it. The empire waist hid the swell of her belly.

Beside her, Nick gasped. And Nikki grabbed his arm in case he toppled over. He wasn't in pain, though. He was in awe. "She's so beautiful," he murmured.

"She is."

The kind of beautiful that radiated from the inside out. As she drew closer, it was clear to see that love radiated from Annalise, as well.

She loved Nick with all her heart—the same way he loved her.

Nikki felt a flash of envy for that kind of happiness. But she didn't need love. All she wanted was to be taken seriously. She had that now—thanks to Nick.

So she pushed aside that momentary lapse and focused on being the best man. She handed over the rings with a steady hand.

Nick slid a diamond band on Annalise's finger. She slid a silver band on his. They repeated their vows in strong, certain voices. They had no doubts—only love. They would love and honor each other forever.

Epilogue

Hours had passed since their wedding. It was all a blur to Annalise, a kaleidoscope of color and music and voices. But she remembered staring up into Nick's handsome face as he pledged his love and devotion.

She would never forget that. She would never doubt his love. He had given her his heart—like she had given him hers so many years before.

Fingertips trailed over her naked skin. He hadn't left her alone in bed this time. He lay next to her, staring at her in the moonlight. "I am the luckiest man in the world."

She laughed. "That's the same thing your surgeon said."

A fraction of an inch to the left and the bullet would have paralyzed him. He had been so lucky.

"You're the reason I'm so blessed," he said. His fingertips trailed over her belly now—where their son moved beneath his father's touch.

She smiled. "We both are." She was so happy she felt almost guilty.

Now Nick touched the furrow that had formed between her brows. "What? What are you worried about?"

"Not us," she assured him. She had no doubts they would be happy. "About Gage…"

"He made it back," Nick said. "Both physically and mentally. He's doing great."

He was better. But he still wasn't whole. It was as if a part of him was still missing. He'd lost something. And she suspected it wasn't in Afghanistan. He'd lost something before he'd left: his heart.

"I want him to be as happy as we are," she said.

Nick sighed and pulled her into his arms. Holding her close, he murmured, "Me, too…"

* * * * *

Look for the next thrilling installment in the
BACHELOR BODYGUARDS *series, coming soon!*

*And if you love Lisa Childs, be sure to pick up
her other stories:*

*BODYGUARD DADDY
THE AGENT'S REDEMPTION
AGENT TO THE RESCUE
AGENT UNDERCOVER
THE PREGNANT WITNESS*

Available now from Harlequin!

REQUEST YOUR FREE BOOKS!
2 FREE NOVELS PLUS 2 FREE GIFTS!

✦HARLEQUIN®

ROMANTIC suspense

Sparked by danger, fueled by passion

YES! Please send me 2 FREE Harlequin® Romantic Suspense novels and my 2 FREE gifts (gifts are worth about $10). After receiving them, if I don't wish to receive any more books, I can return the shipping statement marked "cancel." If I don't cancel, I will receive 4 brand-new novels every month and be billed just $4.74 per book in the U.S. or $5.49 per book in Canada. That's a savings of at least 12% off the cover price! It's quite a bargain! Shipping and handling is just 50¢ per book in the U.S. and 75¢ per book in Canada.* I understand that accepting the 2 free books and gifts places me under no obligation to buy anything. I can always return a shipment and cancel at any time. Even if I never buy another book, the two free books and gifts are mine to keep forever.

240/340 HDN GH3P

Name _____ (PLEASE PRINT)

Address _____ Apt. #

City _____ State/Prov. _____ Zip/Postal Code

Signature (if under 18, a parent or guardian must sign)

Mail to the **Reader Service:**
IN U.S.A.: P.O. Box 1867, Buffalo, NY 14240-1867
IN CANADA: P.O. Box 609, Fort Erie, Ontario L2A 5X3

Want to try two free books from another line?
Call 1-800-873-8635 or visit www.ReaderService.com.

* Terms and prices subject to change without notice. Prices do not include applicable taxes. Sales tax applicable in N.Y. Canadian residents will be charged applicable taxes. Offer not valid in Quebec. This offer is limited to one order per household. Not valid for current subscribers to Harlequin Romantic Suspense books. All orders subject to credit approval. Credit or debit balances in a customer's account(s) may be offset by any other outstanding balance owed by or to the customer. Please allow 4 to 6 weeks for delivery. Offer available while quantities last.

Your Privacy—The Reader Service is committed to protecting your privacy. Our Privacy Policy is available online at www.ReaderService.com or upon request from the Reader Service.

We make a portion of our mailing list available to reputable third parties that offer products we believe may interest you. If you prefer that we not exchange your name with third parties, or if you wish to clarify or modify your communication preferences, please visit us at www.ReaderService.com/consumerchoice or write to us at Reader Service Preference Service, P.O. Box 9062, Buffalo, NY 14240-9062. Include your complete name and address.

HR:

With the pregnancy test long ago thrown in the trash, Trevor paced from one end of the living room of Jocelyn's condo to the other. She sat on her gray sofa before the stacked gray rock wall, a fresh vase of yellow lilies on the coffee table, reminding him that her chosen profession missed the mark. What hit the mark was what had him pacing the room. Her. Pregnant. Raising babies in a warm, inviting home like this one, in a gated community with a pool and clubhouse.

He knew what he had to do. He just couldn't believe he actually would.

He stopped pacing in front of the sofa, looking at Jocelyn over the tops of cheery lilies. "We have to get married."

That blunt announcement removed her annoyed observation of him digesting the idea of his impending fatherhood. Now shock rounded her eyes and parted her lips with a grunt.

"Will I be at gunpoint?" she asked.

She felt forced into this. He understood that. So did he.

"Love isn't important right now. The baby is what's important. No child of mine is going to be raised in a broken home."

She stood up. "Nothing's broken in *my* home."

She kind of went low on that one. His home was broken. Did she mean him or his dad? Both, probably.

"I won't get married just because I'm pregnant," she said. "I want love. Love is important to me, equally as much as this child." After a beat, she added, "And I thought you didn't mix personal relationships with your professional ones."

"I don't, but a baby changes everything. I won't be my father. I won't tear apart a family and destroy the lives of my children. I'll give them support and the best chance at a good life as I can."

Nothing in the world held more importance than that. He'd do anything, go to any length to avoid turning out like his father. He was no murderer. He had sanity. And he was on the opposite side of the law from his father. That was where he'd stay.

HARLEQUIN®

A *Romance* FOR EVERY MOOD™

JUST CAN'T GET ENOUGH?

Join our social communities
and talk to us online.

You will have access to the latest
news on upcoming titles and special
promotions, but most importantly,
you can talk to other fans about your
favorite Harlequin reads.

Harlequin.com/Community

THE WORLD IS BETTER WITH

Romance

8193

Harlequin has everything from contemporary, passionate and heartwarming to suspenseful and inspirational stories.

Whatever your mood, we have a romance just for you!

Connect with us to find your next great read, special offers and more.

 /HarlequinBooks

🐦 @HarlequinBooks

www.HarlequinBlog.com

www.Harlequin.com/Newsletters

 **HARLEQUIN**

A *Romance* FOR EVERY MOOD™

www.Harlequin.com

SERIESHALOAD: